Forgotten Nightmares and Sullen Fantasies

A. C. PERRY

Visit our website at
www.StillwaterPress.com
for more information.

First Stillwater River Publications Edition.

ISBN: 978-1-965733-07-3

1 2 3 4 5 6 7 8 9 10
Written by A. C. Perry.
Front cover illustration by cattle house / Adobe Stock.
Back cover illustration by croisy / Adobe Stock.
Section divider illustration by Y. L. Photographies / Adobe Stock.
Cover & interior book design by Matthew St. Jean.
Published by Stillwater River Publications,
West Warwick, RI, USA.

Originally published by Domesticated Primate of New Bedford,
Massachusetts in two volumes. *The Lonesome Dark: Forgotten
Nightmares* was published in the fall of 2017 and *The Lonesome
Dark: Sullen Fantasies* was published in the spring of 2019. "The
Talley Incident" previously appeared in the Tell-Tale Press
Library, December 2019. (The site has since shut down.)

*The views and opinions expressed in this book
are solely those of the author and do not necessarily
reflect the views and opinions of the publisher.*

For Rachel

CONTENTS

FORGOTTEN NIGHTMARES and SULLEN FANTASIES

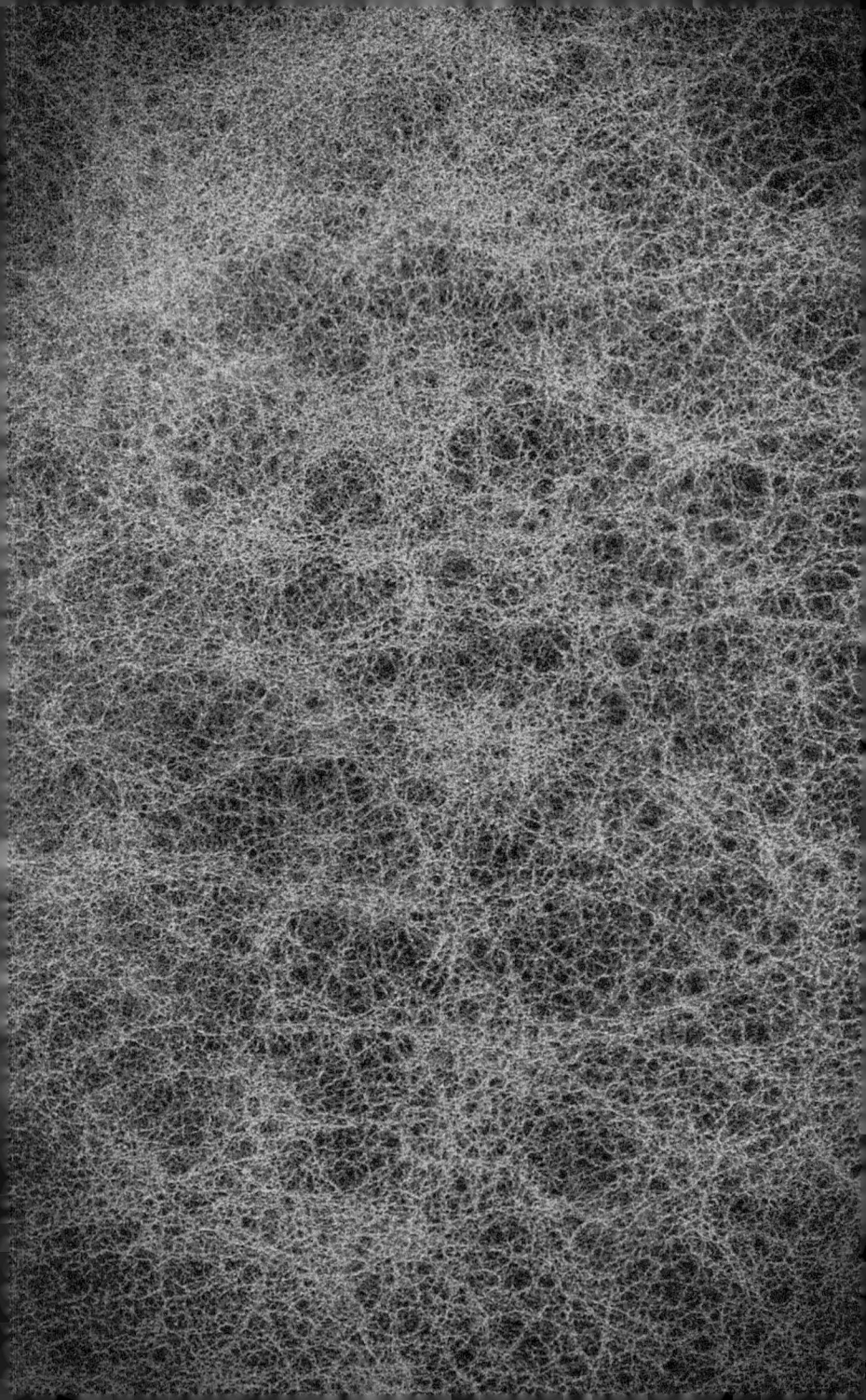

The Talley Incident

Marty clicked his blinker on, got off the highway, and onto a well-maintained dirt road. From the dirt road he pulled into the dusty parking lot of a derelict diner. There were no cars in the lot, and he had seen no other cars on the highway. Marty didn't mind being alone, but the absence of human activity made him nervous about the task that was ahead of him.

From the glove box of his ministry vehicle, Marty pulled out a wrinkled, coffee-stained map. His route was drawn in fine red pen from the little office in Ashland to the town of Talley, the crimson line winding and twisting along back roads and wooded areas. It was as though Talley wasn't important enough to be connected by a main road. Marty was still nervous about getting lost despite his hundred or so checks of the map. He tossed it into the passenger seat and got out.

The little diner was dark inside. Marty put his face to a grimy window and did his best to penetrate the gloom. Chairs sat upside down on tabletops and a layer of dust covered everything. He tried the door, but it was locked. As he walked back to his vehicle, he heard a car approaching and ran up to the road to flag the motorist down.

As the vehicle came into view, Marty saw that it was a park ranger—another government employee. He pulled out his badge and held it in the air, the sun glinting off of it like a beacon. He waved his other hand frantically. The ranger pulled his beast of a truck into the parking lot beside Marty's car.

The ranger rolled the window down and took his sunglasses off. His face was sallow, and his eye sockets were darkened with sleeplessness and worry. He was a young man, but his stubble had hints of gray in it.

"You a cop?" He asked.

"I'm an agent with the Ministry of Decay." Marty said, approaching the ranger.

"Never heard of the Ministry of Decay."

"That's probably a good thing." Marty gave a nervous laugh.

The ranger's neutral look didn't change. "What can I do for you?"

"Well, I'm headed toward Talley. I have some business there and I was hoping to confirm that I was heading in the right direction." Marty said.

He went into his car, grabbed the map, and handed it over to the ranger. The man took the map but continued staring at Marty as if trying to discern some ulterior motive. Marty met his gaze and smiled until the ranger finally glanced down at the map. He pulled a pen out of his pocket and made a mark on the route.

"This is where we are right now. Up ahead there's a dirt road on the right. That's not this road, okay? Go past that and the next dirt road is the one I marked on your map here.

I don't know what your business is, but I don't recommend you goin' to Talley."

"Thank you. Really, thank you so much. Unfortunately, it's my job to go to Talley." Marty took the map back.

"Well, if you insist on going, there's an inn just outside of town. Good people own the place and last I checked they were still there, despite... well, despite what you're probably here for." The ranger smiled for the first time. It was a weak and hopeless smile.

"Good luck." He said and then drove back onto the road with a spray of dirt.

Marty watched him disappear down the road before setting off again.

$\mathcal{T}$HERE WAS STILL plenty of daylight left by the time Marty reached the inn. An agency car was parked in front of the old colonial home, and at first Marty was heartened by the sight. When he got closer, he saw that the car sat on four deflated tires and the body was gutted by rust. Upon exiting his car and examining the other, it seemed as though the hulk of metal had been parked there for decades, but it was the same year and model as his own.

Confusion gripped him. The agent he had been sent to find had only disappeared a little over a month ago, and the car was most certainly his. The identification badge hanging from the rearview mirror was faded, but the name was still legible: Baines.

Marty went to the trunk of his car and popped it. He withdrew a black briefcase and a respirator. He donned the mask and pulled the straps tight. His hand went under his suit jacket to check the safety on his custom Beretta Compact. He clicked it off. He spent a moment focusing on his breathing to calm his heart rate before entering the inn.

As he expected, the place was covered in dust, metallic items were rusted, wallpaper was peeling and moldy, and wooden items were rotted and crumbling. He set the briefcase on the bowed surface that had once served as the front desk and pulled on a pair of latex gloves.

"Hello?" He called. The front room swallowed his voice up like a thing hungry for any notion of life. Something crumbled and fell somewhere deeper in the colonial to answer his greeting.

Marty went over every detail of the front room looking for any evidence of Baines. The inn was full of a desolation on a scale Marty had never seen before. He took samples of materials that were rife with the rot that gripped the place. Little glass test tubes full of every kind of powder, particle, and putrescence were placed delicately into the briefcase.

When he was done with the front room, he moved on to the kitchen and then the dining room. When the downstairs had been fully examined, Marty went on to the guest rooms upstairs. The locking mechanisms in the doors were so rusted that a good yank broke them open. It was in the second room where he found what he was looking for.

In the closet on the floor was a moth-eaten suit, the type that agents wore. On the desk below the window was a handheld tape recorder and a notebook ruined by mold growth. Marty approached the object as though it would disintegrate if he moved too quickly. His heartbeat quickened and he reached for it. The cassette seemed to be intact despite the tape player slowly disintegrating in fuzzy green battery acid.

Marty took the tape to his car and popped it into the cassette deck. He turned the car on and hesitated, his finger hovering over the rewind button. He pressed it and the tape rewound without breaking. He blew out a sigh of relief and pressed the play button. He couldn't believe his luck in finding the cassette intact and playable.

"BEGIN AUDIO DIARY of Agent Baines. The date is February 24, 1989 and the time is 11:30 in the morning. HQ dispatched me to investigate strange reports of a town called Talley. The bulk of the calls about the town were from the few merchants who passed through the area attempting to sell their wares to people so far removed from the cities.

"It has been reported that the townspeople have come to resemble walking corpses, and the structures and infrastructure seem to be crumbling at an alarming rate. It all points to a decay that the MoD has never seen before. As of now, I am still driving though backroads pressed by dense woods. The trees are a spectacle—there are no living things as magnificent in the cities. The great green pines have lulled me into a calmness that I have not known for quite some time.

"My plan is to find a decent place to stay, somewhere on the outskirts of town to minimize my exposure to the decay. This audio tape will serve as my report to the ministry. The sun shining down through these great pines truly is something to see. I'll have to come back this way after we put this incident to rest."

"IT'S A LITTLE after four in the afternoon. Things are worse here than we could have imagined. I'm standing on a hill overlooking the town. Through my binoculars, I can see some disturbing sights. The residents of Talley are gaunt, dead-looking things shambling about the cracked and crumbling sidewalks. I watched one for a few minutes and she stumbled and fell, leaving an arm on the ground when she stood back up.

"Their homes are collapsing in on themselves. The roofs are covered in great swaths of mold. The stuff seems to be thriving as the wooden frames of the buildings are dying. Even the buildings made of stone—the church and town hall among others—are falling to pieces. I watched a few of the stones shift and give in to gravity, falling into yellowing grass lawns.

"I shudder to think that I'll be down there in person, among the decay, but it is part of the job. There does look to be a place offering lodging on the way into town—I judge it only by the vacancy sign hanging loosely below a sign too faded to read. The building appears to be in better shape than the rest of the town."

"THE INN WAS certainly vacant—I was the only guest they had seen that month. The innkeeper was a hobbled old woman. She told me that the town had become quieter and she and her husband had fallen on hard times with the absence of the usual traveling merchants. Her husband had gone into town once and returned with none of the supplies she had sent him out for, only a pasty look of horror on his face. He had refused to talk about what he had seen and began keeping his hunting rifle loaded and leaning next to their front door.

"The man had also taken to sitting in front of a window in a room overlooking the road into town. His behavior frightened her, and she let her feelings out to me. I did my best to empathize while sipping on the neat glass of bourbon she had poured me. Wasn't it the job of the barkeep to listen to the problems of their drunken patrons and not the other way around?

"She let me go eventually, claiming that she had to clean up the kitchen in order to prepare my dinner. I took my chance and headed up to the room she had given me with another glass of bourbon in my hand.

"The room is relatively clean, a bit dusty, but good enough for a comfortable night's sleep. There's a creaky little desk where I can set up an adequate workstation. I think, though, after so much driving, I'll head to bed. I'm setting my alarm for seven in the morning. I'm hoping to get an early start on the investigation. I do hope that in such an advanced state of rot, the town will be slow to wake, and I'll have some time to myself before interacting with the locals."

"It's two in the morning. The moon is shining through my window and giving me a clear view of the same road into town that the innkeeper's husband looks out upon. At first, I wasn't quite sure what had woken me—I'm usually a sound sleeper—but I saw the innkeeper's husband out in the street with his rifle aimed at a figure cloaked in darkness. The figure was approaching him, and he fired a shot into the air. I'll be honest: firearms scare me, and I jumped when the man's rifle cracked. The figure retreated toward town, and the innkeeper's husband returned to the inn after making sure the figure had truly gone.

"I'll attempt sleep again, but this case is already proving to be an exciting one."

"GOOD MORNING. The dim light of dawn is spilling through the window and prying my eyes open. It woke me before my alarm could chime and the day already feels fresh, despite the rotting town nearby."

"THINGS ARE certainly far worse here than the ministry had led me to believe. I found the remains of a few townspeople laying in drainage ditches along the road into town. I could no longer identify their genders, the flesh and clothing were in such advanced stages of decomposition. It's hard to say when they actually succumbed to the rot. I took tissue samples and made sure to place them in the formaldehyde-filled containers rather than the evidence baggies.

"When I heard activity around one of the buildings on the outskirts, I stole into the woods and continued my approach in stealth. I took shelter in a small wooden shack to collect my thoughts and formulate a plan to enter town unnoticed.

"Leaning against one of the roof supports in the shack caused it to creak and begin to buckle. I made it out with a racing heart and sweat-soaked brow. I headed back to the inn after my near-death experience. I felt as though the decay was creeping into my body.

"The innkeeper fed me, and we drank together. I'm going to turn in and try to get into town again tomorrow."

"**J** DON'T KNOW the time; my watch has stopped working. There's no moon, but in the starlight I can see figures out in the road, four or five shuffling bodies. The inn is quiet. I'm going downstairs to have a look."

THE RECORDINGS ended there.

Marty sat in the hissing silence as the tape ran. The cassette deck clicked and began to play the B side of the tape, and still Marty sat listening to the hiss. There had been no evidence of anyone in the inn. He looked over toward the road leading into Talley. There was no evidence of any bodies in the street. He and Baines hadn't been close, but they did chat over beers every once in a while, when they were both working out of the same office. But Baines' fate looked grim, and Marty worried about his own future. Never had he seen a decay so severe and he was afraid that his body would feel the effects of it. The sooner he concluded that search, the better.

The inn was a dead end and that left Marty with only one choice—he'd have to venture into Talley and search for evidence of the missing agent there. With the sun setting, he got back on the road. Despite the looming twilight, Marty wanted to be done with the adventure as soon as possible. The tired colonial inn faded away in the rearview mirror, its sunny windows like sad eyes watching Marty leave.

The road was much the same as those that had led him there, but as he neared Talley the surrounding trees became sicklier and more decrepit. None of them held any sign of life; even the evergreens were devoid of needles. The golden light of the setting sun cut through the spaces between the trees and motes of dust swirled in the breeze. He passed a sign and though the name of the town was faded, it clearly said TALLEY on the rotten thing. Marty took a deep breath and continued on.

It became hard to distinguish between the road and the blasted ground that met it on either side. The trees opened into a gargantuan clearing big enough to hold a town. It took Marty a moment or two, but soon he realized he had reached Talley. He slammed on the brakes in surprise. His breathing came in ragged gasps through the respirator.

There was nothing left of the town.

When he had been briefed, he had seen pictures of Talley. It was quaint, barely bigger than a village, nestled in the woods. It was the kind of place where everyone knew everyone else and life went by day after innocuous day. The quiet little utopia was gone, disappeared into oblivion by anomalous decay.

Marty got out of the car and stared around in wonder. He took a few steps in the gray lifeless dirt and felt as though he were on a different planet or some moon that had withered away after many eons. There were areas of gray dirt that were like little hills, and Marty deduced that they had once been where buildings had stood. Even the sky over the land had a sick gray tint to it.

Marty heard a faint noise out in the otherwise hushed woods. There was a slight breeze and he thought that maybe it was only a trick of the wind through the trees, but then he heard it again. It sounded like a weak, gurgling cry. There couldn't possibly be anything alive out there, unless some rabid animal had wandered into the contamination zone. Or could it be Baines? Against his every instinct, Marty put on gloves and grabbed a few clean glass tubes for samples, then took off into the darkening woods.

Whatever it was cried out again—this time louder—and he veered toward the sound. He traipsed through the springy rotten forest floor, heedless of the branches grasping at him. He heard the cry and it sounded as though he were right on top of it. Marty slowed and began a thorough search of the area.

A weak voice said something unintelligible, and Marty found himself staring into the darkness of a great hollowed-out stump. The dim sky made it impossible to penetrate the gloom held within the stump. The voice moaned pitifully, and Marty felt an icy chill creeping up his spine. He reached into a pocket and withdrew a flashlight. He clicked it on and pointed the beam into the shadowed hollow.

A body not quite alive sat slumped in the darkness. The remnants of Agent Baines were only vaguely recognizable amongst the pile of flesh and rot he had become. His chest rose and fell and he made a guttural wet sound in its throat. His spirit was not quite dead. One good eye rolled up to look into the beam of light, the other already dead-white and wandering. The thing's jaw opened and clicked shut.

Marty gasped and shivered. He was slow to draw his custom Beretta Compact from its holster. He trained it on the thing in the stump.

"I'm sorry, Baines."

The shot echoed in the quiet woods. A tree gave up and fell somewhere close by as if responding to the gunfire. Marty leaned into the hollow stump and wrinkled his nose at the stale smell of rot. He took fresh samples from the messy corpse and returned the glass tubes to his jacket pocket.

There wasn't much to be done about the remains. Marty could see that any attempt to remove them would result in them crumbling into a moist ashy substance. He stood, peeled his gloves off, and began to walk in the dark back toward his car. Gooseflesh crawled up his arms as he thought of the decay spreading farther. The investigation into the disappearance of Agent Baines was complete, however the Ministry of Decay had bigger problems. As he quickened his pace under twinkling stars, the world was quiet as though it were already dead.

THE END

FORGOTTEN NIGHTMARES

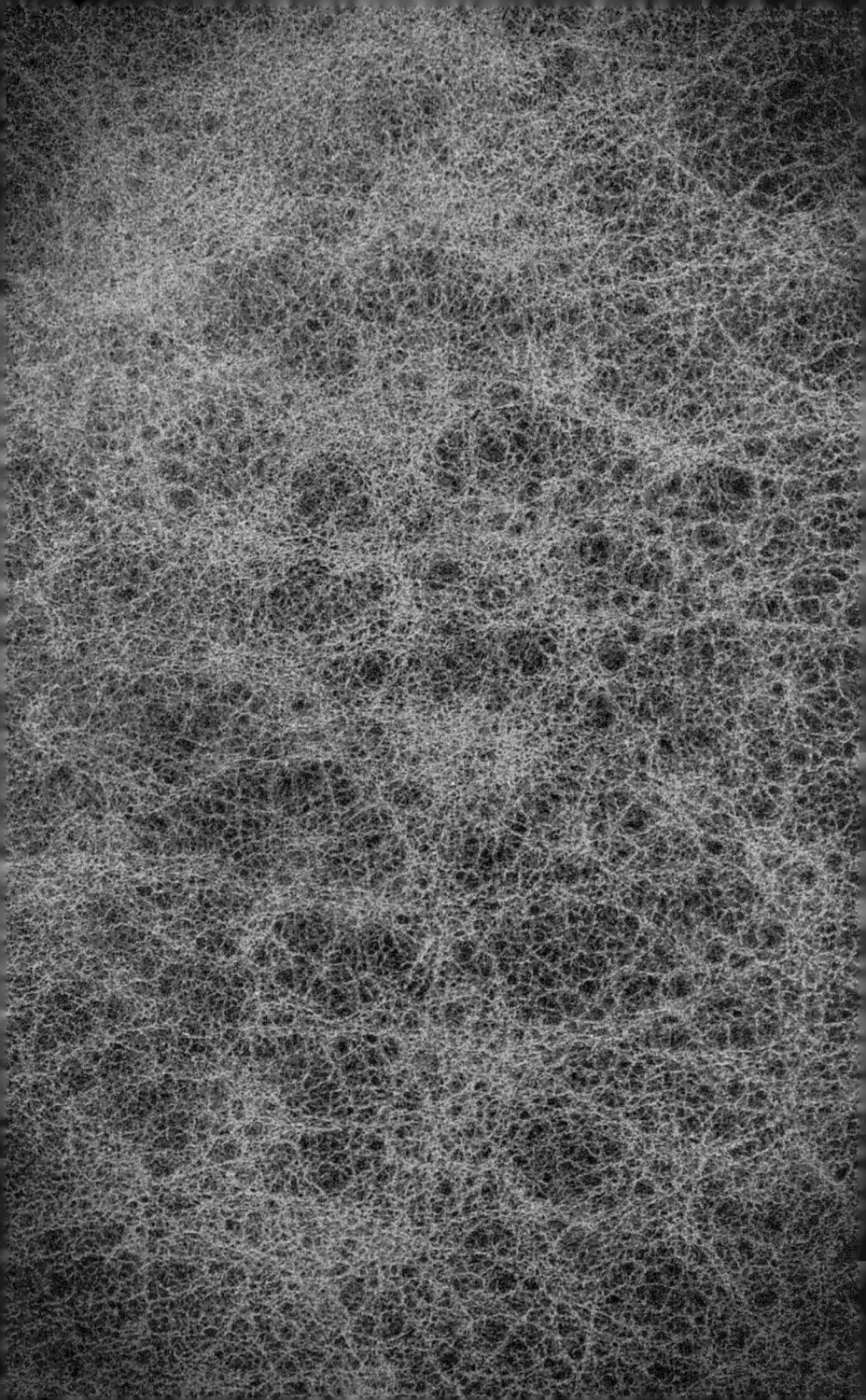

Hunter in the Night

YOU MAY THINK me an evil man when I tell you I enjoy scaring children. It is not at all that they are terrified of the dark and the monsters inhabiting it that brings me joy. It is their belief. Those credulous stares keep me sane. For I personally have seen the thing that they are most afraid of. After hearing my tales I know that they lay awake with blankets pulled up to their chins and eyes on the closet. I know because I have spent countless nights in the same paralyzing condition.

A bump, a whisper, crunching on the gravel, or the rattling of a window are enough to induce a panic attack. Any one of these sounds could be that loathsome being returning to take its revenge upon me. I, who thwarted its plans to take a child in the night for a nice meal. The pudgy little one would have satiated the thing's hunger for a time and left the rest of us in peace.

I could never live knowing that I had stood aside as a child was taken. I remember the scene vividly. The being retreated with the darkness as my flashlight blazed to life. The fat boy stood dazed in the beam, clearly ensorcelled by the thing. I woke him and led him back to his home, the house diagonal from mine. Once safe inside, I left their lawn and prowled the neighborhood for the monster, vowing that I was now its nemesis.

I made flyers for the neighborhood to inform the good people that I would be acting as a one-man neighborhood watch. A few families scoffed, and fewer were supportive, but most stayed silent. It was the silent ones that worried me the most. Did they think I was crazy? Maybe they had caught a glimpse of the creature themselves and knew what I faced. The little boy who I rescued assured me he was just a sleepwalker, but I remember the shadow of the thing fleeing into the black night.

It was at this point that my insomniac episodes became a gift rather than a burden. I was alive at night. A hunter, a defender of humankind! The first few nights were quiet. My flashlight revealed nothing. I also had with me a disposable camera to acquire evidence for others to see, when I finally revealed the purpose for my nightly hunts. A few young faces would peek out of the windows and wave as I strolled by.

During the daylight hours, I gave increasingly grotesque descriptions of the thing to the children. It was the summertime so most were home, frolicking about the neighborhood oblivious to the danger that lay dormant. Some of the older ones laughed it off but I could see tears in the younger ones' eyes. The little fat boy I had saved never appeared outside, however. In fact I hadn't seen him since the night of the rescue.

I trudged up to his home and rang the bell. There was no answer. Most likely they had gone away on a trip. No doubt they felt confident to leave their abode with me watching the streets at night. Things were going well and that day was simply beautiful.

The night that followed it, however, was full of horror.

Just after sunset I woke up from a little two-hour nap. Plenty of sleep to get me through the night. I gathered my gear and went out the front door. The last giggling children were being called in for the night as I strolled down the sidewalk. A few of the kids called out a goodnight and good luck to me. I waved and thanked them.

The hours ticked by quietly. I took a seat on the curb and immediately was taken by an unexpected sleep. I was conscious of time passing while I slept, yet it was strange. I could think, but I wasn't dreaming. The night came back in a rush as a wispy voice awakened me. In front of me stood the boy I had rescued, pale with dark circles under his eyes. His face was dimly illuminated by moonlight.

"Leave us alone," he said in an unsettling voice. It was as if two people were speaking at once. One was his voice and the other was a whisper.

Without thinking I aimed the camera in the boy's direction and clicked off a picture. The flash was blinding. The boy yelped with the same dual voice and stumbled backwards. I was unable to see anything with the ghostly afterimage of the kid burning in my eyes. I felt a different burning sensation in my hand. I fumbled for the flashlight and clicked it on. The boy was gone. My arm was leaking blood and my index and middle fingers were gone. The camera that was between them was also gone. I was in shock as I tore my shirt off to wrap around my arm.

The next morning there was a knock on my door. My neighbor stood on the porch looking very worried. Apparently she had followed drops of blood all the way back to my house. We both looked down at my arm, still wrapped in my shirt. I was a mess and it seemed I had slept through the night after that episode, I must have passed out.

She led me to her van telling me that she was taking me to the hospital. On the way I tried to describe what happened which only led to confusion. She assured me that the neighbors I was referring to had moved months ago after the death of their only son. I shook my head, feeling a little groggy. In turn, I assured her I had seen him in the past week. She looked at me with a deep sadness in her eyes. Almost as if she pitied me. When I began to describe the being in the black of night, her eyes grew fearful. Not of it, but of me. We drove the rest of the way in silence.

After a brief stay in the hospital, I was discharged with pain medication and instructions on how to care for the wound and prevent infection. I flexed my three remaining fingers and gazed out the window. I noticed a 'for sale' sign on the neighbor's house, the same neighbors who had disappeared. Had that always been there? I had seen the boy. I had seen the thing. My fingers were gone along with the camera that had captured an image. What happened that night? What happened that week? The neighborhood seemed to be in much the same joyous mood as it had always been. Perhaps I was losing my grip on reality. I laughed.

I awoke from a nap just after sunset. I gathered my gear and dressed myself. I was ready to resume my nightly hunt for the creature, ready to return to my position as the defender of humankind. I resolved to be more alert, however, as I looked down at my three remaining fingers.

The darkness was nearly absolute. Clouds hid the stars and celestial bodies, the only illumination was from the odd light left on here and there among the homes reflecting onto the dark pavement of my street. The silence was almost complete and together with the darkness I felt as though I was sealed off from reality. But I knew there was something out there inhabiting our peaceful realm, something that had harmed that boy, and stolen my camera...and my fingers. I moved out onto the sidewalk to begin my search and heard the howl of sirens echoing in the distance.

As I patrolled the neighborhood, the sirens howled closer, soon painting the dark houses in silhouettes of red and blue. Two cruisers screeched to a stop in front of me, blinding me with their headlights. Guns drawn, two rough-handed officers took me into custody. From their accusatory banter I learned that my fingers had been found in the mouth of a dead boy that had been discovered decomposing in the woods just outside of the neighborhood. The crime lab confirmed that the breaks in the bones matched the boy's teeth and there was no doubt the fingers belonged to me.

I didn't kill anyone. Someone or something had set me up. I was sure of that.

From out of the darkness came an unsettling laugh that only I seemed to hear. It was as if two people were laughing at once, one a boy's voice and the other a disconcerting whisper. Driving towards the police station, I became very afraid for the other children in the neighborhood. They had no one to protect them now. The thing was scared of me and it had done what it needed to make me disappear. Hopefully the children's fear would instill a policy of self-preservation. I began to weep in frustration, tears running through the spaces in between the three remaining fingers of my mangled hand.

THE END

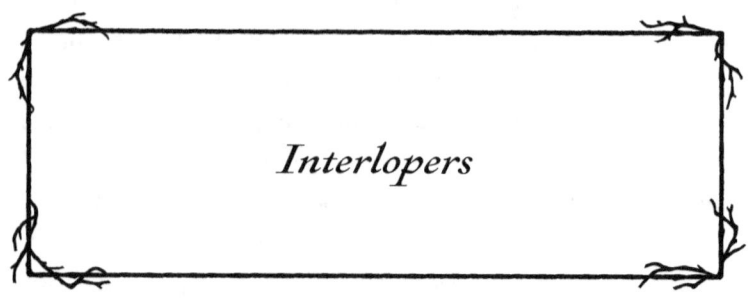

Interlopers

I ARRIVED BEFORE sunrise and took in the scene that swept out before me. There was an abandoned barn; its door creaked and banged as the breeze battered it. The grass was dark green in the haze of the early morning light. The sky was a calming indigo, painted with peach clouds. Those wispy apparitions in the sky floated coyly in front of the bright full moon, hanging there as if it had arrived before its cue. It was the moon that really took my breath away. Its sickly yellow glow captured my gaze and held me right where I stood. I breathed out one word: Beautiful. I wasn't alone. There seemed to be small creatures lying in the shadowy emerald grass. A few were cozied up to the leaning wall of the decaying barn. But none of them stirred, for it was too early for them to greet the day.

Over my shoulder I could see the seemingly infinite amber fields spreading out towards the horizon. The sky was a pale blue and I knew the sun would be up before long. The moon was starting to sink. It was leaving me alone with the task at hand, not wanting to be a witness to what I had come to do. I picked up the jerry can with a grunt. Full of gasoline, the thing was heavy at the end of my frail arm. My other hand slid into my jacket pocket to confirm I had brought the lighter.

I moved along the fence like a shadow at midday. None of the animals took notice of me, even those that had begun to slowly awaken at the setting of the moon. I arrived at the abandoned barn and slipped in through one of the great holes in its side. I opened the can and poured the pungent gasoline all about the rotten hay littering the floor. Dried shit and dead rat carcasses absorbed the liquid like thirsty sponges. I poured the last little bit in a trail from the middle of the floor to the door of the barn. The liquid was cold and strong. I turned the lighter over in my fingers.

I heard the trespassers beginning to move about in the upper reaches of the barn. I had come to destroy these inhuman beings. They had infiltrated our small town one night and unleashed a spree of murder and madness. I may have been one of the first to encounter them. Two of them had entered my store late one night dressed as vagabonds. They didn't quite threaten me, but I heard the promise of death in their sour words. They left the store with assorted knickknacks and some food items without offering any payment. Their pale faces and lidless black eyes haunted me in my sleep.

The next day, two of the local homeless were found eviscerated on the front lawn of the town hall. The entire street was taped off and bustling with police activity. I passed the town hall on my daily walks and was forced to take a different route. I caught a glimpse of the bodies. Fear was frozen onto the pale dirty faces of the dead men. They were stretched out on the bloodstained grass, their clothing and flesh peeled back like the skin of a fruit. Their faces visited my dreams, swirling and dancing with the pale inhuman strangers.

The next week brought more chaos to our quiet little island community. Our church was badly vandalized. Beautiful stained-glass windows were broken, the altar was desecrated with animal excrement, pews were smashed, and lewd phrases were painted on the walls in and out. Upon further investigation, they deduced that the paint was human blood, the blood of the preacher who lived in an apartment in the back of the church. They never found his body. He remained a name in a thin manila folder marked "Missing." Whoever had destroyed the church had done so gleefully, I could feel it.

I would pass by the church on my walks as well. Once again I was forced to take a different route, one that led me down a cramped alley. The alley was dark in the daytime, shaded by ancient leaning homes. I grew uneasy as I moved through this darkened pass. It felt as though I was walking into oblivion, directly into the clutches of those inhuman interlopers that had been inhabiting my nightmares. I arrived at the end of the alley and strode into the warm sunlight, my worry falling away.

I heard a gibbering behind me. I spun around and backed away, my fear rising as a black shape shifted towards me. Out into the sunlight came another vagabond, this one still with his skin. It was a man the locals called Singer. The homeless Singer panhandled by serenading those who would listen in the hopes of receiving a few dollars. He dropped to his knees in front of me.

"I saw em man. Saw em. They grabbed Bob and Tick and unzipped em, ate em. They just walked away all casual, covered in they blood."

I looked around, paranoid that the things might be watching us. Singer began crying and fell prostrate, as if begging to be saved. I turned and hurried home, not wanting to be out in the open for any longer than I had to be. I barricaded my home that night. Mere locks did not put my mind at ease. I drifted into a fitful sleep, waking up in a sweat every few hours. I could not recall my dreams.

In the morning, my radio brought reports of various break-ins and burglaries around town. There were not any more murders, but some residents had awoken to find parts of their homes destroyed. It seemed like the perpetrators were looking for something or someone. Nothing was reported missing, but residents were badly frightened. I turned the radio off and went out to stretch my legs and clear my mind.

Deep in thought on my morning walk, I suddenly spotted one of them. It was walking swiftly down the other side of the road with a hood pulled up to disguise its monstrous face. I caught a glimpse of those inky black eyes darting around in the darkness of the hood. It was shifty, moving as if it were scared. More importantly, it was alone. I stopped and watched it hurry away.

The thing had not seen me, I made the decision to follow, staying a few blocks behind and making use of telephone poles and mailboxes to hide myself. The thing was heading toward the farmlands on the outskirts of town. I tailed it all the way to an old farm that I didn't know the name of. The land was lonely, and beautiful. The thing gave a look around, missing me lurking behind an apple tree, and slipped into an old broken barn. I waited a few moments to make sure nothing was going to emerge before creeping to the barn myself.

A moaning drifted out of the dark top floor window as I approached. The air about it smelled wet and coppery. I peeked inside and saw only the remnants of life in the barn;

rat droppings, rotten hay, and a few dead rodents. The moaning continued above me. I couldn't back out now. I was sure I had found their lair and I meant to confirm it. Against the back was a ladder. Carefully I climbed until my eyes peeked above the hay loft. The scene was seared into my mind forever; unidentifiable raw meat hung everywhere from chains used to move hay. Strange symbols were painted on the wall in dried blood. The two things were engaged in a carnal ritual. They were stripped naked and were sliding all over one another, it seemed like they were trying to mate.

A cold sweat spread over my body and fear clutched my heart. I left that demonic place as quickly and stealthily as I could. I held myself together until I was safe at home. Once inside I tried to wash that scene out of my consciousness with a scalding shower and some strong bourbon. Afterwards I paced about my house trying to process everything. I had wandered into the garage when a plan jumped into my head. The large can of gasoline resting on the shelf above my lawnmower whispered to me. I had just filled it. I could almost hear it saying, "Burn them. Remove them from this world." I chuckled at the thought at first, but, with each subsequent gulp of whiskey, found myself warming up to the idea.

I woke up in a sweat around 3:30am. I was going to the barn and I was going to burn those things. Our little island refuge would be cleansed of those chaotic beings, whatever they were. I dressed for the cool predawn air and loaded the rusty old canister into my truck. I grabbed a lighter and flicked it, checking its potency. I chugged a cup of black coffee—day old and acrid—and I was off to the farm. The world was asleep, watched over by the blackness of space. The infinite stars stared down at me, wondering if my plan would work. I shrugged off their questioning cosmic eyes and pressed down on the accelerator.

Then I was at the door of the barn, turning the lighter over in my fingers, admiring the pools of gasoline that covered the barn floor and the long thin stream that led right to my boots. I flicked the lighter on and held it to the end of the trail. Within seconds the barn floor was ablaze and blinding flames tore up the walls toward the rafters. I could hear nothing over the roar of the great conflagration. The flames had crawled up the rafters and begun weakening the upper floor. Then, an inhuman scream. I backed up, shielding my eyes from the roaring flames. Two shapes dropped to the floor as the hayloft gave way.

The shapes were screaming and screaming as they rolled across the floor like wild beasts. They stood and stared out at me, the flames licking their ghostly white bodies, leaving black and ashy patches on their porcelain white skin. Their screams bubbled out and turned into laughter. I stood paralyzed as they began to pick their way through the rubble towards the door. Their skin was repairing itself, they were practically shining white! I turned and ran as the invincible beings calmly exited the collapsing wreck of a barn. The light of the blaze cast shadows from the farm animals on the lonely fields. Sheep and goats and cows stood transfixed, hypnotized by the attractive dance of the blaze.

I ran until my lungs were on the verge of giving out, scrambled into my truck and sped off. I left the island. I drove until my gas tank was almost empty. By then I was nearly in Maine and I pulled into a rest stop to refuel. I had friends up north, perhaps I would stay with them. I stood pumping gas and struggled to come up with my next move. I felt defeated.

I felt defeated for my entire town. How could they survive that blaze? The chaos and violence of a furious fire had only caused them to laugh. Those creatures had to be unkillable. And they were going to reproduce. I shivered and drove on. I don't think I'll ever go home again, for what is there to return to?

THE END

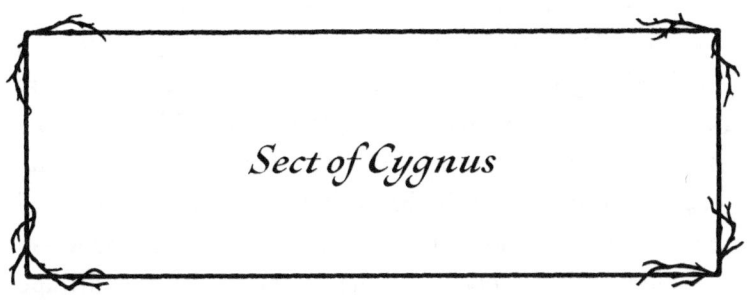

Sect of Cygnus

L IGHTNING FLASHED and the gods struck a drum, filling the valley with the rumbling echoes of thunder. Another crash, and again the light, and then the sound spilled over the emerald peaks in the distance. The massive sound wove its way through the air, bombarding my ears with a warning of impending rain. A sweet summer rainstorm was characteristic of these hot sticky Southern afternoons.

In front of me lay the sidewalk which ran along the small main road. Little businesses lined the street, each offering their own brand of southern nostalgia or tourist trinket. Big bright signs denoted the wares held in each shop. Folk art, guns, knives, boiled peanuts, and homemade jams were the livelihood of these humble Maggie Valley folk.

It was mostly quiet, save for the occasional rumble tearing through the rain. I watched the pavement ahead of me blacken with rain. Suddenly the front of the storm rushed towards me, seeming to swallow up everything in its path. I ducked into the closest shop with a blazing neon "OPEN" sign. The little old man behind the counter gave me a nod before going back to packing his pipe with a pinch of tobacco.

I glanced around, taking stock of what kind of shop I had stumbled into. Taxidermy animals stared back at me with unblinking glass eyes and fearsome toothy snarls. The rain was relentlessly beating on the metal roof. I felt a small pang of dread knowing that if I wanted to remain dry, I had to accept my imprisonment in this strange little shop. A few naked bulbs hung haphazardly from the ceiling, giving the space an eerie dream-like glow. The blue smoke of the now-lit pipe added to the effect. The haze wove lazily from the glowing pipe, procrastinating before it disappeared into a vent on the wall.

The old man seemed to be appraising me like a piece of art, thoughtfully chewing on the end of his pipe. I smiled and dipped my head a bit before feigning interest in a raccoon with its teeth bared. It had a little brass plate attached to the wooden base proclaiming it to be a North American Raccoon, *Procyon Iotor*. I walked around the corner to escape the man's questioning gaze, praying the rain would let up soon.

A meager selection of dusty mugs and shot glasses lined the sagging shelves. They read, "The Great Smoky Mountains" or "Maggie Valley, NC." The yellowing price tags were peeling off, attesting to the amount of time the empty vessels had been sitting out of use. The next section held an assortment of local magazines, newspapers, maps, and books. I thumbed through them, scanning the titles, before one of them captured my gaze: a skinny little volume tucked between an outdated collection of hiking trail maps and a manual on gun maintenance titled *The Godless Rituals of Maggie Valley 1890-1910*. The yellowed tag read $4.99. Flipping through the pages revealed to me that the tome was a quasi-history of a mysterious group that had come to inhabit the area now known as Maggie Valley. Toward the end, there were symbols and descriptions of rituals. Always a sucker for occult literature, I was intent on purchasing it.

I made my way to the counter without bothering to glance at the rest of the merchandise. I placed the book down and the old man squinted at the title before donning a pair of cracked spectacles. He looked back up at me with a wild grin as yellow as the aged price tags. He confirmed what I had gleaned from skimming the text. Half history, half "spell-book," he grunted in a tobacco-deep tone. I didn't bother to reveal my excitement and remained unmoved in appearance as I paid and asked for a plastic bag. The book was now the only thing I cared to keep dry.

Back out into the storm I went. The ominous sky let thin slits of light through, highlighting the sheets of endless falling rain as I trudged off in the direction of the motel I was staying in. The Scottish Inn huddled in the storm, its guests standing on their balconies, staring out with empty expressions into the dull gray. A few eyes followed my approach as I passed under the sign proclaiming that bikers were welcome and the HBO was free.

The musty motel room welcomed me with its relative cleanliness and dryness. I threw the book on the bed and peeled off my wet clothes. Despite the pleasant temperature, I shivered. I started the cheap little coffee pot and filled it with the bland grounds that were present in every room before hopping into the shower. I washed the rain away, hoping the slight chill would go with it. With the coffee done and steaming in a little paper cup, I sat down on the bed, toweled myself dry, and began my journey through the book.

It seemed that in the late 1800s, a group of settlers from

New England had struck out for new land after their strange beliefs had been shunned. Religious freedom was a bit of fallacy then; you were free to practice as long as it was one of a select few denominations. The group claimed to have roots in Eastern Europe during the time of Gothic barbarian rule, but even then the sect was on the fringes of Germanic paganism.

The history seemed hazy— I had never heard of such Germanic fringe groups. The sect seemed to have an obsession with the constellation Cygnus, known more modernly as the Northern Cross. Most paganism involved sacrifice, but those who worshiped Cygnus hinted at a more torturous brand of ritual slaughter.

One particular passage stated, "The offering to sweet Cygnus was to be left conscious to experience the raw power of the flames." If this sect really had Germanic roots, how had they kept alive as the barbarians moved through the Roman Empire, and subsequently the aggressive Christianization of Europe?

The phone rang and snapped me out of the trance-like state that I had entered with the text. I picked up the plastic receiver, but the other line simply clicked and went dead. The glowing green display of the clock read 10:21pm. Hours had passed unnoticed. The rain had stopped. But when?

I pulled on some jeans and stepped out onto the balcony. The unpolluted night sky was crystal clear, cut off only by the looming black mountains in the distance. The Milky Way was a broad brush stroke across the infinite blackness of space.

I sucked the fresh humid air into my lungs as I carefully scanned the sky for the Northern Cross. My eyes locked on to it— the neighboring stars seemed to lessen in magnitude as the stars of the constellation grew brighter. They seared themselves into my vision, sending ripples of nervous excitement through me.

I rushed back inside to the book, flipping to the latter half to search for any more information on the constellation. There was a crude drawing of the stars, their names scribbled almost incoherently next to them: Deneb, Sadr, Gienah, Delta Cygni, and Albireo. I spoke the names of the stars aloud and felt something, almost as if the night sky had seemed to call for me.

I shuffled back onto the balcony. The constellation was blazing still, brighter than the other stars. Soon it was all I could see in my mind when I shut my eyes. The words of long dead adherents whispered to me. The sounds whirled in my head dampening the waking world around me. A great sleepy heat washed over my body causing euphoric pleasure. The pleasure began to move into the realm of pain as the heat began to burn like fire. The pain snapped me out of whatever waking dream I had, and I stumbled back into the room. I sat down hard on the squeaky bed and wiped sweat from my brow with a shaking hand. I glared at the book.

The phone rang again and I lunged at it. This time there was someone on the other line. It was Professor Leonard Bath, a colleague and friend. Twenty years my senior and energetic as ever, he asked all about my retreat into the mountains of the South. We chatted for a little while, and slowly the strange occurrence that had followed my reciting the stars had all but slipped from my mind. Yet, just before we said our goodbyes, I mentioned the book to him. He went silent on the other end for a moment.

He wanted me to send the book to him. His voice was a perplexing mix of restrained excitement and anxious worry.

Bath, being an expert on the arcane and esoteric, most likely knew something about the text I had stumbled upon. After all, it was through attending his lectures on the mystery cults of antiquity that the two of us had become such good friends. Bath was the kind of man I could stand behind— I trusted him almost as much as I trusted myself. I agreed to mail it first thing in the morning.

Bath seemed to let go of his breath as if he had been holding it throughout the entire conversation. He thanked me and promised to call again once he had taken a look at the book. As soon as I hung up the phone, the feeling of the stars searing my flesh surged back in my memory. I took the book down to my beat up Subaru and stored it in the glove compartment. I didn't want to open it again. I wondered if I should write a little note to warn my friend about my experience before he opened the mysterious booklet.

I went to bed with the stars spinning about my body, in the hypnagogic passage from the waking world into the one of dreams. I floated endlessly in space as the stars, every one of them, took hold of my body with their gravity. I heard Bath somewhere out there, laughing to himself excitedly. Then my dreams winked out into blackness until the morning.

The sun snuck over the highest peak and made its way into the room to pry my eyes open. The warm light beams between the blinds lay upon me as if feeling for a pulse. The sun was worried about me. I shook the silly thought out of my head and made myself some coffee. The machine bubbled and popped while I dressed myself for the day. I decided that once I mailed the book to Bath, I would go for a little hike on one of the mountains. I gathered my things and left the room to mind itself in my absence.

At the meager little post office, I bought some paper to wrap the book. I quickly scribbled a note to place inside, detailing my experience the previous night. While the clerk tapped information into the computer screen, I asked if she knew of any good hiking spots. She looked at me as if I had offended her and went back to her typing without an answer. I elected to overnight my package. I felt a weight that I had not noticed before lift from my shoulders as I exited the brick building. I forgot about the book and went about enjoying my vacation again.

The next day I received a call from Bath. He could barely contain his excitement as we spoke about the book. He never mentioned my note and only speculated on the origins of the strange sect. Eventually the conversation ran dry and we hung up. It was late afternoon by then and I went out to find myself something to eat. Upon returning to my hotel room I found that there was a message waiting for me.

It was Bath. He still sounded excited, but it was mixed with that tinge of anxiety, which I had originally detected when first I mentioned the book. I could follow most of his quick-paced musings, but he began to lose me as he began to hypothesize how one might replicate rituals detailed in the book. How had he even deciphered the second half of the book already? I didn't call him back. He could wait until tomorrow to speak to me. At that moment all I could think of was lying as comfortably as possible in my uncomfortable bed. I clicked on the TV and allowed the free HBO to drone in the background as I drifted off to sleep.

I heard Bath in my dreams again. This time he was screaming in agony. I called out to him and rushed around the black nothingness that held me. He was nowhere in that nowhere place, which meant he was actually somewhere. This line of thought brought me into wakefulness, though I realized I was dreaming. It was dawn again. I was scheduled to leave that morning as my retreat drew to a close. I attempted to phone Bath before I began packing, but there was no answer.

I spent the entire day driving nonstop to arrive home in Rhode Island by dusk. Once in the door to my modest little apartment, I relieved myself in the bathroom, then immediately made a call to Bath again. There was still no answer, and this time it began to worry me slightly. The old man had retired from lecturing and rarely left his home these days, preferring to dive into texts and theories. He never missed phone calls. I planned to drive to his house the next morning, and a quiet dreamless sleep overcame me

Upon arriving at Bath's residence, I saw a disturbing sight. The charred and cracked body of a man stood on the front lawn with its arms raised up in a prayer to the sky. There were police and medical examiners, reporters and neighbors. I stepped out of my car towards the back of the scene, but I didn't need much confirmation to know it must be Bath there on his lawn, burned raw by perhaps the same heat that I had felt that night not too long ago.

My heart grew heavy knowing that I had set into motion events that had stolen the life of my friend. The Sect of Cygnus was long gone, but it seemed Cygnus still demanded tribute. I moved among the onlookers to get closer to the body of my friend. There was no question that it was him. His wire spectacles were melted onto his cooked flesh, the glass dripped down his cheeks like comical tears. I saw the volume there, in his hand, charred and dropping ash as the breeze jostled it. I recognized what was left of the cover and breathed a sigh of relief knowing that no one else could be swallowed up in its pages.

Bath had longed for understanding and knowledge so deeply that it had killed him. My gaze lingered before I turned away, whispering a silent farewell to my friend.

THE END

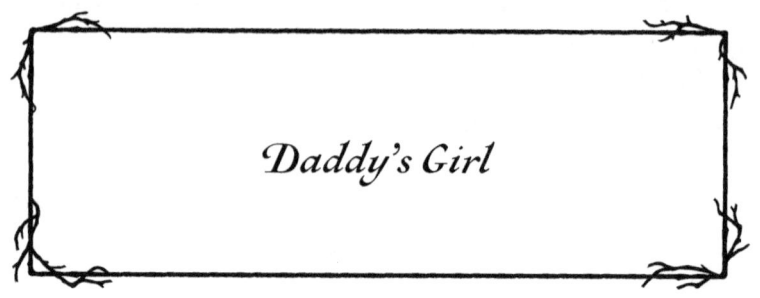

Daddy's Girl

IT'S ON NIGHTS like these that I truly relish the dampness of island weather. It's about midnight now— I heard the church bells not long ago. The streets are almost deserted, save a few bar patrons quitting early and the odd homeless panhandler. They stare at me hungrily, but they know I am untouchable. The quiet of the night is only broken by the soft sounding of fog horns penetrating the miasma. I stop at the statue of Rochambeau and attempt to gaze out at the bay. As the wind switches, it carries with it the clanging of the markers out on the water. Such a peaceful rendition of this island, which crawls with tourists during the daylight hours.

I pick my way down to the shoreline, taking care to avoid the slick black rocks. They lay around like inky black creatures, hunched over in the soft light of the street lamps. A few of them shift here and there as I step on their drier brethren. My father always told me to keep off of the black rocks. That was his first rule. His second was to never turn my back to the sea. Even now on this quiet foggy night I am hesitant to take my eyes off of the water.

The gentle lapping of the waves keeps the infinite swirls

of seaweed convulsing like some colony of rudimentary organisms. A few crabs scuttle in and out of the weed, flirting with the danger of exposing themselves to the giant looming over them. I smile. My father would catch the biggest crabs and cook them in a fire on the beach. Softly I make my way along the water's edge, admiring the toil of all the nocturnal life.

Finally I see the cliffs peeking out of the mists. The rocks at the end of the beach escalate quickly into a sheer cliff topped by the homes of the wealthiest residents of my island. Little do they know of the joys that lay beneath the very foundation of their homes. I strip my clothing off and tie my wild hair into a knot. I savor the cool beads of moisture left on my skin by the fog. It cleanses me of all the negativity and cynicism that has plagued me for the weeks leading up to this moment.

As I tiptoe into the chilly bay water, the full moon makes its presence known. Its gargantuan yellow face shines down on my position, giving a pleasantly eerie light to navigate by. I shiver briefly. I can barely contain myself. The night is too perfect. Despite the warm summer air, goosebumps from the thrill cover me. I plunge into the sea.

The cliffs loom tall as I swim in parallel. There is no bottom where I am swimming. Even I, intrepid shoreline adventurer that I am, cannot fathom what is living below. I feel a kind of nervous excitement that at any moment some leviathan could take me into the depths. I actually giggle to myself and double the speed I am swimming. My father would be proud of his daughter. I see him in my mind's eye, gazing down from the cliffs with an approving smile.

At last I see the dark maw in the solid stone. I paddle

slowly towards it and pull myself into the seaside cave. If the tide was higher I could have swam right in. The pebbles are soft beneath my feet and cushion me as I move deeper into the lightless cave. The moonlight can no longer aid me on my quest. After a few minutes of walking up the slowly inclining path, the cave widens into a cavern. It is as pitch black as the farthest limits of space, but I know exactly where I am headed.

I drop to my hands and knees and crawl forward now, my heart beating faster the closer I get to my destination. The suffocating stench of decay climbs its way into my nose and my hand lands on his withered foot. Tears burst forth and I crawl the rest of the way into his cold dead arms, breathing in shallow gasps. The bugs and crustaceans scatter as I snuggle into the familiar position my father cradled me in when I was a child. He was lost a few weeks ago when the unforgiving waves pulled him off of his habitual night fishing spot. They never found him, but that doesn't matter. He was always there for me when I needed him and now I'll be here for him. I'll always be here.

THE END

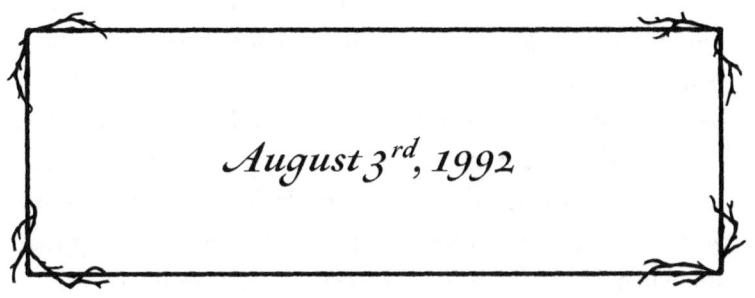

August 3rd, 1992

AUGUST 3RD, 1992. That is the date when the humming started. I remember it well, I was in the middle of reading some short stories when, at approximately 3:00PM, a deep humming buzz began. It was enough to stop my thoughts cold and urge me to get up to discern its source. I assumed I had left the stereo on. It was dead silent when I held my ear close to the speaker. Confused, I moved to the slider leading out to the back yard and threw it open.

The sticky air was laced with the singing of cicadas, yet underneath droned the mysterious constant humming. It seemed to come from everywhere, sounding near and far at the same time. I moved back through the house and exited through my front door. My neighbor was coming up our quiet street led by her new dog, a rambunctious yet somehow noble husky puppy. She had a concerned look on her face, unsettled by the mysterious sound. I waved to her and she and the pup headed towards me.

We spoke briefly while I crouched and tousled the dog's thick ears with gentle hands. He was soft and comforting, antithetical to the ominous sound. The neighbor explained that they had been heading back home when it had started. The puppy seemed unfazed by it. She was going to call her husband, who was across town meeting with a client, and ask if he could hear it from where he was. I told her to let me know.

We didn't speak again that day, and as darkness finally descended the sound stayed uniform. It charged the night air with an uncertain madness. I had no trouble believing that some legion of mutant insects was pouring over the town, destroying everything in its wake. The real insects had changed their tune from the buzz of cicadas to a symphony of crickets. I found it hard to sleep with my ears honing in on the interloping sound. Defeated, I got up and plugged my ears with cotton and popped a valium. The night dark faded into dream dark.

The next few days passed without incident, yet the sound was still there, hanging over my small New England town like a promise of doom. I tried to go about my days as usual—writing, running errands, exercising, but the sound was there, preventing me from focusing fully on anything. At night I could only sleep with cotton stuffed in my ears and a valium in my stomach. Then, on the third or fourth morning, I was thrown out of my black dreams like a car crash at seventy miles an hour.

When I pulled that cotton out of my ears, the full roar of something filled me with dread. It was like wind whipping a flag at the top of a mountain peak, whistling and whizzing. It was separate from the humming sound though, which I could still hear under this new sound as if hiding in the cover of this new sonic intruder. From my bedroom window I could see acrid black smoke rising and swirling in the wind. Were we under attack? Was it a bomb? I clicked on the TV and flipped to the local news.

An unused fuel tank had exploded on the nearby Navy base. So far it seemed that no one was injured by it. The reporter on the scene was talking to a twenty-something-year old who had been in the woods close by when it had happened. His pupils were dilated and he looked paranoid. First he stammered through why he was in the woods by himself, and it became clear to me that he had been out there on a hallucinogenic drug trip— I had done the same when I was his age and I knew how he was feeling.

He then went on to describe a scene that I would eventually become quite familiar with. He spoke slowly, sweat dripping down his temples, trying to make sure his words came out correctly. "The ground just sort of opened up, you know? Like a secret missile silo, it was huge, man. And then this, like, giant truck backed up to it out of the trees and dumped a whole bunch of bodies you know? It was freaky, man." The reporter looked increasingly incredulous, realizing the disreputability of this witness. He asked the stoner about the explosion again.

"Oh I don't know about that, I didn't hear that. I was just tryna bug out of there you know?" The reporter took great care in trying to contain his frustration at this embarrassing turn of the interview. I clicked the TV off. An explosion of a fuel tank. Normal enough, but that humming was still there, filling the air with its stealthy sound.

In the following days, the stories about the explosion died down, but the stories about the mystery sound rose. Scientists were interviewed by local stations about the phenomena. There didn't seem to be any clear consensus on the source. I spent every night with my ears stuffed and in a drugged dream. Nevertheless, the sound found its way in, sneaking through small cracks in my subconscious mind. It took strange forms and danced around my black dreams. I woke up every morning unrested and bleary eyed.

It affected me to such a great extent that I finally decided to go search for its source myself. Yet my drives around town yielded no clues to the source, as the hum remained constant the entire time, never fading and never swelling, taunting me.

That same incessant pitch and note were enough to drive me to anger and violence. In fact, one day after tripping over the carpet in the hallway, I literally put my hand through one of my walls. I seriously thought about leaving town, maybe for good. Anything to find relief. There were others who felt the same as me. I listened in on a town hall meeting that consisted mainly of jeers and exasperated shouting.

The next day, I went out to the woods where the stoner had been. I wanted to have some peace and quiet—well, relative peace and quiet (the humming was still present). I walked through the great pine trees listening to the baseline sound of my world. Eventually I came to a rusty fence that separated the woods from the land of the Navy base. I walked along it for a bit until I came to a hole in the interlocking metal. There was fur stuck in the broken links. A pathway for the deer. I ducked through to the other side.

The trees quickly gave way to a circular clearing of dead grass about the size of a football field. There were large pipes and fantastical metallic mushroom structures sticking out randomly everywhere. Most likely they were a ventilation system for whatever underground buildings the military had spawned. They seemed so strange and alien in the middle of the woods. I continued on, suddenly nervous in the relative quiet. I had not seen a single animal on my walk. There were no squirrels, no rabbits, and certainly no deer. No birds sang. I stopped in my tracks to scrutinize the surrounding scenery. That is when I felt a rumbling in the ground, accompanied by a harsh mechanical squealing.

I took off in its direction, heading back into the cover of trees. It was not long before I came upon the exact scene the stoner had described. A rough dirt road terminated where the ground was opening into a massive black maw. As it did, the humming sound that had plagued me swelled up and spilled out of the pit in the earth. I laughed now, considering that the great mystery might be solved as easily as asking the Navy base to stop whatever machinery was causing the noise, as it was severely affecting my small town.

I looked around and up the road to make sure I was alone before moving to the edge of the pit. It was deep black and there seemed to be some kind of movement far below. Suddenly lights blazed to life down in the pit, causing me to flinch. That is when I saw the source of the humming sound. It was like a massive blender with several wicked scythes spinning endlessly. The chunky blood red liquid it stirred is what put me into a panic. Then I saw a mauled face, one eye still intact, look up at me before being sucked back down into the liquid.

I fell back hard; my legs were numb. I emptied the contents of my stomach off to the side and crawled back past the tree line. Then I heard a far off beeping sound that could only be a dump truck backing up. I was too stunned to move, so I crouched low amongst the trees in an attempt to hide myself. The truck rolled slowly backwards down the dirt road. It had no license plate and no discernible markings. It stopped short of the edge and the driver and passenger exited. They both wore hazardous material suits.

The truck bed rose and a hundred naked humans tumbled out of the truck. Some were screaming, some were obviously dead. A few clung to the edge of the truck and the hazmat men yanked them from the bed and tossed them roughly into the human blender. When the bodies reached the blades below the humming stuttered and the blades revved and powered through the mass of meat. The pit then reached its uniform hum again.

They got back into the truck as the earth began to close back up into its perfectly camouflaged position. After the truck had pulled off, I stood up, nauseously clutching the nearest trunk and sweating profusely. Before I could gag out more bile, the bark next to my head exploded, sending splinters into my face. Warm blood trickled out of my wounds as I ducked. The bush next to me exploded.

Someone was shooting at me. The gun must have been a silenced sniper— I couldn't hear the shot nor see the muzzle flash. I took off running and hoped I could find the deer path again. Luckily I did and I made it back through the woods to my car parked on the side of the road. I got in and sped off without looking back. My engine roared to match my heart as I made it back into town.

Once home, I stumbled into the shower and broke down in tears, having witnessed such a gruesome act of a mass killing. Once it was all out, I felt like I could think, so I dried off and began to write down what I had seen. Halfway through my account I realized how quiet it was. There was no buzzing hum, no giant blender grinding away anymore. I continued to write with even more urgency. I wasn't sure who to go to with the information yet. Maybe the news? The police?

I decided to make a copy of the information and gave it to my neighbor for safekeeping, with specific instructions on where to send the info should I wind up dead or missing. I could tell that I was scaring her and I implored her not to look at what I had written if she didn't want to be deeply disturbed. With that, I left for the police station. On my way there, I was stopped at a light to let a seemingly endless convoy of military vehicles pass by. I grew cold in the summer heat when I recognized among them the unmarked dump truck.

The police did not take my story seriously. I asked them to rewatch the interview of the stoner kid following the fuel tank explosion so that I could point out similarities to my account. I tried the local news who refused to even meet with me. Their broadcast that night spoke of the military concluding some tests that had been going on at the base, thus ending the strange hum. I sneered at the thought of the military conducting tests. Human tests. The people I spoke with seemed to be satisfied with the media's explanation, trusting them and the military completely. I knew better. I had seen things, experienced things.

I attempted to find my way back to the camouflaged pit, but a new fence had been erected— one with razor wire curling like vines. Something had been going on out in those woods. With no answers, I left the events that had transpired alone. Now I hope and pray that that convoy of unmarked trucks never comes back to my town.

THE END

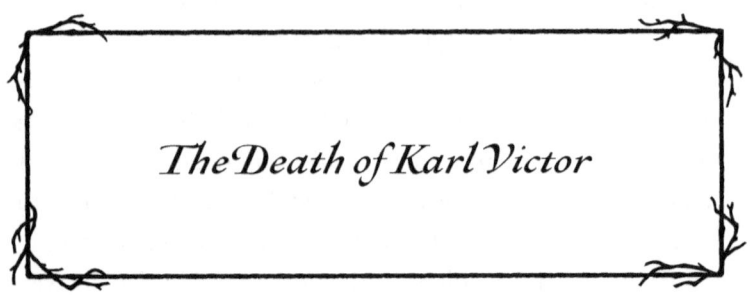

The Death of Karl Victor

My CURRENT mental state is thanks in part to Karl Victor. The morning I offered him some work set into motion events that I do not see myself escaping. My only reprieve would be a nice quiet death. I can't fathom the insanity that awaits outside of my apartment. There is still a cop outside keeping watch, but I don't know what good he'll do. My cheap furniture is stacked against the front door and my television lays on the floor, the screen smashed to pieces.

Karl Victor was always a quiet man. Some would describe his quietness as strange, but I enjoyed his company. He was a career handyman, always around Newport picking up odd jobs here and there. The jobs he took didn't pay much, but he made enough to pay his rent and buy his beer.

We were just arriving home from a week-long fishing trip when I convinced the captain to offer Karl some work unloading our unusually large catch. I liked Karl's work ethic and he was always friendly towards me, so I tried to throw him jobs when I could. We called him up, and an hour later Karl arrived by bicycle. He approached me and I noticed that his eyes were bloodshot. His face was pale and he seemed apprehensive. I had never seen him like that before. Probably just had a late night drinking, I thought.

We exchanged a brief greeting and went to work. He worked as hard as ever, but he seemed off, distant somehow. His arms and legs moved mechanically and his eyes were unseeing. When the day's haul was finished, I offered to buy him a beer. He politely refused, so I asked him if everything was okay—Karl never turned down a free drink. He nodded glumly. I shrugged and, as I turned to walk away, he grabbed my shoulder, his fingers digging into my muscle.

With a wild look in his eyes he whispered feverishly, "Something's gonna happen man, they don't tell me much. I can't leave. They pulled me in and took hold. Leave man, get the hell out of Newport!"

He loosened his grip and stumbled backwards into a jog. He ran off, his bicycle and pay forgotten. I stared after him. The captain came over with a questioning look on his face. I shrugged and told him I'd get Karl's cut to him one way or another. He nodded and handed a sealed envelope over.

Later that night I made my way to Karl's apartment. It was only a short walk from the bar I had just stumbled out of. He lived in a room that had been converted into a studio. The house was ancient and no doubt it was carved up into as many apartments as possible. Newport was full of petty real estate barons who bought ancient homes and partitioned sections of the house into tiny living quarters. They used the location of Newport to jack up the prices. You had to know someone to get a good deal.

I swayed a bit as I waited for Karl to answer my knock at his door. No answer. I could hear his television hissing static, so I went around to an open window. Karl was kneeling on the floor in front of the television, his eyes transfixed on some grainy image. A woman in a dark robe stood in the center of the screen, chanting in a language I couldn't place. I lightly tapped on the window and called out to him. No response. I called again, louder. The television snapped off leaving him only faintly illuminated by the moonlight, frozen in place. The scene was eerie. Suddenly, he stood, spun, and came to the window.

A dramatic change had taken place in his demeanor since this morning. Karl was calm, relaxed. His eyes shone clear. He smiled and said a friendly hello. I held up the envelope containing his cash from the captain. He slid the window screen up and took the envelope with an enthusiastic thank you. He shut the window, and a moment later I heard his apartment door unlock and open.

Out of the darkness he came and stood next to me. He put a friendly arm around my shoulders and asked if I would like to accompany him on a walk around town. It was a little past one in the morning, but I didn't have anywhere to be tomorrow. I had never spent time with Karl other than working a job with him or having a beer at his favorite pub, but there was always a first for everything. So I went. Karl was more talkative than I had ever imagined he could be. He lost me a few times as he moved into deeper topics of conversation.

He spoke philosophically about humanity's place in the universe and hidden knowledge he had immersed himself in when studying the more historical districts of Newport— the ones that had survived the British destruction during the American War of Independence. He spoke of the founding fathers and the secret rites that supposedly led to their seizing of power in the colonies. Newport apparently had been a hub of trade in secrets with ships coming and going at all times.

It really surprised me, hearing Karl speak so intelligently. I knew a bit about history—it was always my favorite subject during my brief fling with community college—but his monologue was revealing an interconnected past far beyond what I knew of my hometown. While I listened to him speak, Karl guided me down twisting, claustrophobic side streets that I had never dreamed existed here. There were broken down vacant houses and ancient dilapidated buildings leaning into each other at dizzying angles. A few windows here and there were lit and a few more held air conditioning units that hummed at the summer heat.

Karl stopped us on a one-way street that had no name. It was more of an alley than a street. There was a rotting Chevy Nova parked on the curb, leaving barely enough room to squeeze another car by. The street didn't look like it was heavily traveled—garbage swirled in the slight breeze. I had lived in Newport my entire life and never had I thought an area like this would have existed. I felt as though I was in a foreign town in a foreign land.

The house we stood in front of was tall and white in the soft starlight. Its roof was sunken in and the windows and doors looked to be boarded up. Karl glided into the narrow gap running between the house and its neighbor. He pulled open a squat door that must have led to the basement of the ancient home. He beckoned me to come closer with a welcoming smile. I was overcome with an intense feeling of dread. Perhaps I had sobered up enough to see the strangeness of my nocturnal adventure. This quiet loner who I barely knew had led me to an abandoned house in the middle of the night after giving me a cryptic warning earlier in the day. And then there was the strangeness of the television scene in his apartment.

I glanced at my watch. The luminescent hands told me it was almost three in the morning. I declined Karl's invitation and told him I was going to head back. He grew irritated and took a step towards me. He looked suddenly monstrous in the moon beams. I turned and began to walk quickly back the way we had come. He followed behind me, his footsteps echoing mine in the stillness of the night. The menacing old buildings passed me by as I picked up the pace. My chest thudded as my heart hammered and my mind was now only focused on losing the man and returning to the safety of my home.

The moonlight grew dimmer as clouds moved in to cover my escape. Turning down an unlit street, I threw myself into some bushes, barely noticing their clawing branches trying to toss me back out. I held my breath and begged the clouds to hold position. Karl stomped by my hiding place without noticing me. I heard him cursing under his breath. I made out one line he spoke— *almost had him.*

I stayed there in that tangle of brush until the edge of the world was lit by the coming dawn. The more time passed, the more at ease I felt. I moved and stretched to thaw out frozen limbs and began a tired search for some scenery I recognized. Barely able to keep my eyes from closing, I made it home practically falling through my front door.

The daylight could not wake me until the early afternoon. The hot sun beams pried my eyes open and willed me to get up. I shuffled into the kitchen to grab a much needed glass of water. There was a hurried knock at the door. I filled a mason jar and downed it before I moved to answer. The knock sounded again before I reached the door. I wondered if it was Karl coming to take action against my leaving him in the early morning hours. Just thinking about his behavior was unsettling.

I cracked the door open. It wasn't Karl. Two portly women, one in a red dress, the other in black, stood on the other side. Their eyes were dark and mysterious. The one in black had a trickle of blood streaming down her forehead. It leaked from under her curly hair. The one in red told me there had been an accident and demanded the use of my phone. Something about them made me nervous, perhaps that they were so calm despite one of them being injured. I told them I would call 9-1-1 on their behalf.

As I went to shut the door, meaty fingers appeared around the edges and the door was shoved back in my direction. Like crackling thunder, my heart leapt in my chest and I threw all of my weight back in their direction. One of them threw their own considerable weight to counter mine. The fat hand still held fast. In a frenzy, I smashed at the hand until it gave up and I rammed the door closed with a final burst of strength. Panting, I clicked the lock home.

The women continued to bang on the door until I heard shouts coming from a neighbor. Then silence. I stood in the living room, afraid to move. At any moment someone or something was going to break down the door. Minutes ticked by, devoid of all sound, until a soft knock shattered the calm. I hesitated before calling out, with a crack in my voice, that I had called the police. Perhaps I should have. A man's flat voice answered. It sounded like Karl.

I moved like a cat to the threshold and peered out through the peephole. Sure enough it was Karl behind the door. Bleary eyed, haggard Karl. His dim gaze darted back and forth before settling on the little portal I spied him through. I jumped even though I knew he couldn't see me. Exhaling, I opened the door.

We both began to awkwardly apologize for last night. I stopped speaking to let him say what he had come to say. He told me to get out. Now. They knew who I was and they would come for me. That's when I noticed the gun in his hand. I thought it was a toy at first. I had never seen a gun and it was as if my brain couldn't process that this man held a firearm.

I could do nothing but watch as Karl brought the pistol to his temple and squeezed the trigger. The whining in my ears convinced me the gun was real. Karl lay dead on my doorstep. Paralyzed, I stood in disbelief of the violent suicide I had just witnessed mere inches from me. Then I ran for the phone. I held the thing in both hands in an attempt to stop myself from shaking. The operator pumped me for information like a machine and before long I heard sirens screeching their way towards my apartment.

The scene was alive with movement as the investigation and cleanup got under way. I despondently gave my statement, which included the events from yesterday and early that morning. I was in shock. After clearing me of any suspicion, a cop asked if I would ride along to identify the white house on that hidden side street. I went with him.

The two of us sat in silence, save for my hesitant directions. Officer Murphy. A good Irish Newport cop. He probably lived in the Fifth Ward, I mused. After what seemed like hours I spotted the Nova down a side street. He pulled onto the street and I extended my arm and a finger to indicate the decaying residence. Murphy left me in the car as he approached the house, his gun drawn and a flashlight held in his off hand. He disappeared into that little side door Karl had attempted to lure me into with his friendly gestures.

I stared at my watch. Officer Murphy had been in there for fifteen minutes before he came out as pale as a ghost. He opened his door and abrasively told me to get out of the car. I got out, unsettled by his sudden change in demeanor. I felt heat in my cheeks thinking that I had done something to implicate myself, but the officer told me to go. I stared at him dumbly for a second and he repeated himself. He wanted me out of there.

As I walked away shaken by the events, I heard him on the radio. I caught him pleading for backup and the state police and medical examiners and the FBI. He became visibly frantic when he was sure I was out of earshot. The scene scared me. My stomach dropped into a blackhole and I felt a numbing sensation like I was losing control of my bodily functions. The suicide of Karl Victor had not been processed by my mind, but whatever had shaken the cop, the dark connections were swirling through my synapses.

I walked home in a haze of contemplation. A few police cars and a crime lab van whooshed by me, but I barely registered them. I looked up and I was home. The bloodstain lay waiting like a welcome mat. I tip-toed around it and entered my apartment, still in a fog. I picked up my phone and called the police station.

The officer that I spoke with assured me that she would send a car to hang around my place. She only offered after I made clear to her my connection to the ongoing case that seemed to be now more than a suicide investigation. I set the phone back down and a few moments later I watched through the half-closed blinds as a black and white auxiliary police car pulled up in front of my house. I could see the officer inside. He popped open a thermos and produced a chocolate doughnut.

I felt a little better, but not much. I decided to relax and see if a little television would keep my mind off of things. Before I could touch the remote, the television snapped on. It was that woman I had glimpsed on Karl's TV screen. I thought I had lost it. I pressed the power button on the remote and nothing happened. She began to dance a suggestive dance, and that same inane chanting I had heard the previous night began to invade my senses. My hands painfully crushed my ears and I shouted. My boot-clad foot went straight into the TV.

The screen exploded in a hiss of static and the entire unit rocked and fell forward onto the carpet, spilling its guts all over the floor. Before I knew what I was doing, almost every piece of furniture I owned was stacked haphazardly in front of my door. I ran around the apartment securing windows and letting the venetian blinds fall. With all of the direct sunlight snuffed out, my apartment was lit by the dull streaks of light slipping between the slatted shadows. Yet I felt no safer. I heard a helicopter somewhere above and heard more sirens pass by. And then all was quiet. Insanely quiet.

I moved to a front window and parted the blinds. The cop car was still there and my heart was still beating at a nightmare pace. I sat back on the floor. A terrible madness had gripped me. The chanting woman, the fat women, that house, Karl's volatile moods, and ultimately his suicide ate away at my sanity like acid— severing brain matter and breaking down the chemicals which made up my consciousness. I stood shakily and went to the kitchen to find some kind of alcohol to ease my mental burden. A quarter bottle of cheap bourbon stood on top of the humming fridge. I reached for it and drained it. I returned to the living room and sat down on the floor.

And I was there—sitting patiently while the sun set, waiting to see what fresh horrors the night would bring. Karl Victor was a friend; he had tried to save me from whatever was coming. He was also my enemy, leading me right to the den of whatever horrible rites those women had used to gain power over him. I could sense it coming like the smell before a rainstorm. The air was charged and I was waiting. Waiting for what? An end to this? The hours passed and I sat decaying in my apartment. My mind thought more and more about Karl's answer to the problem and what my own answer would be. Then I remembered the box of razor blades under the bathroom sink.

THE END

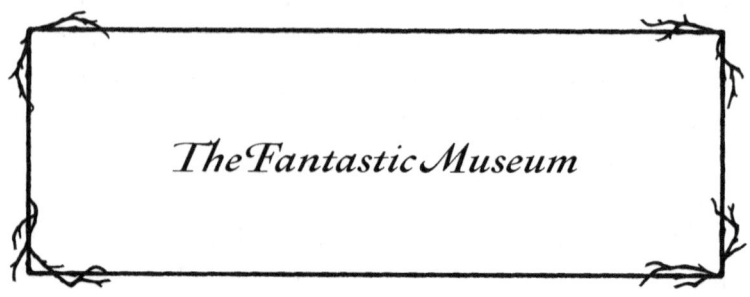

The Fantastic Museum

𝕴 FIND MYSELF in some strange places due to the nature of my line of work. What I do for a living does not matter to this story, but one place in particular altered the course of the rest of my life.

In my younger days, I fell in love with a menacing house that looked as if it had been ripped from a gothic horror novel and dropped onto the shore of a quiet bay. A narrow path cut through tall grass that surrounded the area like a wall. There was nothing nearby besides a quiet little town so common on the New England coastline.

One chilly fall morning, I blundered down an unmarked dirt road and found myself on the verge of my discovery. I had missed the ramp onto the highway and was anxious to turn around. The bends in the path and the tall grass made it impossible for me to see where I was headed, until suddenly the house loomed up, as if sprouting from the marshlands. The bay was nestled deep between the land, so that its treasure was not visible from any of the main roads. Taking in the sight of the place and its thrilling architecture made me almost forget my pressing engagement for the day.

Although aged, the property looked as though it had received regular maintenance. After taking one last look and attempting to backup, the owner appeared at the front door. A skinny old man with more hair in his beard than on his head gave me a tentative wave. I pulled forward instead and rolled my window down to tell him how much I appreciated the look of his home. His eyes grew friendly and asked if I would like a look inside, as the facade did the contents no justice.

I paused in the car for a moment. I was already late for the meeting I had set up with that strange art dealer. What was a few more minutes? The old man could probably give me directions as well, so it made sense to visit with him for a bit. I cut the engine and approached the brooding property. The place felt as though it was emitting some grand unseen presence the closer I got. It was magnificent. Every window and door frame on the outside was a work of art. The man introduced himself as Charles Nicholas and motioned for me to follow him.

The entranceway was decked with impeccable antique jackets and boots, hanging from ornate hooks and tucked into carved cubbyholes. I was hesitant to even step on the fine Persian carpet that lay on the floor so casually. I hung my own coat up over one of his and felt embarrassed at my lack of dressing in the aesthetic of my career. We moved into the main hallway while he began to convey the history of the light fixtures and the staircase and the beautifully gruesome paintings that hung on the wall. Scenes of violent medieval execution and renaissance spectacle caused feelings of awe to well up within me, as I never had experienced art that grandiose before.

We paused at the threshold of a large room packed with medieval artifacts. Priceless relics. Rust-gutted swords and slash-marked shields decorated the walls and tapestries hung about between. The intricate weaves depicted hunts and battles and the odd mythic story. From a cursory look around the room, it seemed as though everything could be dated from the ninth to somewhere in the fifteenth century. Beautiful. Finding it tough to tear my eyes from that room, we moved on.

The next chamber contained occult objects of the Renaissance. Glass display cases lined every wall interrupted only by the doorway and a bookcase here and there. Strange religious paraphernalia sat safe behind glass and the bookshelves contained rare one-of-a-kind grimoires. Most were in languages completely dead and untranslatable, Charles Nicholas explained eagerly, gushing over the room's collection like a proud parent. The memories and energy held within all those objects floated as a miasma to my extrasensory perception. It was I who pulled my host away this time as I moved on to the next room.

It was as if Darwin's theory of evolution had crawled its way into this house and reproduced in this room. Infinite specimens of seashells and dried shoreline critters lined lighted dusty display cases. There were books in this room too: field guides and journals, some no doubt originals, written by the very explorers who brought scientific knowledge to the masses. The vibrancy of life swam around me in the room. My head buzzed as I tried to grasp the priceless contents of this museum of a house.

We floated through the rest of the rooms, becoming more comfortable in each other's presence as we conversed. He claimed to have collected every single specimen himself. I explained to him what I did for work. He laughed and said it was destiny that I got lost and found his home. We went into every chamber save one. It was at the front of the house and I noticed earlier that it was the only window with curtains drawn. The door was shut and I waited to see if he would bring me to it. He never did.

With the day's itinerary forgotten, my host and I settled into comfortable antique chairs in his parlor. They felt more like thrones. He built a fire and poured us each a glass of bourbon—of the finest quality, of course—to chase the chill of the morning away. He had lived alone here for almost his entire life. It was his secret hideaway, his castle. He had no family and no friends, a true introvert. I would have been suspicious of his welcoming attitude had I not been so enamored by his house.

As the conversation went on, I finally saw fit to pose the question of the door we had not traversed. His jovial smile faded into a grave line cutting across his wrinkled face. He made me promise to never attempt to enter the room in question nor mention it ever again. His demeanor was one of deep concern for me, or perhaps something greater—a weighty warning rather than a simple agitated admonishment. His curious answer only stimulated my interest in the unknown chamber more so. I made the promise to him while at the same time resolving to enter the room before I left for the day.

After another glass of fine liquor in the sun-drenched sitting room, I excused myself to use the bathroom. I passed the marbled bathroom wrought with gold and continued on towards the forbidden room, all while staring over my shoulder to make sure I wasn't being monitored. The door was a heavy dark wood, cold to the touch. The knob was glass, loose in its fixture like most antique doors. The knob turned uselessly in my hand, though the door did rattle in its frame a bit. I pressed my ear to the arcane barrier. The house held its breath when I did, deadening the world around me. A quiet insectoid buzzing vibrated through the door and danced about my head.

And then my host was there, at the end of the hallway with a menacing antique rifle. There was a look of regretful terror painted on his face with a frantic brush stroke. He raised the gun. I backed up with my hands in the air, immediately remorseful, praying the old man would not fire at me.

"You've doomed us," He snarled. I started to apologize, but he kept on, "That is no room in this house! It is a tether, a gateway, the roots of our very existence! Whatever it is, it was keeping us anchored to our plane of existence, our universe! You have doomed us, for I fear we are no longer anywhere." His voice lost some of its fire as he finished his words. He lowered the gun and produced a key.

The door swung open and a metallic darkness like a film negative spilled out between us into the hallway. The man disappeared into it. It was a kind of anti-light painting the ceiling, floor, and opposite wall with blackness. The dream-like doorway threatened to swallow me up, to pull the very fibers of my being apart as if it were some black hole. He called for me to follow him back to the sitting room. Carefully I stepped through the negative light, doing so only because it seemed to have not affected my host. I watched my body disappear into blackness and reappear on the other side. The old man stood waiting for me with a white-knuckled grip on the gun. A shiver racked my spine when I turned to scrutinize the strange anti-light.

We returned to the sitting room and I made for one of the

comfortable thrones. My mind was busy trying to process the events unfolding and before I sat, the view from the window caught my eye. An astonishing change had taken place— instead of the calm bay and marshland, an infinite field of dead grassy plains spilled out before us. There was no sun nor moon in the sky. There was no light per se, but there was a general ambient brightness illuminating the landscape. Turning to question my host, I realized he was gone. I made my way to the front door attempting to cut my losses and leave the museum-turned-madhouse.

The front door swung open and revealed the same nothingness I had glimpsed from the sitting room. I walked a little farther out and turned to view the house. There was nothing visible but a rectangle where I had left the front door open. I felt as though I was physically in a dream—not just my subconsciousness, but my conscious mind and body as well. Yet a part of me still reasoned that logically there had to be a way back to wherever we had come from.

Back through the rectangle cut into space I went. I found the old man in his occult room, tearing books from the shelves. He was flipping through them and then tossing them to the ground like rotten vegetables during a harvest. I offered to help him with whatever he was doing. He stopped abruptly as if my sudden appearance had snapped him out of a trance. I was worried his mind had fractured and for that matter I wondered if mine had as well. There was a fire in his eyes and a hopeful grin on his face. "A book with a secret compartment, wherein lies a looking glass. Also another book with blank pages. Yes! I was instructed many years ago on how to go about reconnecting the planes, but I let it slip my mind as countless years wove on. My masters saw this far into the future. We are not doomed my friend, we are not."

Ancient tomes lay about the room in piles by the time we found the pieces to the obscure puzzle. With the book and looking glass in hand, we made haste to the room that was not a room. The old man held the silver dollar sized glass up to his eye and let out a triumphant laugh. He handed it to me excitedly. The circular glass washed away the negative light, revealing what looked like an ordinary four-walled room with a simple podium in the center. I handed the glass back, impressed with its fantastical nature.

The old man then pressed the blank unassuming book into my hands. I looked at it and began flipping through the pages. I was suddenly shoved with more strength than the old man could have ever mustered into the ink black room. I felt as though I was dead, the only sound was the door shutting and locking behind me. The old man raised his voice. "I'm sorry to do this to you." His words sent me into a panic. I dropped the book and began to beat the door with my fists, compelling him to let me out. I stopped and the outside was as devoid of sound as the black reaches of space.

The insectoid buzzing started up again, seeming to shatter the deafening silence. I tried to remain calm when my stomach dropped as that dreadful sound continued to increase from no particular source. I felt for the book in the darkness, and upon grasping it, opened it again, though I knew I couldn't even see my own hands in front of me. Amazingly it now had text on its pages—unusual characters emitting a phosphorescent glow. I could read none of it but I was suddenly aware of some voice reading it to me. Despite the strangeness of the words, I comprehended the information being conveyed. And then I heard bloodcurdling inhuman screams from somewhere outside my prison, inside of the house. The voice reading suddenly stopped and told me the lighthouse keeper had been punished. It made clear that I was an innocent party in the events of today. The lighthouse keeper had betrayed an oath to guard the tether.

The door swung open. I could see real light beyond the anti-light spilling from my prison. I went quickly to the sitting room and was relieved to see the familiar scenery of the calm bay and tall marsh grass. The parlor however was a dilapidated moldy ruin of a room. Every room in the house was devoid of its treasures, replaced by cobwebs, mold and all things relevant to decay. The old man was nowhere to be found. I called a few times and only received creaks and cracks from the rotten house. Dismayed, I wandered out of the house in a sort of daze. My car was right where I had left it. For a moment I was afraid of what I would find outside, but I moved forward automatically. I never even turned to look at the house again. I knew it would only be a ruin of its former beauty. I turned the car around and drove, all while averting my eyes from the property.

Now that I am old myself, I often dream of the treasures housed in that wonderful museum of a mansion. Occasionally I reflect on the friendship that could have blossomed between the old man and I. Where had he disappeared to?

I think I'll hold on to my memories of that chilly fall day. My own collection of objects from my travels has grown significantly, and the house I keep them in is almost as fantastic as that old man's gothic mansion, albeit somewhat safer.

THE END

The Toymaker

GORE DECKER SMILED at his work as he finished up the last little gruesome details of the sculpture. The pint-sized monster that sat before him was inspired by vicious nightmares the previous night. Gore always woke from his nightmares panting and sweat-covered, but he felt satisfaction immediately afterwards, like the dull ache of stretching a tight muscle mixed with the nostalgia of seeing an old flame. Nightmares were Gore's livelihood. Every sneaking creature and every fleeting feeling of horror were poured into the art that he produced.

The little sculpture sat off to the side, forgotten for the moment, and stared at its creator with a multitude of bulbous orb-like eyes. Its python limbs were poised and ready to wrap their prey and fracture bones. Gore mixed a two part silicone with great care. The gooey liquid bubbled and clung to the side of the cup, ready to embrace the sculpture and create a negative mold.

The artist then gently placed the sculpture in a paint splattered wooden box. Next came the silicone folding and diving into itself as it filled the surrounding space.

The monster drowned and spit up a few last bubbles of air. The whole box went into a pressure pot, which was also covered in paint. Gore flipped the compressor on and the chamber did its work, crushing any air pockets that would mar the surface of the mold. These actions had been performed countless times by the artist, with hands that moved automatically. He rarely made mistakes anymore. The second floor studio apartment, which functioned more as an art studio than a living space, was relatively quiet.

The mold would take about six hours to set fully, so Gore pushed himself to fill customer orders in that time. Each of his past creations had slowly gained popularity in the relatively small community of custom toys and collectables. He found himself thinking of hiring an assistant to keep up orders. He had around twenty to package that day. Each figure was delicately wrapped with colorful tissue paper. A thank-you note and stickers that read "Gore Customs" were also thrown in the box. They were then taped up, addressed, and moved to the outgoing pile.

It was a lot of work, but the money that was slowly accumulating in the bank was worth it. The figures being shipped out all stood before him on the table like a hideous army—nightmares brought to life in four-inch figures. The paint jobs had gotten better. Beautifully sleek faces and eyes shone darkly in the light. Gore gazed at his own collection of figures lining the wall as he finished packing up another order. There was a knock at the door that snapped him out of the repetitive task.

As he approached the door, a wrinkled and stained piece of paper was shoved under it. He bent to read the messy words scrawled on it. "Down the fire escape NOW!" Gore stared at it dumbly, not sure if it was some weird joke or prank. He reached for the door handle just as something huge threw itself up against the door. THUMP. Dust fell from the frame and wood cracked. The suddenness of the sound caused Gore to recoil. THUMP. More wood cracked and splintered.

The frightened artist went quickly to his lone window. He pulled the screen up as the being-turned-battering-ram threw itself against the door more frantically. He was halfway down the escape when he heard the door explode inward. He didn't wait to see if whoever or whatever it was followed him to the window. The night swallowed Gore up as he moved into the shadows of the alley. There was an inhuman roar of rage and then silence. The artist, with his back against the cool brick apartment wall, panted and tried to pull himself away from the edge of a panic attack.

He stayed in the blackness and stench of the garbage-filled alley for a long time. There were no sounds, as if the world was dead. Slowly Gore moved back to the fire escape and began to climb hesitantly. He hazarded a glance into his room. It was the same as when he had left it. The door was still shut, the air compressor still hummed, and the monstrous army still stood at the ready on his table. Confusion hit him like a migraine. He had hallucinated. That's the only explanation that made sense. The clock showed 3:21am. Lack of sleep; that had to be it.

Laughing, the beleaguered artist climbed back into his humble studio and shut the screen again. He made a move to the bathroom to splash some water on his face and he saw that same piece of paper lying on the floor. "Down the fire escape NOW!" He stopped and felt unease creeping underneath the relief. He picked the paper up and turned it over.

There was another message. "They'll be back. They need your nightmares." This time he opened the door and sprang out into the hallway. His fear fueled an anger that rose in his throat. The building was as quiet as the night outside.

Once back inside, Gore locked the door and continued back to the bathroom. He flicked the light switch and his reflection stared back at him from the mirror. Seeing his blood-shot eyes and dark circles suddenly made him feel very tired. His reflection blinked. He hadn't blinked.

"Please," whispered his reflection in a glassy faraway voice not unlike his own, "please leave and don't come back. They'll do to you what they did to me. You will be nothingness."

Gore pounded the mirror with both fists in a tired fearful rage. The glass shattered and his hands bled from tiny shards that fought back on the mirror's behalf. His reflection stared back with an eerie teeth-bared grimace. What was happening? Gore decided he desperately needed sleep. He suddenly couldn't remember the last time he had slept. He washed the blood from his hands and did his best to pick glass out from the wounds. Bandaged and washed, the sleep-deprived artist went to his bed.

He didn't dare turn the lights off. He was afraid of what his mind would manufacture in the darkness. It was one thing to experience nightmares in his subconscious dreams, but it was too much to handle in wakefulness. Sleep would make him feel better and the mold would be done curing by the time he woke up. Eventually, with no more hallucinations manifesting, he fell asleep with a pillow over his head.

Morning came like a violent storm; Gore was soaked with sweat and feeling feverish. He stumbled to the bathroom and turned the shower on. He gazed into the cracked mirror warily as if his reflection would reach right through the compromised barrier. The shower made him feel better, but not much. Maybe what he needed was some fresh air and a coffee. There was a coffee shop not far from his apartment and Gore was a regular. They'd fix him up a sweet caffeine cocktail. He shut the compressor off and pulled his cured mold out. That would be his job for the day; casting some tests with resin. He was looking forward to seeing his otherworldly monster come alive.

Gore's footfalls were distant thuds in his feverish head. He felt strange and there was something about the world around him that was a little bit off. He stopped and appraised the swaying trees across the street. His anxiety grew when he realized how still the air was. The trees were swaying, independent of any wind or breeze. He averted his eyes and kept walking towards the coffee shop at a quicker pace. At the door he glanced behind him. The trees were still swaying. The door opened to admit him into the safe little shop.

The windows of the coffee place were covered and the lighting was dim, creating a moody atmosphere. The place was devoid of people. The barista wasn't behind the counter. Perhaps they were in back? What time was it? Gore approached the counter and leaned over it, trying to view the back room area. There was slight movement back there. A subtle sound like cloth rubbing against cloth was steadily rising. Gore called out. "Hello?"

The subtle sound stopped and a different more unnerving sound began. Like the tearing of flesh. Someone or something began crashing through the kitchen towards the front of the shop. Gore froze. Around the corner appeared a gigantic bulbous creature, multiple limbs and multiple eyes all moving in different ways. Somewhere within the thing came a guttural call like a bull gargling water. Gore screamed and fled from the monstrous thing. The thing pulled itself over the counter, knocking the register and cups all over the place. It stood to its full height, almost touching the ceiling. Gore gagged on the thing's stench.

Outside the trees still swayed and somewhere behind the sprinting toymaker, the door to the coffee shop exploded, birthing the otherworldly being into the universe. He ran screaming for help. Nothing living existed besides the waving trees, Gore, and the monster. Then there was a whisper in his ear.

"I told you to leave." It was his own voice.

"Who are you?!"

There was no response. Gore was back at his apartment. He exploded into his studio and slammed the door behind him. He crouched by the window, heart beating and lungs sucking air. The street was empty. The trees waved. There was a deadly quiet in the world and then the horrific flesh ripping sound of the impossible being as it went lumbering by Gore's apartment. It had lost him and let out that guttural gurgling roar once more.

He carefully picked up his phone with the thought of calling the police. There was no dial tone. What was going on? The toymaker sat at the window, defeated. Had he gone insane? He got up slowly and went to the fridge. Despite the insanity of the morning, he was hungry. The refrigerator door opened up to a humid menagerie of mold and insects covering the entire inside. There were no recognizable food items among the purple, blue, black, and green molds. The smell assaulted his nose and stomach and he slammed the door before any of it could escape.

Gore laughed. It was the laugh of a man cracking up. He reached over to the sink and twisted the faucet on, hoping for at least a drink of water. There was a bang in the pipes somewhere below and a grotesque fat centipede dropped out of the tap. It scuttled up and over the edge of the sink before disappearing under the microwave. Gore wasn't even surprised in his broken, defeated state.

"Steal my nightmares? They made them real." He went to his kitchen table and sat in front of the wooden box that held the sculpture in the now-cured mold. The mold came apart easily, revealing the details of his recent sculpture. It wasn't too far off from the thing that had chased him. He put it back together and began to mix up a two part resin that had a five minute cure time. He poured the liquid into the mold, minding the heat it produced from its chemical reaction. Five minutes later he pulled the mold apart, and a marvelous white miniature of the beast from the coffee shop sat before him.

Gore moved to the window with the still warm and slightly pliable figure in his hand. He clutched it to his chest like a protective talisman. Upon reaching the window, he saw the insane beast standing in the middle of the street staring up at him silently. Something within him urged him out onto the fire escape. The monster didn't move from its position, almost waiting obediently for orders from its creator. Gore realized he had created the thing. It was the sculpture he had crafted and birthed into reality.

He continued with purpose and descended the fire escape. The whisper sounded in his ear again. "They were afraid of your nightmares. They were afraid of your power to create." He moved closer to the monster and its ominous stink. It made no sound and made no moves towards the artist. Gore laughed as he began to touch the thing. It was warm and slippery. He held the white miniature aloft while touching the creature.

Gore dashed the miniature on the ground, shattering it into hundreds of resin slivers. The being screamed out, gurgling and growling as it fell backwards. Gore backed up as it thrashed. The trees no longer swayed and Gore began to hear sounds of the city off in the distance. The thing dragged itself with the last of its strength into the darkened alley before dying. The monster's body splashed onto the ground and rapidly drained away like the remnants of a quick summer rainstorm. The artist cackled maniacally. He had created that thing somehow.

A car drove around him and honked, trying to scare him out of the street. To be sure the insanity was over, Gore headed quickly to the coffee shop. He found it bright and full of people talking, laughing, and quietly reading. He ordered his usual coffee and the barista asked about his health, with a look of genuine concern. He was fine. Finally fine. He laughed and paid and headed out of the coffee shop.

A few weeks later, after some noise complaints and a steadily ripening smell of decay, the cops were led to Gore's apartment. They found his dead body curled up on the floor in a fetal position, his hands clasped around his ears. Around his body and littering the house, they found hundreds of grotesque resin figures. Yet the autopsy revealed no apparent cause of death. Gore Decker had just died. They were unaware of Gore's newest creation, however. Had they seen it as the toymaker had seen it (in the flesh), they would have likely suffered a similar miserable, screaming death as Gore Decker.

THE END

The Island Murders

$\mathcal{T}$HERE WERE FOUR of us in our little flotilla of kayaks headed towards our favorite private island. Blake's parents owned it and Theo, Daniel, and I invited ourselves out on an exclusive camping trip. The 'yaks were loaded with a couple of tents, a cooler of food, a cooler of beer, and all of the other odds and ends essential to camping. It looked like we were in for some pleasant weather and the bay wasn't too rough on our voyage. The water lapped and splashed as we paddled. Its emerald depths contrasted beautifully with our red and orange vessels. At some point, we wordlessly challenged each other to a race out to the island. I let the other three get ahead of me. They didn't know that I had been planning to kill them all.

The race was good. They'd tire themselves out and sleep well tonight. The first to go would be Theo. The little shit had always been hard on me about my stutter. I wasn't so bad these days, but in school it still impeded conversations at social gatherings. I would be hitting it off with a girl despite my struggle with words and Theo would burst in. "D-d-d-do you think I'm ca-ca-ca-CUTE?" The girl would blush, I would blush, and all of my *friends* would laugh. Maybe I would cut his tongue out. He snorted and laughed in front of me while splashing water back with his paddle. "Come on, you loser!"

I smiled and continued paddling methodically. Next would be Blake. Blake killed my cat, the only being in this world that gave me one-hundred-percent unconditional love. Penny would trot into my bedroom and see me staring glumly. She would immediately jump up onto the bed and push herself into my lap, purring. She would know I was hurting and she would ease the hurt. Blake and Daniel were at my house after school one day. We were building rockets in the backyard. Blake had the biggest and best rocket, since his wealthy parents bought him whatever he wanted. I had gone inside to get glue to repair my own modest creation. Upon returning, I found Penny with Blake's massive rocket tied to her back. He was giggling maniacally. "You ready to see the first cat in space, man!?" Daniel shied away, not wanting to watch.

I was in tears as I lunged forward to save my best friend. Blake pushed me back and lit the fuse. He whooped and hollered as my cat was carried along the ground bumping and screaming a banshee wail. I swung a fist at him and he knocked me down. "Relax man, my parents will buy you another one. It's just a dumbass cat." I didn't know how to explain to my parents the sudden disappearance of our cat. I feigned ignorance and suggested that maybe she had run away.

Blake reached back with his paddle attempting to knock mine away. I dodged it deftly and smiled at him.

Daniel was last. Quiet Daniel. We grew up together and were close from day one. We were neighbors and we were best friends. At least until we met Blake and Theo. Daniel would stand aside as they tortured me. At first I justified his behavior, thinking that if he spoke out, he would get the same treatment. I could understand that. Eventually Daniel joined in with them, seeking their approval. He betrayed me and left me alone. I was their friend they could pick on. They must not think that any of their taunting broke me down, but it did. I came close to killing myself once. I had my father's revolver loaded and cocked, ready to go. I cried. Thinking about death and the finality of life led me down a darker path. Revenge.

Daniel glanced back at me with hesitant eyes. He always looked at me apologetically these days. Perhaps he sensed the impending carnage.

The neat little island drew ever closer as they raced and I lagged behind with my rhythmic paddling. The quaint little place was shaped like a crescent and had a luscious little forest at the center of it. It took maybe about an hour to walk all the way around on the beach. There were signs sticking out randomly warning curious adventurers to turn back. 'Private Island, Trespassers Will Be Shot!' A bold warning from a snooty family that may have completely forgotten about the island. Theo was first to hit the sand. For his prize, he didn't have to do any of the work setting up camp. He moved to the cooler of beer and snuck one out. He cracked it with glee and chugged it between exerted breathing. "First place, bitches!"

I smiled and the others rolled their eyes. I took my sandals off and sunk my feet into the warm sand. It felt good. I allowed myself to feel the pleasant sensation briefly before sealing the sunshine out. I needed dark thoughts now to help me carry out my plan. Deep black thoughts, like the space between stars. Those thoughts made me feel good as well, despite the nauseous taint of evil. I turned back to the kayaks and us guys who lost the friendly little race went about setting up camp. The tents were up, the coolers were buried in sand, and the fire pit had been dug. I went back to my kayak and pulled out my hatchet. It was a wicked looking thing with a half moon blade and a spike to balance it. The handle was dark mahogany and felt smooth in my hands.

"Holy shit, whadya bring that for?" asked Theo, almost choking on his beer.

"I'm gonna kill ya." I answered him, calmly and truthfully.

The three of them laughed and I laughed with them, though for darker reasons.

"We're gonna need firewood, dipshit," said Daniel, as he eyed the deadly weapon in my hand.

I trudged past them and into the modest woods to find the right specimen for good burning firewood. I found a long skinny tree that had died ages ago and was well seasoned. Perfect wood for a fire. I chopped at its base like a surgeon and began to dismantle it section by section after it fell. I took some twine from my pocket and wound it around the bundle. I slung it over my shoulder and trudged back under the heavy load. When I came back through the tree line, all of the work was done and the sun was beginning its rapid descent. Daniel was tying the last kayak up to prevent the tide from taking it. Blake was the first to acknowledge my presence.

"Hey look! A faggot!" That set the three of them laughing again.

"Very astute observation, Blake." I smiled again at the idiots.

We went to work making a fire and beers were passed around. They had gone through three while I was still sipping my first. I needed to be coherent and ready for tonight. We cooked steaks over the fire and talked about women. When I say we, I mean they, they spoke about women. The conversation made me uncomfortable. They confessed their sins gleefully, detailing sexual harassment committed and borderline rape that went unreported. I held my smile though, and laughed at the right places, swallowing my disgust. The drunker they got, the more they seemed to forget about me. I began sneering at them and answering their occasional inquiries evilly. Only Daniel seemed to catch on, his eyes bright and fearful in the glow of the fire.

The darkness was now complete around us. Insects sang in the interior of the island and the occasional gull called out. The three of them were plastered. Not one could keep his eyes open or lips moving enough to be deemed awake. Only Daniel made it to a tent. The other two passed out right next to the smoldering embers of the fire. Their faces glowed with the dying heat, seeming to reflect the hatred radiating from me. I moved silently to the tree where I had leaned my hatchet. The silver moon had begun to rise and it painted the island with a ghostly glow. It was like we were the only inhabitants existing on an ocean of nowhere. The last four humans left in the galaxy. The stars winked at me and urged me on to do the deed I had been planning for so long.

Guided by the moon now, I reached the very tree where my hatchet would be. It was gone. Perhaps I had placed it somewhere else, or one of the idiots had moved it. I looked around the camp. Theo and Blake lay motionless next to the fire and Daniel's feet stuck out from his tent. I couldn't find it. In the relative silence of the night I heard something slide through the sand and then a light splash in the water. I stopped moving and tried to slow my heart down so I could hear over its thumping. All three guys were still where they were. Another sliding in the sand and a splash followed by a third and then a fourth. I called out nervously. There was no answer.

I crept in the direction of the sound. There was nothing. I stood and strained to hear something in the darkness. Then I realized the kayaks were nowhere to be seen. I fumbled for the flashlight I had in my pocket. It came to life and displayed four eerie oblong shapes floating out into the bay. They seemed to be propelled by some unseen force. I swore to myself and looked back at our camp. The guys were still there. I was frightened at this point. Shaken enough that I began to reconsider if I could murder these three and then stay alone on the unsettling island by myself for the night. Breathing heavily, I moved back to the camp.

The hatchet was gone and the kayaks were gone. There had to be someone else on the island with us. That was the only logical explanation. It scared me, not knowing who or what was out there. It truly scared me. Defeated, I crawled into the tent next to Daniel. I tried to sleep, but it wasn't happening. Every little sound caused the hair on my neck to prickle and my heart to pick up its pace. Then I heard a clear footstep in the sand— soft and stealthy. And then another and another and a vague shadow appeared on the wall of the tent. And then the shadow came crashing onto the tent.

The thing collapsed and I screamed. Daniel awoke thrashing, but the two of us were trapped under the thing that had attacked us. Daniel did his best to try and wriggle his way out of the tent. I managed to get my pocket knife out, cut a hole in front of me and pull my way to freedom. Once out from under the thing, I backed up defensively. Daniel was on his hands and knees vomiting into the sand. The thing on the tent was Blake. He was laying on his back with the whites of his eyes showing and his dick hanging out of his shorts. Lost his balance pissing.

I started laughing at the scene. Idiots. Daniel had passed out again after depositing the unwanted contents of his stomach. It would make a tasty meal for the crabs and creatures of the shore. Theo was gone though. Probably went into the woods to relieve himself. I crawled into the other undamaged tent and zipped it shut. My plan for the night was completely abandoned. Investigation into the missing kayaks and hatchet would have to wait until morning. I finally dozed off with thoughts of "The Willows" by Algernon Blackwood dancing in my head. Our current situation was uncannily similar to the plot of that otherworldly story.

The dream I had was a nightmare. A pale skinny man dressed in black approached me out of infinity. He gave me a toothy grin and knelt.

"Why do you waver, my disciple? Your actions surely are justified. These three men are scum. Their souls should serve no purpose but nourishment for me."

"Who are you?" I was afraid of the answer I would get.

"I am known by many names, by many different peoples. I am nothing and I am everything. I am the meaning of life and the futility of life. Human consciousness was an accident and I draw strength at the winking out of each little light buzzing about your planet. You humans are the only ones. You alone grew a consciousness, alone in the infinite void you call the universe. One day all of the little lights will wink out and I will be complete again. So do what you need to do my disciple. Help me douse the lights of those near you."

The specter moved swiftly to me and I was thrown out of the dream. The warm sun was shining down on the tent and moisture dripped from the ceiling onto my face. Before I could move I heard what sounded like my hatchet burying itself into a damp log. I unzipped the tent and sprang out. Daniel stood covered in gore. My hatchet was in his hand, dripping blood and in his other hand was Theo's surprised head dripping the same thick blood. I retched and tripped backwards.

"Good morning, friendo. I knew what you were up to. I was afraid. Not of you, but of the phantom that had been visiting me in my dreams, urging me to kill. Did you think you were the only one humiliated in life? The only one who suffered? The only one who had shitty friends and shitty parents who showed their love by throwing money at you?" Daniel was pointing the hatchet at me.

Blake was still passed out where he had fallen onto the tent and was now beginning to stir. His bleary eyes took in the site of Daniel the monster.

"What the fuck man? What did you do?" He cried out in a small panicked voice.

Daniel dropped Theo's head and advanced on Blake. He buried the spike of the hatchet in Blake's chest. Blake coughed up blood and began to cry and beg like a child. With his attention on Blake I got up and made my way to the water. I dove in and began to swim as if a shark gave chase. I heard two more sickening thuds and the beach was silent. Daniel had made sure the kayaks would be taken by the tide, Daniel had hidden away my hatchet, Daniel was a cold-blooded murderer. He screamed in rage back on the beach. The hatchet splashed into the water near my shoulder and sank rapidly and then I heard him dive into the bay.

A plan popped into my head. I could dive down and hide beneath the waves until he was over me. I could hold my breath for that long. Then it would be a desperate fight between the two of us. It was the only chance I had. Thalassophobia gripped me, but I also feared my psychotic friend. I dropped myself like a stone into the emerald doom. I could see him on the surface, a thrashing blur against the sun. Unknowable things brushed up against me and I nearly lost my mind. I held for a moment more and then kicked my way hard up to where Daniel was treading water.

I climbed him like a ladder and burst into the fresh salty air. It filled my lungs with a sweet sting as my assailant filled the void I had left. I brought a knee into his bewildered face and I felt a crunch. The water around us became bloody very quickly. Daniel coughed and sputtered and went below again. I took the opportunity to swim back to the island. He tried to give chase, but he had to maintain a focus on keeping himself above the waves. He cried out in a sad hoarse voice, sputtering on half swallowed seawater. As I swam back to the gore-stained shore, my head swirled with memories of Daniel and I when we were kids.

I felt my throat tighten with emotion as I watched him out in the water struggling to breath. We were so close once. He was desperately trying to make his way back to shore when I saw his end approaching. A shark can smell blood from three miles away. This one must have been close by. With a thrash and a confused yell Daniel disappeared into the depths with the appearance of a cutting dorsal fin. I laid back and allowed myself to rest.

I spent a week on the island. With sharks in the water, I didn't risk trying to swim again. The camping trip was only supposed to be three days. Anyone else's parents would have been worried the first day we didn't return. It took our parents four days to realize we were missing. A rescue party arrived to find a very hungry me dozing on the beach a little ways away from two corpses pulsing with maggots. I told them everything that had happened with Daniel's sabotage, his murderous rage, and the shark taking him to the bottom of the bay. A few days later they even found half of Daniel's water-logged corpse, confirming the shark attack. I was truly shaken, but the ending I had planned for remained the same. It was an even better ending than I had hoped; they were dead and I was an innocent man.

THE END

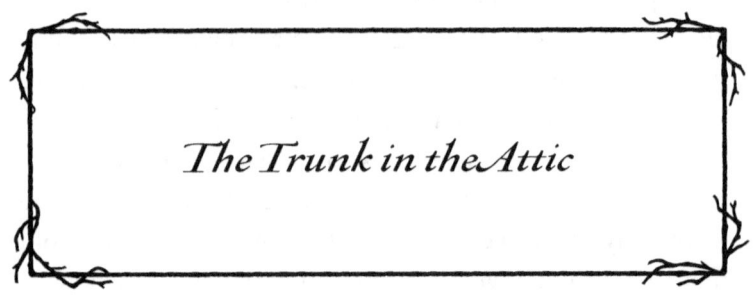

The Trunk in the Attic

*T*ALON SAT IN HIS grandfather's chilly attic. Earlier, he had been implored to go outside and join the cousins playing football. Talon agreed, but then slinked off to the room that led to the attic. He could take the cold and the dying leaves, but the thought of interacting with the other boys in the family revolted him. For the ten years he had been alive, his cousins had caused him nothing but grief. They locked him in dark rooms, abandoned him in the woods, squished his pet spider, pushed him into the brook, and did whatever they could to make him miserable during family gatherings. The adults didn't know all that had happened, but what they did know, they chalked up to boys being boys. Talon went off to his grandfather's attic to escape the realities of boyhood.

The November air penetrated the walls and caused Talon to shiver more than once. The attic was a special place, for it was filled with treasures collected throughout his grandfather's long life. Talon walked carefully, trying to keep his step light. He did not want the adults to hear the stealthy footsteps of a child above their heads. Every single thing in the attic was amazing to the imaginative boy. He sat staring wonderingly at an antique globe with a few differences from the one he had in his own room. Then he heard a whisper.

It was a whisper in the attic. He heard it above the shouts and giggles of the boys outside and the roaring laughter of the adults below him. Those sounds seemed to fade and he heard it again, clear as crystal. "Talon," the whisper said. His name. His special name, not the one his parents gave him, but his own secret code name he had given himself.

In his mind he was Talon of the Northern Border, a heroic Germanic warrior he would make up stories about. Talon of the Northern Border was strong and helped his people survive the dastardly Roman Empire. He did not let anyone who crossed him get away with it. Talon took the name for himself in the hopes of feeling a little power within his ten-year-old self. He did not feel powerful as the whisper reached his ears.

Talon called out in a quiet unsteady voice, "Hello?"

His eyes fell on an antique trunk at the far end of the attic. He cautiously moved towards it, willing himself forward courageously like his barbarian hero would. As he approached, he became aware of a whispery muttering, like someone speaking to himself in a closet. It was coming from the trunk. The trunk was wooden and held together by rusty strips of iron. It was locked shut with an outrageous padlock.

Then he heard his name. His real name this time, his Christian name. He lost his nerve and began to back away from the chest. He heard his name twice more before realizing it was his mother calling outside for him. Talon panicked and descended the attic stairs into his grandfather's office. His grandfather stood in the door waiting for him. The hard old man glared with icy blue eyes set in a sunken wrinkled skull of a face.

"Do not ever enter the attic again, my boy. Do not EVER go near that chest or speak of it to anyone. Your parents are leaving." He moved aside from the door, content with his reprimand. Talon gulped and fled to the living room to find his parents. Somehow Talon had been in the attic long enough for the day to grow dark. His mother and father were collecting their things and saying goodbyes. The little family left.

Talon could not stop himself from thinking and dreaming about the strange trunk in the attic. He imagined Talon of the Northern Border snapping the massive lock right off and pulling out whatever had whispered his name. He would teach it a lesson for trying to scare him. The boy became obsessed with it and attempted to question his parents about its origin. They had no helpful answers. A month later the little family was getting ready to head to the same house to celebrate Christmas.

Now that a biting winter had set in, Talon would be locked up inside the house with his dreadful cousins. The adults banished all of the children to the basement straight away. Talon followed the other boys down into the dark dungeon, hesitantly. Once at the bottom of the stairs he was immediately put into a headlock. He could feel hot tears already welling up behind his eyes. "I have to go pee!" he yelled out. The other boys laughed. The headlocker let go, disgusted that the kid may have an accident on him.

Their laughter chased Talon up the stairs. Waiting for him in the hallway was his grandfather. All he had to do was glare at Talon to make his will known. Stay out of the attic. Talon knew, but he was going to go there anyway. He snuck by his grandfather and went into the bathroom. He stayed there for a couple of minutes planning his route to the attic. He didn't actually have to pee, but it felt right to follow through with his lie. Before they had left their little home, Talon had hidden a pry bar under the back seat in his father's car.

He slipped out of the bathroom and tiptoed to the front door. Adult laughter roared and glasses were clinked. It was not hard to go unnoticed with all of the noise. Out into the icy night Talon went and returned with his weapon, a long yellow pry bar he had found in his father's tool shed. He tiptoed back through the house and peeked into the room where the adults had gathered. His grandfather sat in his recliner grinning over a glass of wine. He seemed distracted enough, but Talon still feared his grandfather would somehow know that he was in the attic.

A few more stealthy moves and Talon was back in the icy attic room. It smelled stale despite the fresh winter air pouring in through the uninsulated walls. The trunk stared at him. He moved toward it and heard its muffled whispers again, just as he had a month ago. He steeled himself and closed his eyes, envisioning himself as the hulking barbarian brute, Talon. He jammed the pry bar behind the lock and threw all of his weight onto it. Nothing budged. He put a foot onto it and stood on the yellow bar. He began to jump up and down and there was a crack.

The lid had moved a little. He removed the pry bar and stuck it underneath the lid and did the same dance on top of the thing again. There was a louder crack and a pop and a rushing of air as if a vacuum seal had been broken. Wispy gray smoke began to pour from the cracks the pry bar had made. There was a muffled laugh that grew and morphed into an agitated growl. The trunk thumped and slid toward Talon who had dropped the pry bar and began to back away. His temporary bravery had completely faded and he was scared enough to wet himself.

Talon ignored the wet spot on his pants and scrambled down the attic stairs. He folded the staircase up and carefully pushed it back into the ceiling. He quietly and carefully snuck his way back to the basement, ready to submit himself to the torture of the other boys to serve as an alibi. Once in the basement, it took his cousins a little while to notice that he had in fact peed himself. They all laughed and uttered exaggerated cries of disgust. Talon stood in the center of the damp basement letting tears stream out. He barely noticed the bullying, he was entirely consumed by what he had experienced in the attic. One of the boys ran upstairs and returned with Talon's mother.

His mother attempted to calm him down with a gentle voice while admonishing the other boys for making fun of him. They grew quiet and spoke half-hearted apologies. Along with his mother and father, Talon fled the party prematurely. He sobbed on the way home. His father looked back at him uncomfortably and his mother spoke about the other boys making fun of his accident. Talon tuned them out. His anxiety had reached levels he never knew existed. Something was in the trunk and he had almost let it out. He felt overwhelming guilt at not heeding his grandfather's warning. No doubt his grandfather knew exactly what was in that trunk.

Talon had nightmares when he finally got to sleep that night. He woke screaming as the trunk opened, swallowing him up into complete blackness. His grandfather came to him pleading for help. The boy's parents did their best to comfort him and get him back to sleep. In the morning, Talon awoke from one last fitful bad dream to find his mother crying softly in the kitchen. She saw him and motioned for him to come give her a hug.

"Sweetheart, your grandfather isn't with us anymore." Talon pondered on the meaning of that. Did she mean he was dead? She did. The little family went later that day to start packing his house up and choose a suit for him to be buried in. Talon overheard the adults talking. His grandfather had died in his sleep, seemingly of natural causes, after everyone had left the Christmas party. Talon's stomach sank. He wandered away from the adults and came to the stairs leading up to the attic. They were pulled down and the dark threshold seemed to beckon him up.

He began to climb the stairs slowly. When his head was in the attic he quickly scanned with darting eyes for any creatures loose. His eyes fell on the trunk. It was thrown wide open. Talon shakily pulled himself up into the attic and approached the trunk for the third and final time. The padlock lay shattered on the floor and the wood of the lid was splintered in places. A thick musty smell of death and decay wafted out from the velvet lined box. "Talon..."

An echoing whisper sounded behind the boy and he spun in time to see some dark shapeless form disappear down the folding staircase. He screamed and was paralyzed. He couldn't move until his father appeared in the attic and took him by the shoulders. Instead of comfort, his father reprimanded him for playing in the attic before dragging him down the stairs and out of the house. He sat him in the car and told him to stay there.

Talon stayed. He sniffled away some snot and tears and

tried to comprehend recent events. Out of the corner of his eye he saw the same dark form, untouched by the bright crystal sunlight, disappear into the adjacent woods. Talon screamed again and locked the doors to the car. He fell to the floor and shivered while hugging himself tightly. Something was out there. Something his grandfather had kept. Something Talon had let out. Something that had taken his grandfather. Something he couldn't comprehend.

THE END

SULLEN FANTASIES

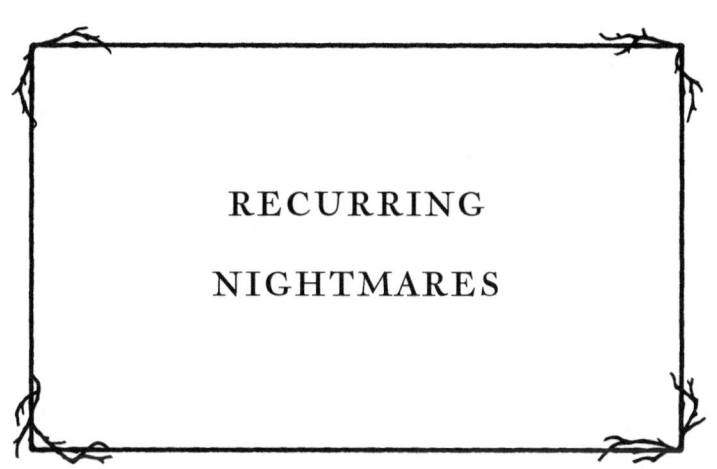

RECURRING

NIGHTMARES

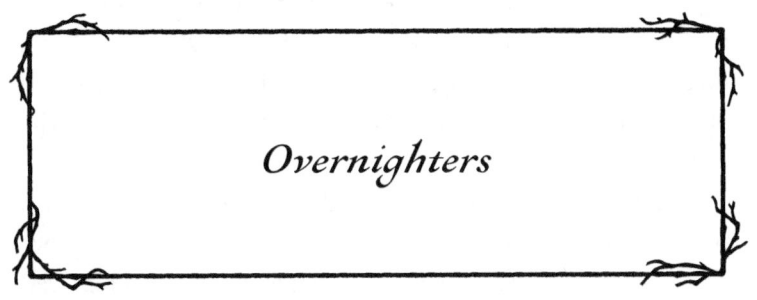

Overnighters

FLOYD LOOKED UP from his book as the mechanical doors banged open to admit one of his late night regulars. Every Saturday morning around 3:00 am Pavel would stop in after his last pizza delivery and spend some time shopping and chatting with Floyd. Occasionally, Pavel would even bring Floyd and the overnight pharmacist free pizza. Working the overnight shift was rough, but it did come with a few perks.

"Floyd buddy! How you doing tonight?" Pavel exclaimed breaking the silence in the store with his heavy accent.

"Hey. I'm tired, Pavel. How are you?"

"Oh, me too man. Happy to go home, you know? Hey, I got a pizza for you guys."

He held up a box that had escaped Floyd's notice. A smile crawled across the cashier's face and he moved around the counter to take the box.

"I don't know if you saw, the lights are out in your parking lot, buddy."

Floyd peered out the window into the inky blackness, the moon hidden behind thick clouds. All of the parking lot lights had gone out at some point in the night. The only cars outside were Floyd's F-150, Pavel's little shitbox Nissan, and Liz's Beemer. Liz was the overnight pharmacist. Floyd shrugged and went back to reading as Pavel moved into the aisles to shop.

The arrival of the Pavel and the pizza gave Floyd a much-needed jolt of energy. He hadn't been able to nap before his shift and caffeine wasn't having an effect on his tired mind anymore. He reached over and sucked down the last few sips of an iced coffee out of the styrofoam cup that held it and tossed the empty thing into the trash can.

His eyes scanned the page to find his place again.

A few minutes later the doors banged open again causing Floyd's eyes to snap open. He had started to doze without realizing it. A tall long-haired man with deep purple bags under his eyes had entered looking around wildly before he spotted Floyd and raised his arm. The man held a gun. Floyd stared dumbly, his tired mind trying to process what was happening.

"Get over here. Now. Lock the doors. Do it!" The man demanded.

Dazed, Floyd moved automatically to the doors and shut and locked them. The man moved behind the counter with the gun still trained on Floyd and unplugged the phone. Pavel wandered up to the front with a gallon of milk in his hand and a questioning look on his face. The armed man trained the gun on Pavel.

"You, get over here. Both of you give me your cell phones."

Pavel dropped the milk and it exploded all over the floor. He looked over at Floyd who swallowed hard and nodded. They both obeyed and held out their phones to be collected. The armed man grabbed Pavel and held him close.

"Please, I have a family. Please don't do this, please!" Pavel cried.

"Shut up. You," he pointed to Floyd with the gun, "go get the pharmacist's cell phone and unplug the phones back there. Do it or I'll shoot this bastard." He pushed the gun into Pavel's neck and the pizza man began to whimper. "Is anyone else in here?"

Floyd shook his head.

"Good. Don't do anything dumb. Bring the pharmacist back here when you're done."

Floyd moved back toward the pharmacy and the gunman turned his attention to the darkness outside. Floyd heard him muttering and cursing under his breath as Pavel blubbered and prayed.

Liz was tapping away at the computer and cracking open bottles of pills to count. It took her a moment to notice Floyd standing there. She was cheery despite the same overnight tiredness in her face that Floyd had so recently shaken off—nothing could have woken Floyd up better than the appearance of the gunman.

"Sup, kid." She said with a tired smile. "I saw your pizza friend. Does that mean we've got something to eat?"

"Liz, there's a guy with a gun. I need your phone and he wants us to unplug all the landlines. He said he'd shoot Pavel if we try anything." Floyd's voice quivered.

Liz's smile dropped. "Did he say what he wants? We need to comply with everything he says."

The two of them unplugged all of the phones in the pharmacy, Liz shrugged out of her lab coat, and they approached the front with their hands up. The pharmacist held her phone out to the gunman and he took it. The man seemed to relax when he had all the phones. He released Pavel—who now had a dark stain in the crotch of his jeans—and shoved the gun into his waistband. Pavel sat down on the ground and hung his head weeping.

"I can get you all the money in the safe upstairs and—" Floyd began.

"I don't want the goddamn money, kid."

"Are you looking for drugs? I can—" Liz began.

"No! Just shut up. Hand me that pizza box."

No one moved. They didn't know how to respond to a demand for their free, lukewarm pizza. Had he asked for money or drugs the overnighters would have rushed to comply. The gunman rolled his eyes, pushed past Floyd and scooped up the pizza box.

"Y'all can call me Tommy. Who are y'all?" He pointed with a piece of pizza.

"Floyd."

"Pav-Pavel."

"Liz."

"Good, we're all acquainted now. Have some pizza and relax, I'm not gonna hurt you."

None of the hostages made a move for the pizza.

"I bet y'all are wondering why I'm here." Tommy said as he bit into his third slice.

No one spoke.

"There's something out there. Chasing me. It doesn't like the light and y'all are the only 24-hour joint in this hick town."

One of the fluorescent lights overhead flickered, startling Tommy. He stared up at it and the light went out. He looked at each of them gravely.

"Shit." He said.

"I don't see anything out there, sir." Said Liz who had her nose pressed to the glass.

"I saw it." Whispered Pavel, his eyes downcast. "Three little glowing red balls."

"Its eyes." Tommy said.

Another light flickered and went out. There was something moving outside underneath the window, tapping and scraping against the concrete sidewalk.

"What is it?" Floyd asked.

"I don't know," admitted Tommy who had drawn the gun again. All of them stared outside trying to pierce the darkness with tired eyes. "My plan was to stay here until morning and then move again, but I don't know if we'll last that long with the lights already going out."

Two more lights in the middle of the store flickered and died. The silence was suddenly too much.

"What should we do? Why not call the police?" Asked Liz who still seemed skeptical.

"I don't want to go to jail. That's why not. I already shot someone on my way here. I missed that goddamn thing and hit a guy walking his dog. So, I'm a murderer now. And what do you think would happen when the cops got here? They'd open the door and the damn thing would be inside in an instant tearing all of us apart."

Shadows began to take hold of the store as another few lights went out. At the rate the lights were dying, it wouldn't be long before the store was plunged into total darkness.

"Shit." Tommy swore again at the lights. "We have to barricade ourselves in your stockroom. Once it's dark in here, those doors won't keep it out for long. Let's move."

The hostages moved toward the back of the store with

Tommy bringing up the rear. The front of the store was now lit only by the neon 24-hour sign. It began to flicker and went out as they reached the stockroom door. The dim emergency lighting flickered on and bathed the store in a strange other-worldly glow.

Floyd fumbled with the keypad trying to put the right code in but kept hitting extra numbers. The light blinked red again and again. Liz grabbed his arm and put the correct code in with her own steady hand. Floyd looked at her and gave a meek, thankful smile. They all went through the swinging door.

Tommy directed them to start piling shelving and boxes up in front of the entrance. The grating of the shelving being pulled from the walls was ear-shattering. Heavy products were piled in front of the door and the shelving was wedged against the mountain of debris.

Through the window in the swinging door they watched as the emergency lights flickered off. Something began beating at the front doors. Pavel whimpered. They worked rhythmically with Tommy watching over them until they heard glass shatter.

Pavel began gibbering to himself and he turned and sprinted to the fire exit and threw his shoulder into the door which didn't open. In his panic he failed to notice the bar that said push. He smote the door with his fists and cried words in his native language. He gave up and sprinted farther into the stockroom as some of the lights illuminating the overstock began to flicker. Pavel found another fire exit and began to beat it. Tommy was right behind him.

"Hey get back here! You open that and I shoot." Tommy shouted.

Tommy took aim at the panicked man with his gun. He squeezed the trigger without waiting to see if Pavel would comply and the shot echoed strangely through the stockroom.

The delivery guy fell against the door and slumped to the ground wheezing ragged breaths. Tommy stood over the body in shock as something threw its weight against the stockroom door. The pile they had used to barricade it shifted.

Liz and Floyd made a run for the receiving door which lay in the opposite direction of Pavel's body and the crazed gunman. The cashier yanked on the chain to pull the door up and the pharmacist dropped to her stomach and rolled underneath as a shot rang out. The lighting in the stockroom died all at once and the only light came from the pale moon hanging over the world now free of its cloudy veil. Once both of them were out of the building, they took off running into the silvery field abutting the back of the plaza.

Another shot rang out and then a scream that was cut off by an audible crunch. The escapees turned to see three glowing red orbs peeking out from under the receiving door. When they turned to run again their hearts grew heavy. Out in the distance they saw four or five more groupings of the same three glowing red eyes parting the tall grass. There was more than one of the creatures out in the inky darkness.

They ran, but it was no use. The overnight shift had tired their bodies and before long their muscles gave into exhaustion. Floyd fell and screamed as the creatures pounced on him. Liz fled for a while longer, though she eventually took a bad step and twisted her ankle. The creatures were on her before she could attempt to stand.

The police never found any bodies, only the blood of

Pavel on the door and Tommy's gun. All four missing persons cases remained open. The store opened back up two days later with a fresh help wanted sign in the window.

Business went on as usual.

THE END

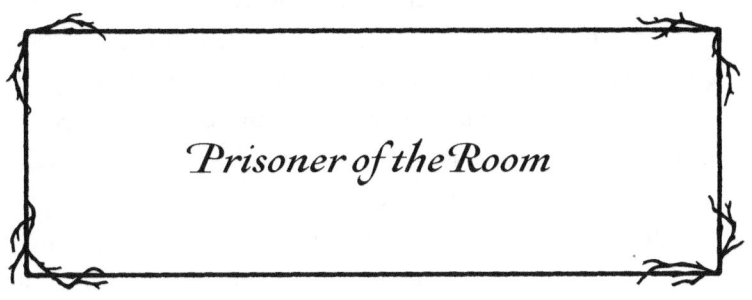

Prisoner of the Room

S HE OPENED her eyes and came to the horrific realization she was trapped in a tank of bitter-tasting water. Her hands flew forward and were met with thick glass and she screamed, countless bubbles of air pouring from her lips. The screams sounded almost dreamy to her submerged ears. She was going to drown, she was sure of that.

She sucked in and gagged on the water. It meant to kill her. Before she lost consciousness, there was a mighty rushing sound and the thick glass in front of her slid down into the floor. The water flooded the room before disappearing into a drain at the center of the floor. She fell to her knees and then flopped to her belly, vomiting up the fluid she had unwillingly consumed as the drain sucked it down greedily.

The small room she was in was harshly lit. She pulled herself up onto legs that did not seem willing to support her and surveyed her new prison. Directly across from the chamber that had held her captive was the mummified remains of another human. The body hung on the wall with arms outstretched and various wires and tubes embedded in the thing's paper-like flesh. The corpse was female.

She shuddered as a familiarity she couldn't understand crawled into her thoughts. When she pulled her gaze from it, she saw that the floor was littered with bones. She gasped, and her eyes moved back up to the remains on the wall. Next to the corpse's head was a message scratched into the metal.

"Break the mirror! Get out before—"

Whoever wrote the message didn't get a chance to finish. To her right was a mirror that occupied the top half of the wall. She stared at her nude body and touched her face. Bright blue eyes stared back. She was completely hairless, smooth as a newborn...what had happened to her feathery blonde locks? She slid a hand over her bald head and couldn't help but stand in awe of herself. It felt strange to be standing there, alive. Memories began to push through her clouded thinking like germinating seeds in the spring.

A mechanical noise caused her to forget her reflection. She spun to meet the new threat. A three-foot by three-foot section of the wall opposite the mirror slid up to admit a one-armed robot on treads. It was a glaring orange machine that looked as though it belonged on the assembly line in a car factory. It drove towards her innocently enough with its one arm and claw bowed in deference.

Break the mirror, break the mirror, break the mirror. The instructions echoed louder in her head as the thing moved toward her at an easy pace. She looked around for an object, settling for a strong-looking femur from the pile of bones before her. She swung it at the mirror once, then again. On the third hit, it shattered inwards revealing a vacant office dimly lit by one red emergency light bulb. The sounds coming from the robot behind her caused her to look back as she crawled through the broken glass.

She spun to see that its one arm had split into five. She screamed and four of the thing's limbs shot out and deftly caught her wrists and ankles. She thrashed and struggled against the thing, but to no avail. It backed up and rotated so her back was to the mummified remains hanging on the wall. There was another mechanical noise and she heard the corpse slide from its place to crumple onto the floor amongst the bones.

She fought, thrashed, and screamed, but there was no one to hear her pleas for help.

"You bastard! Let me go, please let me go!"

It pinned her against the wall. She began to whimper and cry as she felt wires and tubes penetrating her. Metal bonds slid around her neck, wrists, and ankles. Once the robot was done inserting all it had to, it retreated back into its hole. She hung there on the wall, aching in the areas where wires and tubes had invaded her body. Hanging there, she again felt a cold familiarity.

When she blinked her tears away she saw the sign bolted to the wall above the chamber that originally held her.

"Bob's Cloning Facility: Trade in your old model for a new one!"

The chamber across from her resealed itself and filled back up with the same bitter fluid which she had been birthed out of. She understood now. This cycle had happened many times before, and it would surely happen again.

THE END

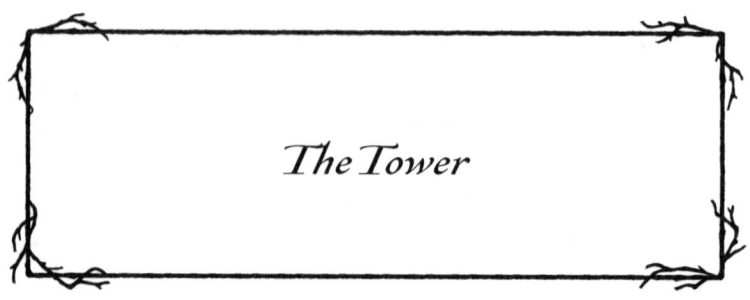

The Tower

I KNOW I'M GETTING close to death when every financial publication wants to interview me about my billions. They all want the same thing; the secret of how I did it. It's not like I built my empire up from nothing. Like Alexander the Great, I inherited what my father had built and maximized its usefulness. But you're different. You want to write about my personal life. Why is that? When we spoke, you were specifically interested in what happened to my marriage. It's actually quite a story, and I don't expect you to believe it, but what reason would I have to lie? From what I remember...

My driver had trouble finding the place. Specifically, he had trouble finding the road that led to the massive tower which stood above all else in the vicinity. It was a hard building to miss on the coast of that sleepy little New England town. Long ago it had been a wire factory and, in the years following the decaying manufacturing industry, an enterprising businessman had converted the tower into luxury apartments. I grew up in the area and I remember hearing stories about the factory. Stories that almost ensured that the building was haunted, if you believed in that sort of thing.

A few years before the place closed, a disgruntled worker had brought a pistol to work with him. He shot the foreman and attempted to shoot himself, but only managed to blow his jaw off. He was tackled to the ground by a friend of his who had described the gruesome scene to my father. I was never supposed to hear that story when I was a kid, but of course I eavesdropped on almost every dinner party my parents hosted.

There was a high rate of turnover near the end. Those employed at the factory experienced severe fatigue, even those with less labor-intensive tasks. I once overheard my father's friend—a local doctor—whispering his unease at the amount of prescriptions for sleeping pills he had to write for the factory workers. My mother laughed at that, claiming that everyone needed sleeping pills these days. Others joined in on the joke, but I saw the look on that doctor's face. It was like he knew something else about his patients that he couldn't share.

A few years after the place had closed, some local teens went missing. A year-long investigation dragged on until at last they found the remains of the teens in the basement of the place. I remember my mother and father volunteering to head up search teams in the woods near our neighborhood. Soon after the discovery, details were leaked to the media about the crime. There were reports of runic symbols and strange drawings on the walls where the bodies were found. The Church claimed Satanists had sacrificed the boys. Their killers were never apprehended. I had too much imagination in me and despite my age, I spent most nights sleeping on the floor in my parent's room as the case wore on.

I suppose I always had a morbid fascination with the old

tower. My heart fluttered the day I received a piece of mail cordially inviting me to view the spaces available for purchase in the apartments. Whoever had sent the letter knew that I had grown up in that town. At my wife's urging, we made plans to go and we were on a flight to Boston the next day. I had never taken my darling Elizabeth to my hometown in all our years of marriage, so perhaps her hope was that we would purchase a summer home and spend some time there.

Elizabeth sat across from me in the limousine with her feet in my lap. She stared intently at her phone, vigorously tapping the screen. I pulled her heels off and began rubbing her feet.

"Honey, this is supposed to be like a vacation. Those idiots can wait a few days for their emails."

She looked up at me with the same intensity, but her face softened immediately. She handed me her phone.

"You'd better hold on to this then."

The two of us had taken my father's company and drastically increased its profitability since he gave us the keys. The old man wished us luck with what he had built and disappeared on a flight out to China. The last I heard from him he was somewhere in the Himalayas, living out the remainder of his life as a Buddhist. I think he reached a point where he was content with everything he had done in life—there was nothing left for him but to be at peace with himself. I thought that was horseshit. I like being rich.

The driver finally turned down an unnamed road that wound through old abandoned warehouses. Broken windows full of darkness peered at us. I had to stop myself from staring into them, my eyes would eventually see things that were not there. It was hard, but I finally tore myself away from the scenery when my wife shook my shoulder. Apparently, she had been saying my name and I hadn't responded. Strange.

"You okay?" She asked.

"Yeah, I was just staring at those buildings. Maybe we should buy those properties up and convert them into our own luxury apartments."

I hadn't told her any of the gruesome stories that had been generated at the factory. I thought it best to leave those details out. The narrow road and archaic buildings suddenly gave way to lush green grass; a private golf course for the tower's residents. It was a beautiful day, but only one solitary human was out on the green. He leaned on his club and watched as we drove by. I was never much of a golfer, but Elizabeth put all the guys we played with to shame. Most were indignant at being beaten by a woman and that's why I loved playing with her.

The man on the course raised a hand in a hesitant wave. As the limo rolled downhill towards the tower entrance, I could see the private marina. There were only two or three boats docked. The place didn't really look like it was thriving. We pulled up to the entrance as a woman in a sharp suit stepped out of the gilded doorway. She had to be Jordan. We spoke over the phone that morning when I called to set up a showing.

Once out of the car, introductions were made and apologies for our tardiness were accepted. As the women walked into the building, I knocked on my driver's window. He rolled it down.

"Yes, sir?"

He was a polite kid, very professional. I handed him a hundred.

"Go get us some burgers, grab yourself whatever you want. There's a place we passed in Newport, an old friend of mine owns it. Here's the address."

I typed the address into his phone.

"Right away sir."

"Know what? Grab a six-pack too, some exotic IPA or something. We'll have burgers and beer on the lawn when you get back."

He nodded and proceeded to drive back the way we had come. I turned and followed the women into the tower.

The lobby was palace-like. Marble sculpture and Romanesque architecture pervaded the place. The atmosphere was magnificent. I heard my wife's breath catch as she examined one particularly gruesome marble statue. She ran a company with me, but her true passion was sculpture. Jordan had been explaining the concierge service available to us when she realized we were no longer listening. I joined my wife in appraising the hideous thing.

"You seem captivated by this one, my dear." Her lips worked as I spoke.

"I've seen this before." She whispered.

"Well I'm sure there are others like it."

"Oh sir, there are no others like that statue. It's one of a kind, a gift from one of the tower's first residents." Jordan had joined us. "If you'd follow me this way I can show you the fitness center. We have all the amenities of a private athletic club right here on the tower's grounds."

Jordan walked away without waiting to see if we followed. I grabbed Elizabeth's hand and squeezed it tenderly. I watched her eyes trace up and down the statue's form one more time. I had to admit, it invoked something strange within me, a feeling unlike anything I've ever experienced. It was a sort of dread blended with an intense excitement. The thing's ghoulish eyes still danced in my head as if it had watched us leave. Elizabeth snapped out of her trance as we moved farther away.

"I think I saw it in a dream, but it wasn't marble. It loved me, I think."

I laughed. "It freaks me out. The anatomy of the thing is just slightly inhuman and its eyes are piercing. Like a ghoul in a funhouse mirror."

Elizabeth grimaced at me.

The three of us stood on the edge of an Olympic-sized pool. The water was completely undisturbed. It was as if a sheet of glass had been laid over the whole thing. I crouched and poked a finger into it. Ripples fanned out. We continued past exercise equipment. Rows and rows of machines and weights that all looked brand new and untouched.

"How long has the tower been open?" I asked.

"We're coming up on twelve years in September." Jordan continued with her tour.

"All this shit looks completely untouched. It kind of weirds me out." I whispered to Elizabeth.

"Nothing is weirder than that statue. I don't know if I could come home every night and be greeted by that thing."

We made our way back to the lobby and Jordan explained how the elevator worked. Only two buttons on the panel would function, your floor and the lobby. Each floor had two units, so the elevator had two sets of doors. Only one side opened depending on which key you had. She pulled out an intricate key and pushed it into its home before tapping the button for the fourteenth floor.

"So, you're showing us the thirteenth floor, huh?" The buttons skipped from twelve to fourteen, so the fourteenth floor was the thirteenth no matter what you thought.

Jordan gave me a patronizing smile, I don't think she liked us very much. It was strange that they still made buildings with silly superstitions in mind. The doors opened, and we stepped out at the front door of 14A. Jordan unlocked the door and pushed it open. Natural daylight flooded into the entryway making the overhead light seem dim. Massive glass windows gave way to a breathtaking view of the ocean. We walked slowly over the lush carpet ignoring everything but the view.

"Some of our residents say the view alone is worth the price tag." Jordan watched us like a hungry coyote.

Elizabeth grabbed my hand and tore open the sliding glass which led to the balcony. She pulled me out with her and a sudden gust stole her words. She turned to look at me. I could see the surrounding beauty reflected in her eyes. I kissed her despite the other woman staring at us. As the breeze died down we heard shouting below us. I leaned over to get a look and Elizabeth followed suit. Her eyes went wide.

"No! You won't take me, you can't have me!" A man shouted after a gunshot went off. Glass broke and suddenly the owner of the voice was falling ten stories to his death. He hit the ground below.

"Oh my God." Elizabeth had her hands over her mouth.

I turned to see Jordan on her phone. I was in shock, but I heard the words 'clean up' and 'police.' She pocketed her phone and began to apologize for what we had witnessed.

"I think we're done here. Thank you for the tour, but I don't think we'll be taking a space here." I said once I regained my composure.

Jordan looked angry. Not scared or dismayed or sympathetic, but angry. I took a step toward her and she turned and fled back towards the elevator. The door closed with alarming speed, leaving my wife and I in the apartment alone. I slammed the down button when the elevator reached the lobby, but nothing happened. I gave it some time, but the elevator never came back up.

I turned to Elizabeth who still looked a little shaken. "I don't want to scare you, but I think we may be stuck up here."

I pulled out my phone and dialed 9-1-1.

"9-1-1, what is your emergency?" The dispatcher's voice crackled and popped.

"I think my wife and I are trapped. We were being shown some property and I think the woman showing it to us locked us up here."

"What is your location, sir?"

I gave the operator the address to the tower. There was silence on the other line for a moment.

"Hello?" I thought maybe we had gotten disconnected.

"I'm sorry sir, we have no record of that location. This is an emergency line, please don't call it again."

"It's the giant tower on the coast! You can't miss it, you can see it from..." The phone clicked, and the call ended.

I dialed again and got the same result with a different operator.

"Are they coming?" Elizabeth asked.

"I don't think so. They said there's no record of this location."

She laughed.

"I'm sorry sweetheart." I apologized. "The first time I bring you to my hometown and we get trapped in an apartment. I don't understand why she left us here. This whole situation doesn't make any sense."

I went back out to the balcony and watched as the dead man was being cleaned up down below. They loaded his body into a nondescript black van. Then I saw the limo we had hired winding its way through the trees, on its way back with lunch.

"Oh shit, the limo driver. I can call him, maybe he can get help."

I pulled the little piece of paper with his number on it out of my pocket. He picked up on the second ring.

"Hello sir, I have the burgers and beer."

"Great, great. Listen, the lady showing us the place locked us up here in one of the units. We called 9-1-1, but they're not going to help. Find a way up here, get the key from that crazy bitch and I'll pay you enough to retire right now."

There was silence for a moment. "Are you joking with me?"

"Absolutely not, kid. I don't know what's going on, but someone just committed suicide and the place is freaking us out."

"Uh, ok. Sit tight, I'll figure something out." He hung up.

"This kid's gonna get us out of here sweetheart, don't you worry." I gave her a big hug and a reassuring smile. She only smiled weakly in return.

I paced back and forth in the living room as Elizabeth wandered through the rest of the space. I was dying for a goddamn beer. The only sounds we heard were our own soft footfalls and the occasional howling of the wind as it moved by the balcony. Hours seemed to have passed before I heard the elevator whirring to life. Elizabeth heard it too.

She joined me in the entranceway and we stood tall, ready to face whatever the elevator brought.

The door opened and there stood our driver. Our goddamn hero. He looked scared.

"Quick, we need to get out of here, this place is...is creepy." He waved us in while looking past us into the apartment.

As we rode down, I began to think of all the ghost stories that had come out of this place. I had almost forgotten what this place used to be. Death, there had been a lot of death here. We watched a man die, and that statue's glare was still dancing in my head. The doors opened, and we were in the lobby again. When the elevator closed behind us, it began moving back up. The lights were out in the lobby and the light that came through the windows was casting strange shadows throughout the place. A few of the shadows moved in a sickening way, seeming to shrug away from us independent of any light. I couldn't trust my eyes.

Before we reached the front door, we came upon a body in the dim light. Jordan lay on her back, eyes cast upwards. She had a look of pure terror frozen onto her face and blood leaked from what looked like a bite wound on her neck. Something loped out of the shadows, a crouched humanoid shape. Elizabeth and the kid screeched in unison. I grabbed both of them and pulled them towards the door.

Sunshine and fresh air hit us like cold, sobering water. I pushed the kid and Elizabeth into the back of the limo and I jumped into the driver's seat. The keys were in the ignition, thankfully. I backed the vehicle up as something slunk out of the lobby doors and into the sunlight. I couldn't see it that well in the glare of the sun, but it had about the same proportions as that gruesome statue.

I ignored the figure and spent my energy on driving us out of the area. I didn't stop until we were well into Bristol. I parked at a quiet little nature preserve and turned to check on my wife and the kid. They looked rattled. On the seat next to me was a six pack. I pulled one of the cans off and cracked it. The liquid was refreshing.

"I don't think we're going to be purchasing a summer home here, Elizabeth."

After that, things went downhill quickly for my wife and me. The kid, we put on the payroll. He got a nice fat paycheck every week for doing absolutely nothing. Well, nothing besides saving our lives. He was no idiot though, he used the money to get an education and is now the CEO of his own company. I'm sure you've heard his name. My wife, however, was right about that gruesome thing visiting her in her dreams. She was right about it loving her and she began to love it back. She became secretive and distant. She sculpted countless clay figures of its gruesome likeness and could do nothing else.

She grew to hate me. Eventually I had to have her committed, she wasn't eating or taking care of herself at all. She spent the rest of her days sculpting and drawing that thing. I still remember it as though it were yesterday, striding out of the tower and into the sunlight. I can't explain it, I can only tell you what I saw.

The tower was demolished, but not before a lot more people died. Maybe that's why the thing was so taken with my wife. We had gotten away from it. She died a few years ago. I had stopped visiting her, but I went down there when I got the phone call. The medical examiner said she killed herself. She had bitten into her wrists and bled out. I saw the bite marks and they didn't look human. They looked more like that odd angled grin of that gruesome marble statue.

Sometimes I dream about it, but I hope they're just dreams. Otherwise, maybe the end of my life is closer than I think. Is that what you wanted to hear? I hope that is good enough for you because I'm leaving soon on a flight across the Pacific. It's time I found my own peace and put some distance between me and the haunting nightmares I have about that tower.

THE END

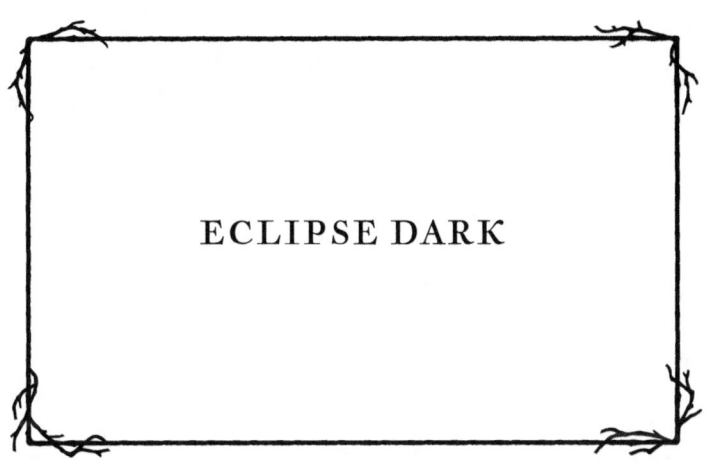

ECLIPSE DARK

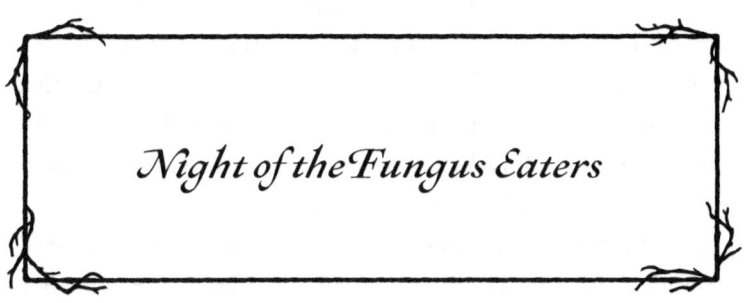

Night of the Fungus Eaters

I T WAS EITHER very late or very early depending on whether one was waking or just getting off to bed. It was that strange time in our twenty-four-hour cycle that feels the most lonesome and horrible no matter where you are or what you are doing. Whether lying in bed next to a sleeping lover or desperately trying to keep awake working third shift, it was an empty time of the night—or morning.

I didn't quite know the time as I had neglected to wear my watch that night, but I can guess that it must have been around three-thirty in the morning. I stood next to my car fiddling with an unlit cigarette and watched Walter as he locked the massive rust-pitted receiving door and descended the crumbling concrete stairs. The wind off the nearby coast caught his hair and jacket and he looked beautiful for a moment.

"Pleasure doing business with you, pal. I'll give you a call when it's all finished." Walter said.

"I await that day with bated breath, my friend." I replied.

He reached out to shake my hand and I paused for a moment. I had to remind myself I only had to keep the act up for a few more minutes. I took his hand and it felt slimy. I urged myself to squeeze his hand rather than recoil. He walked off toward his truck parked under the sole surviving lamp that struggled to illuminate the parking lot all on its own. The truck roared and Walter sped off, bumping and jolting over the massive potholes of the dirt lot.

I was left in the silence of the immense condemned cotton mill that stood before me. It was a great stone L-shaped building resting in the ominous quiet at the end of an unnamed side street. There were neighborhoods close by, but they were in the same state of disrepair and neglect. I imagined a shanty town of drug dens and squatter's abodes. The loading dock was in the crook of the L and faced a pond covered in a putrid algae bloom. Various unidentifiable debris stuck out here and there from the pond. This body of water was a dead one. On the other side of the pond was the highway, devoid of movement at this hour. A sigh escaped my lips, I placed the cigarette behind my ear, and I got to work. This late hour had its lonesome grasp on me.

Entry back into the mill was going to be tricky as the first-floor windows were well above my reach and I saw nothing in the parking lot that would help me to reach them. Had this been a premeditated job, I would have had a ladder with me. I am not that poor of a planner. The windows in the basement looked just big enough to squeeze through, though all were barred with heavy iron. I checked them anyway.

I was in luck, the fifth window I checked did not have bars on it. I pushed the window with my foot and it creaked open when the rust gave way. I went back to my vehicle and retrieved a paltry flashlight from the glovebox. It wasn't too powerful, but it was better than nothing. An owl hooted somewhere close by. The soft sound startled me when it broke the absolute quiet and I searched the skeletal trees for it. It flew off when the beam of my flashlight caught its eyes.

I took one last look at the crumbling facade of the mill, at its shattered dark windows, and vine-choked crevices. I dropped to my stomach and wiggled myself into the basement feet first. I paused for a moment before I let myself drop. Clinging to the ledge with one arm, I swung the other around wielding the flashlight. To my horror, the beam only penetrated the dark beneath my feet and the immediate area. The basement was massive and probably spanned the entirety of the mill. The blackness ate the flashlight beam with fierce hunger.

The muddy floor was not far down, so I let myself go. The impact jarred my bones, but I had done it, I was back inside of Walter's mill. The smell crawled to me and spoke of the sewage and animal carcasses that festered on this level of the mill. The light revealed exotic fungi poking between decaying wood and debris. Mold lined the sweating concrete wall. The ceiling was decorated with rotting pipes, loose wires, and mineral stalactites. I tried again to look out into the basement with my flashlight but there was only the hungry dark.

The dark was the ultimate test of my will and the deafening silence was its steadfast accomplice. All I had to do was keep my wits and follow along the wall until I found the staircase. I was to be Dante, my flashlight, Virgil. I had to trust the little thing to lead me up and out of this hellish basement.

I began to creep along the wall, mud squelching under my boots. I tried hard to keep the silence, but every step shattered it and the open basement sent the echoes back at me. I ceased moving for a moment, wanting to be free of the frolicking echoes, but they did not stop. They kept rolling over me with their boot-in-mud words. It was impossible, echoes didn't work like that.

I made another futile attempt to penetrate the dark of the basement with my flashlight. It reflected off two blind, milk-white eyes that inhabited a human shaped shadow moving through the dark toward me. A scream caught in the back of my throat as though I was in a dream and couldn't utter a sound. The figure coming toward me cried out, it almost sounded like a cry for help, but I didn't wait around for clarification. I shed my caution and took off running.

I kept moving quickly on my route along the moldering wall, my feet squelching in the mud. I ran into something and stumbled, losing my feet beneath me. Luck was on my side and I ended up landing on a drier patch of the dirt basement floor. I shuddered to think of what liquids were mixed with the dirt to make such noxious mud. I pointed the flashlight at the lump that had tripped me and saw that it wasn't something, but someone. A dirty, ragged old man lay there on the floor curled up and chewing on one of the various mushrooms that had found a home in the basement. He drooled and mumbled something while reaching toward me.

The basement had to be full of homeless people. Watching him eat the mushroom was unsettling to say the least. My heart raced, though I was becoming accustomed to my dank surroundings. Not to say that I wanted to hang out with depraved bums, but I felt a little less alone and a little more grounded with my imagination quelled. At least I knew who was down there with me.

I stood and dusted myself off. The other one came into the beam of light and stood there swaying over his brother-in-sludge at his feet. The man was blind and dirty. His thread-bare clothing hosted colonies of fungi all over it. He reached over to his left shoulder and pulled a few pale blue caps off and smashed them into his mouth. He chewed and gurgled, his friend continued in his own feast.

Their combined odors and the image of them eating fungus was enough to cause a roiling in my stomach. I turned and left them. When I stopped to let my echoing footsteps die again, I could hear nothing coming behind me. The last thing I needed was for the bums to follow me up into the mill.

I reached a point where a large circular portion of the first floor had collapsed into the basement, spilling its ancient machines into the primordial soup of the subterranean floor. The decaying wood had just given up and let the mud have the massive hunks of iron adorned with bolts and gears. The mud looked to be swallowing the rusty relics, giving them a proper burial after all the years they had sat abandoned. The floor was still connected to one edge and formed a steep ramp up to the first floor. It was possible that I could climb up and out. Here before me lay a viable path forward. I had not yet located a staircase, though they may have collapsed into ruin as well. I opted to climb.

I reached the top unscathed and searched around the room with my light. To my relief I could see all four walls and the jagged perimeter of the floor that had let go of its burden. There was nothing unknown in this room and it calmed me. Careful not to let the basement dark swallow me back up, I moved around the perimeter to the exit leading out of the room.

When I opened the door, there was a great rending sound and I spun to see the makeshift ramp give way and join the rest of the lost flooring in the basement. It had hung around just long enough to give me passage into the mill before falling into a rotting fungal death. I thanked it with a silent whisper.

Out in the hallway I tried to locate exactly where I was in that old monster building. The hall led off to both the left and the right, each way containing the same swallowing darkness of the basement. There were doors every twenty feet or so, but I preferred to keep them closed. Ignoring what might be in those large rooms suited me better than potentially knowing of something that my mind might not be unable to cope with.

The horrors I had seen in Walter's workshop had nearly caused me to break down. I was using all of my strength to go back there. It was the right thing to do. I was desperate for a cigarette, but Walter had warned me not to light up while in the mill. Something about the chemicals in the air and violent reactions to fire. I could light the place up if my original plan failed.

I took my thoughts with me as I moved off down the right side of the hallway, the same direction I was heading in the mucky basement. It was then that I noticed the dull throbbing in my right hand. I inspected it with my light and saw only a circle of redness. There was no discernible wound, but going to the doctor for a tetanus shot after this adventure didn't seem like a bad idea. I must have grabbed something while climbing. I ignored it and continued.

I found what I was looking for. The immense receiving door that was padlocked on the outside stood in front me. To the left of it was the breaker box. The panel squealed open and I flipped every switch. Dim light flooded the hallway as each set of lights clicked on overhead, chasing the dark into the dreary corners of the mill's innards. I knew where I was going from here.

My hand throbbed, clenching itself to dull the pain. I clicked my flashlight off and shoved it into my pocket, massaging my hand to try and open it. It wouldn't obey my commands. I remembered Walter's slick and slimy handshake. A bubble of anxiety formed in my stomach that refused to shake loose.

I retraced my steps looking for the staircase we had taken to get up to the fourth floor. Everything in the building was crumbling and dying. Above, sagging ceiling tiles tried desperately to hold their guts in, but to no avail. Pipes and wiring hung about like the innards of a human long past the point of any kind of corrective surgery. The floor cried out with every step that I took on its cracked and decaying wooden boards.

At one point I thought I heard something and stopped to listen. A breeze whistled through the place, but other than that there was silence. Then a bang and scuttling somewhere overhead. I swore and told myself it had just been some kind of rodent, though I hadn't seen any evidence of them. It was strange, the floor should have been littered with animal droppings. The air was stale in that place and my hand was still a tight fist.

I kept on until I found the staircase. It was the most solid and complete thing that I had seen in the place and it supported me as I ascended to the fourth floor. It was dark in the hallway. So dark that it seemed to spill out into the light instead of the light spilling out into it. An intelligent darkness that served to keep the unwanted out. I stepped out into the hallway and saw light in only one doorway.

I hurried towards it and in the process put my foot

through a crumbling section of floor. Something sharp tore my pants and ate into my leg like some burrowing insect. I gritted my teeth at the pain and pulled my leg out, being careful not to rip my flesh further.

Blood pumped out of a two inch gash in my leg. The leaking was slow, so the gash couldn't be that deep. I chose to ignore it as I moved ever closer to my destiny. I expected the lit doorway to bring warmth and comfort, but it only made the dark feel like the lesser of two evils. I peered around the corner into the place where Walter worked.

And there I was, staring at the shoddy workshop. The little cubicle of a shop had walls of particle board and a roof of scrap metal scavenged from somewhere else in the mill. Wires ran out of a hole in the side and trailed like a nightmare tail behind the cube. The whole thing sat in the center of one cavernous empty room lit by one single floodlight suspended high above. The door had been taken from a foreman's office as evidenced by the chipped black letters on the frosted glass window. Pale light flickered behind the glass and the bass note hum of the machines within the thing crawled and danced around me.

I approached and pushed on the door. To my surprise it was unlocked and I stole inside. I was aware of the living presence. I took a deep breath and limped to the center. The place was much the same as we had left it not long ago. I spied the massive glass tank containing the phosphorescent liquid and strange abstract shadow at its center. The floating abomination looked bigger than it had a few hours ago and I swear it shuddered and convulsed when I laid a hand on the glass. Walter's "answer to humanity" as he lovingly named it.

I could feel that dawn was on the horizon and directed myself to destroy the equipment. From his workbench I reached for a hammer with my right hand, forgetting that it was paralyzed into a fist and switched to grab it with my left. The gravity of that presence I felt in the workshop grew in intensity and I spun to meet it.

Walter stood there in front of the glowing tank with his hands clasped behind his back. He gave me a warm smile and reached out to touch the tank.

"I knew your mind, Martin. That moment of hesitation when I offered you my hand tipped me off. I gave you a little something." He pointed to my paralyzed fist. "I was hoping that it would have worked quicker, that it would have a chance to take its full effect before you reached me."

"What you're doing is wrong, Walter. You're a madman."

"Is that what I am? How cliche."

I took a step toward him and swung my right fist at him. He held up his hand and my arm stopped in mid-air. It wouldn't move no matter how hard I tried to pull it back to me. I threw the hammer. He snatched it out of the air.

"I can't have you interrupting my work. It's very important stuff, you know. I appreciate the parts you sold me, but I'll have to dispose of you now. Shoulda just kept the money, my friend." Walter said.

My hand flew to my gut without warning and knocked the wind out of me. My hand only obeyed the madman now. Walter reached down, pulled the envelope of cash out of the back pocket of my jeans, and placed it inside of his jacket. With a strength I didn't know he had in him, he tossed me over his shoulder and exited the workshop.

He retraced my steps all the way back down to the room where the first floor had collapsed into the basement. I was still squirming and struggling to breath when he dumped me from his shoulder into the black basement. I fell screaming and landed painfully in the putrid mud. My body had missed the ancient machines that lay in the mud by mere inches. I would have been dead had I hit one.

"Goodbye, Martin." Said Walter as his silhouette left the jagged precipice of the room above.

I laid in the mud with tears in my eyes. My plan had been thwarted. I could feel my right fist finally relaxing and when I opened it, I felt a strange fuzziness on my fingers. I fumbled for my flashlight and clicked it on. It flickered, but it showed me a fungus growing on my hand. I tried to wipe it off on my shirt, but it held fast. I remembered reading somewhere that fungi had lengthy root systems. It was a part of my hand now.

I heard one of the fungi-riddled homeless men moan in the distance of the pitch-dark basement. I reached into my right pocket and brought out my cigarette lighter. My last resort was to burn the place. I prayed to every god that Walter hadn't lied about chemicals reacting to fire.

Suck it, Walter.

I clicked the wheel and the flame appeared. The flame grew before my eyes and in slow motion the entire basement was lit up by a blinding white light. I could see everything, all the collapsed portions of the floor, the skeletons of pipes and the wired sinews. The vision was like an old film reel burning up. The vagrants threw their hands over their eyes and I saw at least ten of them near and far all along the basement. I saw the black pools of putrid liquid and the abundance of fungi along their shores. Then there was an explosion of sound and I saw nothing.

I woke up in a hospital bed with my husband asleep in a

chair against the wall. I could feel that I was heavily sedated. I looked at my hands. My left one had a few bandages on it. My right one no longer existed. There was only a bandaged stump that began to throb when I looked at it. I started to cry as the memory of what happened in the mill came back to me.

Through my blurred vision, I saw that Mark had jumped out of his chair and stumbled to my side. He clasped my left hand with a careful gentleness.

"The mill." I rasped. "What happened to the mill?"

"That mill is gone. Explosion. Very quick burning fire. The paramedics said some homeless men had dragged you out of the basement. I'm so glad you're ok." Mark said. His eyes were bloodshot with sleeplessness and tears.

"Were there other survivors?" It pained me to talk.

"No. What were you doing there? They said there must have been a massive gas leak. Were you smoking again? Maybe this will convince you to quit once and for all." Mark said with a stern face.

I waved him off and his face softened. "I'm sorry, Marty. Your hand was so mangled they had to amputate and your leg was broken. It was—"

I patted his hands. "Can you get me some water? And maybe the doctor?"

Mark nodded and left the room. I closed my eyes.

When I opened them again, Walter was standing at the foot of my bed. His right arm was in a sling and his hair was singed. A blood vessel had broken in his right eye and his right ear was raw.

"Nice move, Martin. You've set me back, but I can start again. All of my research is up here anyway." He pointed to his head.

He exited the room without looking back and I fell out of the bed with wires and tubes trailing behind me, trying to get someone's attention. I couldn't yell and before anyone showed up, it was too late. Walter disappeared down the hallway. Soon there would be another tank of that otherworldly liquid with another of those beings swimming about in it. Walter would be more careful this time. I laid on the cool tile floor and cried.

THE END

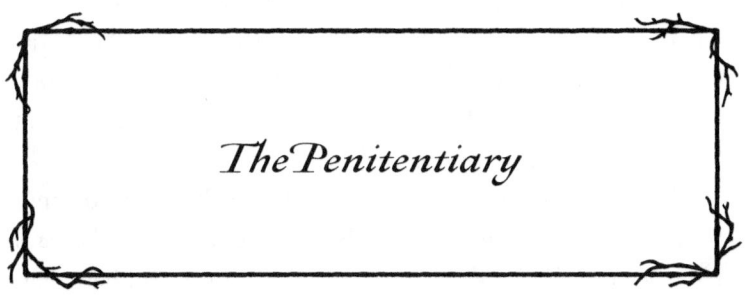

The Penitentiary

BAR-SPLIT BEAMS crept down the cell wall as the sun rose and cast its golden light upon the penitentiary. As the time ticked by, the light came closer and closer to falling on the ugly scarred face of Eugene Lackworth. When it did, the warmth caused the murderer to stir into wakefulness and blink at the barred window.

It seemed he had slept through the jarring morning alarm and had most likely missed breakfast. The guards had left him to sleep and miss meal time not because they hated him, but because it would have inconvenienced them. Lackworth's stomach grumbled and he sat up to shake the sleepiness off.

Once stretched and fully awake, he realized how quiet the penitentiary was. The standard din of screeching, yelling, fighting, and cheering was absent from the prison that day. He didn't even hear the slightest sound coming from the yard. Surely at least one block had yard time already. He almost called out but decided against it. Somehow the thought of disturbing the peace made him feel ill.

Lackworth stood from the cot and relieved himself in his little metal toilet. The sound of his liquids hitting the bowl caused him to jump when it shattered the calm. When finished, he shuffled to his cell door and gazed out. There was only a barred window exactly one foot by one foot and a slot below it for passing things in and out. He could see nothing but the cell door across the hall from his.

He listened through the slot and after hearing nothing, he went to his window and pulled himself up using the bars to look out. It was the same forest scene that he had seen every day since the first day of his incarceration. The pines were still in the cloudless sunny day. The glass beyond the bars was warm with the sunlight and it kept the cold clear winter air out.

Perhaps the most maddening thing about the view from Lackworth's cell was that it never changed unless it snowed or rained. The pine trees were all he could see, and they looked the same every season. Lackworth missed watching the seasons change and that feeling alone moved him to feel remorse for his crime.

A sudden crash and a bang out in the hallway ripped him from his seasonal musings and he flew to his cell door with a thumping in his chest. He pressed his face into the bars hard enough to hurt as he tried to discern the source of the noise. He heard a gurgling cry, then heavy footsteps moving closer to his cell. Whoever or whatever the hulking being was, it had a heavy object that was scraping the ground behind it.

At the last second the murderer pulled himself from the window and sank to the floor. He pushed himself against the door trying to make himself invisible. The heavy footsteps and the dragging sound stopped in front of his door and his eyes watered. Fear was tearing through his body. His bladder felt heavy and ready to empty again.

The flap over the slot below the window suddenly opened causing Lackworth to jump and slap a hand over his mouth to stifle a scream. The flap closed, and the footsteps moved away from his cell still dragging whatever it was dragging behind it.

Lackworth shivered. When he didn't hear the footsteps anymore, he hazarded a peek through the slot again. The floor was covered with a viscous black ooze that had been left by whatever had been dragged down the hallway. The ichor's putrid smell made it up into Lackworth's nose, causing him to gag and stumble back from the cell door.

He sat back down on his bed to think. He pushed the thoughts of what the thing was and what it had been dragging out of his mind. Those were unanswerable questions, his thoughts were only on a way out of the prison.

He pulled his mattress up and leaned it against the opposite wall, revealing the metal slats that crisscrossed the frame of the cot. There was a shout from somewhere inside the penitentiary, followed by a shotgun firing, then a scream. Lackworth kicked at the metal slats until one of them bent. He grabbed it, working it up and down until the metal broke. His hands were blistered, cut, and numb, but he went to work on the other end of the metal slat. Once the other side was severed, he clutched the two-foot-long length of metal in his mangled hands.

He knew it was growing late, the sunlight had ceased to spill into his cell. He set to work bending the slat into a hooked shape at one end using the metal toilet like an anvil. When he was satisfied with the piece, he moved to his door and fed it through the slot.

After a few tries he hooked the bolt that secured his door and with gentle dexterity, eased it up and out of its locked position. He pushed his cell door open but didn't immediately step out into the hall. He wasn't sure that he should leave the safety of his cell.

One deep breath later and Lackworth was out in the hallway walking to the left, away from where the being had dragged its leaking burden. He hugged the wall trying not to step in the putrid liquid painting the floor. At each cell he stopped to peer in, but it seemed he was the only prisoner left. Some of the doors were open, though most were closed.

He had never been down this way, the cafeteria and entrance to the yard were in the other direction. Soon he came to a lone door at the end of the hallway. The cell doors had ceased interrupting the walls a few yards back. He turned and stared toward the other end of the long corridor. It was hard to see the other end even in the glaring fluorescent light. His hesitation was a mistake.

There was a sudden bang of the door flying open at the other end of the hall and a dreadful sound echoed down to wash over Lackworth. He turned away, not wanting to catch a glimpse of what had entered the cell block. He jammed the door's heavy metal handle down and pushed. It didn't give. He threw his body into the great steel thing. It still didn't budge and now his shoulder felt raw and bruised.

He thought he heard the faint echoes of heavy footsteps, but he didn't dare turn to meet what approached. He cried out in frustration. He was drawing himself back to hit the door again while still holding onto the handle when it squealed open. Lackworth couldn't help but burst into terrified laughter, realizing that all he had to do was pull on the door and it would have opened with ease.

He yanked it again until there was room for him to

squeeze through. There was a bar on the other side and he slammed it home, locking the heavy door in place. With his back to the door he steadied his breathing while taking in his new environment.

The hallway looked much warmer and less sterile than his cell block. Wooden walls hung with portraits and great glass windows placed between them made him feel as though he had escaped the prison and wandered into a cushy office building. There were potted plants at the ends of comfortable looking benches that lined the walls. Lush carpet covered the floors. He thought it far too nice for even the administrative portion of a prison.

A heavy weight crashed into the thick door causing it to rattle in its frame, sending Lackworth tripping forward. He caught himself on his hands and half scrambled, half crawled to one of the doors leading into an office. He entered and secreted himself away under a desk. The thudding ceased, but he remained hidden until his butt and legs became numb.

His legs buzzing with pins and needles, he rose and began to take careful steps. The office was immaculate and devoid of any personal touches. There were no family photos on any of the desks nor any kind of decoration, only perfectly aligned workstations with lamps, phones, pen and ink, and filing cabinets against one wall. He picked up the receiver from a telephone at the corner of a desk, but there was no dial tone. He dropped it and moved to the filing cabinets.

He pulled open one and found that it was full of manila folders marked by the names of inmates. He found the drawer marked 'L' and yanked it open. His fingers coasted over the files until he came to 'Lackworth, Eugene' and yanked it out. The file contained his picture, his criminal record, medical records he couldn't quite understand, and notes made about his dealings in the prison. They knew everything about him.

Lackworth wandered out of the office and into the cozy hallway with his file in hand. He walked by a door and stopped when the words on the door caught his attention. It was the warden's office. He found his hand turning the knob and pushing the door open before he had even consciously decided to investigate.

The warden was there. The fat balding man sat slumped in his chair with his elbows on his rich mahogany desk, a bottle of scotch in one hand and a revolver in the other. The man's eyes were glazed and his head swayed a bit attesting to his drunkenness. Lackworth froze, afraid that he'd be shot after all he had been through.

"Who're you? How'd you get in here." The warden slurred.

"What's happening warden? Where is everyone?" Lackworth asked with eyes on the gun.

"I promised 'em. They could have you all iffen they left me alone. They did. Leave me alone, that is. But the dreams. The agony of their image in my mind. Can't live with it. Sorry."

The warden thumbed the hammer back and Lackworth spun out of the doorway. The revolver cracked and there was a thump on the desk. His heart sped in his chest as he turned to look in on the dead man. A gun would go a long way to make him feel better about the strange situation that he had found himself in. He pried it from the dead man's hand, wiping the bloodied grip dry on his pants and tucking the revolver into the front of his waistline. An arm suddenly wrapped around his throat and a lithe hand reached around to take the gun from its place.

"Make a sound and I'll kill you. Come with me." Said a woman's voice.

She dragged him out of the warden's office with the gun pushed painfully into his spine. The woman backed them into a cramped dark closet that smelled of cleaning supplies and shut the door. Lackworth hadn't felt the touch of a woman in years, but the fear and confusion he felt pushed those feelings right out of his mind. He opened his mouth to say something.

"Shush!" She whispered harshly into his ear.

She tightened the grip on his neck, he could hear heavy footfalls coming towards them, coming to a stop outside of the warden's office. They heard what sounded like the warden's fat body hitting the floor and then soft dragging sounds. Lackworth felt ill as the sound of the warden's dead body being dragged on carpet passed by their hiding place. When the sound had stopped, the woman let him go. His first instinct was to spin and throw a punch into her face, but she had already pushed past him and opened the door.

In the warm light of the hallway he saw that she was wire-thin but made of steel. She wore only a white tank top stained yellow with sweat and the standard issue blue prisoner trousers. She wore no shoes—which must have been how she had snuck up on him so easily. Her head was shaven and she had tattoos on her arms. Lackworth thought she was pretty, but figured she was into women. There was a trail of blood on the carpet now.

"Do you know what's going on?" He asked, trying to keep his voice steady.

"I don't know. I was working in the boiler room. I saw where they came in, but it was dark, and I didn't get a good look at them. They're big. Came in through some kind of portal, science fiction shit." She disappeared into the warden's office.

Lackworth climbed out of the closet and looked around nervously. The hallway and the offices didn't seem so cozy anymore. He crept to the doorway and watched as the woman rifled through drawers in the warden's desk. She pulled out a ring of keys, a box of slugs for the revolver, and a flask. She tossed the flask to Lackworth who caught it clumsily.

"Have a drink, calm your nerves. I'm gonna need your help to get us out of here. And take your shoes off, stealth is the name of the game."

She pulled out a handkerchief and bundled up the keys to muffle their jingling. In the closet she found a wrinkled dress shirt that hung loosely on a hanger. She tied it into a sort of pack and placed the slugs and keys into it.

"I'm keeping the gun, you're the pack mule."

She tossed the makeshift bag at Lackworth who caught it despite being off balance removing his shoes.

"I'm Lackworth." He said feeling sheepish in the presence of this natural leader. "Eugene Lackworth."

"Eugene, I have to tell you I don't care what your name is, but I suppose you'll have to call me something. Call me Key. Because I'm your key to getting out of here."

He finished removing his shoes, slung the makeshift pack across his back and stowed the flask. It contained smooth bourbon. Lackworth nearly teared up when he tasted it. Without another word, Key pushed by him and they were off following the gruesome trail left by the warden's corpse.

They moved at a quick pace, Lackworth unlocking doors and Key covering them with the weapon. She claimed to know exactly where they were going and Lackworth put his faith in her. He had no other choice. She claimed they were headed for an emergency staff exit that led directly out into the woods. She didn't know what waited for them at the front gate of the penitentiary and she didn't intend to find out.

They didn't encounter any more survivors or come up against any of the unimaginable beings that had infiltrated the penitentiary. Lackworth felt as though he had been holding his breath the entire time they moved. Hours seemed to have passed, but really their journey from the administration hall had only taken about half an hour.

They were in another cell block now and the kitchens were supposed to be right on the other side. The block looked like a mass extinction event had taken place. The strange black ooze was everywhere, as were chaotic swaths of congealed human blood. The air was damp, and the block was as quiet as an Egyptian tomb. The sun had gone down long ago, and the only light was that of the glaring fluorescents.

"Alright, Lack, through this door is a short hallway which leads to the kitchens." Key said as they reached the end of the block.

"Okay, well let's get out of here." Lackworth said.

"I'm going to grab some flashlights from the guard's office." She pointed up to the little office on the second floor of the block. "Maybe there's a riot shotgun or two up there as well. Stay here."

Lackworth handed her the muffled keys from his pack and watched as she scaled the stairs. Key slipped into the guard's room and Lackworth lost sight of her. He tried to occupy his mind, but there was nothing that could draw him away from the apparent carnage that had taken place in the block. He cracked his knuckles and sang softly to himself.

He thought he heard something from where they had entered the block.

His eyes grew wide as the door at the other end of the block opened and a dark dressed figure that he couldn't quite see clearly lumbered into the block. Lackworth crouched low and shuffled behind an open cell door. He prayed that the thing hadn't seen him, and he prayed that Key would notice the thing before it noticed her.

The lights snapped off and Lackworth's vision was plunged into the very depths of darkness. He imagined that he had just died right then and there of the fear that had held him since the sun shook him awake that morning. And then Key's steel fingers were around his wrist and pulling him to his feet.

Like two black cats in the night they slipped through the door into the hallway that would lead to the kitchen. They heard the being grumble, but it didn't seem to suspect anything suspicious in the power failure.

"That was lucky." Lackworth's voice quivered.

"Luck? I shut the lights off idiot. Let's go."

Key pushed a flashlight and the revolver into Lackworth's hands. They trotted down the hallway, Key unlocked a door, and they were back into the light and hurrying down another hallway. Lackworth saw that Key held a menacing riot shotgun. The bigger gun made him feel a little better, though the labyrinthian nature of the penitentiary was beginning to weigh on his anxiety.

They found the kitchen. It was in much better condition than most of the other areas in the prison they had been through. Lackworth's stomach grumbled and he went looking through the cupboards that held industrial quantities of ingredients.

"What are you doing? We don't have time for this." Key said.

"I'm starving. I need to eat something, who knows when we'll eat again."

Key didn't say anything, but she did help him look through the cupboards. They found a barrel of apples. They each ate one and Lackworth filled his pack up with more.

"That's the best apple I've ever eaten." He said.

She glared at him, but he could tell she had enjoyed hers too. They searched the kitchen for the emergency exit and found it half concealed by boxes of plastic utensils. They moved the boxes and stared at the door.

"You ready to run?" Key asked.

"Yeah."

She pushed open the door and a fire alarm began to blare throughout the penitentiary. She shouldered the shotgun, clicked on the flashlight below the barrel and stole out into the cold night. Lackworth followed with the revolver out and his flashlight pointed into the dark. They rushed out onto the lawn towards the welcome dark of the forest.

A deafening crack sounded off and Key was no longer running next to Lackworth. He slowed and pointed his light behind him. Key was on the ground writhing in agony, her teeth bared.

"I can't. Breath." She wheezed.

Lackworth went back to her as another crack sounded in the night and a searing point of heat went through his shoulder. He took a startled step back and saw wetness spreading in the blue of his shirt. It dawned on him—there was a sniper in the tower. He left Key coughing in the grass and ran in a zigzag pattern as two more shots were fired. He made it to the tree line and got low. Another alarm sounded over the fire alarm that was still buzzing out of the open doorway.

Lackworth had only heard the alarm one other time when a prisoner escaped, it was like an air-raid siren. He panted and held his shoulder which had become a burning, throbbing mass of pain. There were shouts in the night, men's voices mixed in between the barking of dogs. Lackworth saw flashlights dotting the night and moving over the lawn.

Now there are people? Lackworth thought. He hadn't made it all this way away from those unknown intruders just to be taken by guards. He took off into the woods, grinding his teeth against his bullet wound. He threw his flashlight down and tucked the revolver into his pants. There was enough moonlight to make his way through the dim dark woods. Somewhere behind him Key screamed out. They had her.

Lackworth found a hollow tree and pushed himself inside. He pulled a fallen branch and piles of dirt and pine needles over himself as camouflage. The men came close to his hiding place and he caught part of their conversation.

"I didn't think there were any left alive. I thought those things had gotten them all."

"Did you hear they took the warden? What if they decide they're not happy with the contents of the penitentiary and they move outside of it?"

"That's why we're all out here trying to keep everything in."

"But, the warden..."

"The warden's not the one who was paying us..."

They moved off and Lackworth could hear their conversation no longer.

As gray dawn crept through the trees, Lackworth came

into wakefulness. He hadn't realized he had fallen asleep. The alarms no longer sounded and nothing but the slight rustling of the pine trees disturbed the silence. He felt cold and sluggish. It seemed his wound had stopped bleeding and he could barely feel the pain. He munched on a couple apples before climbing out of his hiding place.

He was dizzy due to the loss of blood he suffered, but he was confident he could continue on. The penitentiary was no longer visible through the trees, but he didn't mind. Lackworth shuffled through the undergrowth clutching his wounded shoulder, but his head was held high and he was looking forward to a different view than the eternal pine trees.

THE END

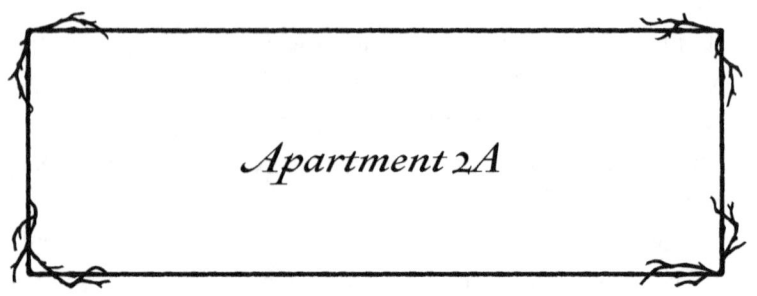

Apartment 2A

𝔄 NEW NEIGHBOR moved into the apartment above mine on the second floor. I know this because I was jarred out of a restful sleep by the tremendous racket that ensued. Being on the first floor next to the stairs meant that I heard every step that traversed the creaky wooden things. It was strange that someone would be moving at that time of night. Footsteps and large objects bumped and jumped up the stairs over and over again. After tossing and turning for a while I worked up the nerve to confront my new neighbor. At that point sleep was more important to me than being neighborly.

I unbolted my door and threw it open dramatically as if I were revealing some villainous character in a pivotal movie scene. The sound ceased at once and I peeked my head out into the hallway. There was not a soul occupying the first floor hallway or staircase. Across the way my fellow first floor resident's door remained shut and quiet as if the noise hadn't woken her. There was a Christmas wreath on that door, the holly and evergreen sprigs bone dry. It was August.

The hallway smelled musty with the humidity and some of the faded and flowering wallpaper had begun to peel from the wall. The overhead light flickered once. All was quiet, so I shut the door. I thought perhaps I had dreamt of the noise and a new neighbor moving in, but it wasn't like me to have such mundane dreams. I relieved myself in the bathroom, drank a glass of rusty brown water from the tap, and crawled back into my bed.

I rolled into the center where I had broken in quite a nice sleeping divot. Sleep began to take me when I heard a tentative footstep above me. And then another. And then something was being slid across the floor. Step, step, step, slide. I did have a new neighbor upstairs. I resolved to introduce myself in the morning. Sleep came.

I woke to the sun streaming through the gap in my smoke-stained curtains. I wasn't a smoker, but the previous resident of apartment 1A had been. My place reeked of smoke, but it did not bother me, nor did it bother me to use the curtains she had left behind. I rolled out of my sleeping divot and went to the curtains. It was a cloudless sunny day. Too sunny for me. I fixed the gap in the curtains and went to the bathroom to complete my morning ritual. Dust swirled around me as I moved.

I returned to my bedroom with a fresh shave and slicked hair. It was time to go knock on my new neighbor's door. I had hoped to wake them as they had woken me last night. I donned a button-down shirt, faded jeans, and a pair of socks. They didn't match—one was black and the other was blue—but no one would see them in my boots which I pulled on next. I exited my bedroom, glided through my sitting room and threw open my front door again, which I had neglected to lock last night much to my surprise. It wasn't like me to leave a door unlocked.

I stomped up the stairs, letting my steel-toed boots announce their presence. When I reached the door to apartment 2A, I hesitated before knocking. There was some vague electric feeling that I felt when I moved my hand close to the door. It was almost as if some unseen entity was trying its hardest to keep my hand from the door. I ignored it and pounded on the door. There was no answer, so I pounded again. Nothing.

I stomped back down to my apartment huffing all the way down. I went in and slammed the door, locking it this time before going back to my bedroom. It was then that I noticed a yellowish stain on the ceiling in the corner of the room. There were stains of all kinds all over my apartment, but this one was brand new. I reached up and touched it. The stain was dry and warm as if the sun had been hitting it for an extended amount of time. I thought that my new neighbor must have spilled something or busted a pipe. What most perturbed me was that it was Saturday and I would have to wait until Monday to call the landlord to get everything sorted out.

I stood there with my hands on my hips, gazing up at the stain frustratedly, when there came a rapid knock on my door. I started and ran to the door, hoping it was my new neighbor coming to confront me about hammering on their door so early in the morning. For a third time I threw the door open dramatically.

There in the dim lighting that flickered every now and then stood my shrunken and wrinkled neighbor from across the hall.

"Good morning, Mrs. Lazenby." I managed.

"Mr. Cooper." She nodded and remained silent.

"Was there something I could help you with? I'm sort of in the middle of something right now."

"Mr. Cooper." She nodded again and remained silent.

"Mrs. Lazenby?"

"Mr. Cooper."

I shut the door in her face, unable to contain my frustration any more. I leaned forward to stare out of the little looking glass in the door. I only saw Mrs. Lazenby's door closing and the dried wreath swinging and dropping leaves to the floor. The lighting flickered. It was strange how quickly the old lady had retreated into her apartment.

It was a peculiar morning to say the least.

From there I left my apartment to complete my usual Saturday ritual. I walked the trail around the park near my apartment eight times, which comes out to about five miles. I ignored the staring eyes of every person I encountered. No one in the park ever said hello to me, I only received unreadable stares or averted gazes. The birds enjoyed my company. They would fly from tree to tree following my progress around the park. It always started with one or two, but by the end of my walk, the final tree would be inundated with all manner of birds.

They were like living ornaments among the dull green leaves of the fog-colored tree branches. It was like everything in the city was behind a dull gray filter that sucked the life out of every image and vision. The birds in the park though—my birds I suppose I could say—were a burst of excitement to break up the morbid monotony of every week. I kissed them goodbye and began my short journey to the old gothic building I called home.

When I entered my building Mrs. Lazenby was standing

at the bottom of the stairs looking up at the door of my new neighbor. She had her hands on her hips and when I moved to my door, trying to escape her notice, she turned her scowl on me.

"Mr. Cooper."

"Mrs. Lazenby."

"Mr. Coop-"

I was inside my apartment with the door shut before she could utter the false name I had given her again. Senile idiot.

I heard the noises that had caused her to scowl up at the door—a rhythmic bass thumping that I felt in my chest. Thump, thump. Thump, thump. It sounded almost like a heartbeat. I sighed and moved into my bedroom. The new stain on the ceiling caught my attention. It had grown considerably in the time that I had been out walking. It had a glossy wetness to it and as I stood there focused on it, I could see it creeping outward as if it were trying to swallow my entire ceiling.

I flew back out into the hallway, past the scowling Mrs. Lazenby, up the stairs, and planted myself in front of the door to apartment 2A. I pounded on the door with no intention of stopping until my new neighbor opened it. The landlord was going to hear about this on Monday for sure, I thought.

There was still no answer. I struggled to calm myself. I flew back down into my apartment and fumbled around trying to open my little bottle of pills the doctor had prescribed to calm me down. I popped one and swallowed it. All I had to do was count to ten and I would be as calm as a cucumber. Or maybe it was cool?

I spent the remainder of the day watching television with the volume turned up loud enough to drown out the thumping noise my new neighbor was making. My favorite program was on. It was an untitled black and white presentation where a man was let loose in the desert and forced to find water before he succumbed to exposure. The previews assured us viewers that everything in the program was real. I fell asleep there on the couch as the setting sun cast red fingers through the venetian blinds covering the cracked living room windows.

I awoke sometime in the middle of the night to a high-pitched whine emanating from my television. The channel had gone off the air and before I clicked the idiot box off I became aware of a whispering that swirled within the high-pitched whine. I strained trying to hear what the diminutive voice said, but I could make nothing out. I clicked the television off and was aware at once that the whispering was coming from my bedroom.

My bedroom door was open just a crack and the soft voice trickled out like a little stream. My breathing was heavy as my medication had worn off.

"Hello?" I said, trying to sound confident.

The whispering ceased. I stood up from the groaning couch and began a slow lope to my bedroom door. The lights were off making the room seem that much more terrifying. I slipped a hand in through the crack and clicked on the light switch. I pushed the door open and revealed my room in the same state that I had left it when I viewed the creeping stain. That stain had almost engulfed the entire ceiling.

"Hello!" I shouted.

A crack in the ceiling—which had always been there but was now part of the stain's territory—split open to reveal a mouth-like maw with nails and wood splinters as teeth. It looked like a horrific grin in the ceiling. And then it moved again, closing this time. It opened again, seeming to be working stiffness out of itself and then it spoke.

"Hello." It was a soft whisper that caused me to fall back against the wall.

"Who...what..." I couldn't bring myself to say anything intelligible.

"The water, the eyes, steal sunrise, hush and die, keep surprise." The crack in the ceiling opened and closed with each splintery word.

"What...what are you doing to my ceiling, what's that stain?"

"I am sorry about that. I didn't know you were home. Sometimes I can't help from leaking through the gaps in the floors. If you can handle it, come on up and I'll show you what I mean."

I didn't know what to say. The crack resealed itself and spoke no more. I thrust a shaky hand into my hair and retreated into the living room, slamming the bedroom door behind me. I thought that I had been hallucinating and decided to sleep on the couch. There was nothing in the living room that seemed to bring on the strange waking dream I had experienced in my room.

I swallowed another pill to calm my nerves and after counting to ten, I laid back down on the couch. As I drifted off to sleep again, I became aware of the thumping, bumping heartbeat sound that persisted above. I tossed and turned fretting about it but sleep eventually settled my thoughts.

In the morning I dressed without shaving or fixing my hair and went—for a third time—up to my new neighbor's door. I calmly knocked, ignoring the tingling feeling which screamed at me to flee from the door. The second-floor hall was quiet and I could hear the whine of the dim lights lining the walls. The door clicked open, startling me and a wet breeze wafted out of the second-floor apartment. The air smelled coppery and wet and bothered me enough that I placed my hand over my mouth and nose. I pushed the door open.

The living room of apartment 2A was a nightmare scene. A fleshy pink substance lined every square inch of the room including the windows. I knew it covered the windows because the sunlight shone through the flesh material exposing intricate veins and capillaries within the substance. The room was filled with a warm darkness. At first, I failed to notice the basketball-sized heart thing suspended in the middle of it. When I did see it, I knew it was the source of the thumping bass sound I had been hearing. There were grotesque sacks of flesh lining the wall to the left of the entrance. I stood in the entrance to the insides of a monster.

"What is this?" I said to myself.

"This is me, your new neighbor." Said a watery voice I couldn't discern the source of.

"This can't happen. This is too much. I'll be reporting you to the landlord on Monday." I said, trying to keep my voice even.

"You mean him?"

One of the great flesh sacks on the wall opened to drop a body onto the floor. It was the landlord. His eyes were rolled back and his mouth was frozen in a permanent scream. I never liked him, but I never wished him dead. My stomach tightened.

"This building is mine now, I *am* the building and if you

try to leave, I will collapse upon you. I will get to you and our other neighbors in time." The disembodied voice said.

I didn't stick around to hear any more of what my new neighbor was saying. I retreated down the stairs and kicked my front door in. I stumbled into the kitchen and ripped open the cabinet door above the sink where I kept the tools of my trade. The black bag was still there, and its presence helped to steady my heartbeat. I yanked it down, struggling under the weight.

From the bag I drew a fish boning knife. It was a bit dull, but it would suffice. I would not let this creature have sway over me in my place of residence. I charged back out into the hallway and saw Mrs. Lazenby peeking out of her door.

"Go back inside Mrs. Lazenby, I'll take care of this."

"Mr. Cooper." She nodded her head and shut the door.

I raced up the stairs and found the door to apartment 2A closed and locked. I threw my full weight against the door again and again. Soon after several tries, I heard the old wooden doorway crack. I hit it again with a shoulder that would surely be bruised and the door gave way.

"You do not know with which you meddle, you are the master of a subtle smile, but it is dangerous to gaze at the stars for too long. Mr. Cooper you will be lost!" The disembodied voice said with a frantic timbre.

I rushed into the damp dark and stood before the massive heart-thing. It convulsed rhythmically. The speed of its pumping increased when I raised the boning knife. I heard a flesh tearing sound from where the bedroom door should have been and saw a withered yellow figure burst through the membranous wall. The figure was humanoid in shape, but its face only contained two deep black holes for eyes and a dripping black hole for a mouth. It moved at a sluggish pace despite the desperation in every step. A gurgling sound rose in its throat.

I brought the knife down, slashing one of the veiny cords that held the heart suspended. The gurgling grew louder and the entire room seemed to move. I slashed again, severing another cord and it felt as though an earthquake had struck. Again and again I slashed until the meaty thing fell to the floor in the chaos erupting around me. I stumbled out of the room just in time to be saved.

In the hallway I saw the living room of apartment 2A collapse in on itself pulling everything that existed in apartment 3A—including the old man and his oxygen tank—down onto itself. The impact knocked me off my feet and I was choked with the dust of the collapsing building. Then the floor in apartment 2A gave way and crashed into my own apartment.

I fled from the building, a dirty and bloody figure frantically searching for a safe place. When I came to the park, I calmed myself down. Those who responded to the building collapsing would find evidence of my work in the rubble and debris. I couldn't be around when that happened. All that was left for me to do was find another city with a similar worn out apartment building to hide out in. There were always people in cities in need of my particular skill set and there were always run-down residences to hide away in. I cursed the monster that had moved in upstairs and I kissed my bird friends goodbye one last time. I had enough money in my pocket to ride the bus out of town.

THE END

The October Theater

BOAR WAS DEAD. His final moments played in my head while I walked as a ghost through the strange and dark streets of that decaying city. The moon was an orange crescent behind hazy clouds and I felt rain on my face, but it didn't motivate me to walk any quicker. I was numb. I had been wandering the city in an aimless trance for over an hour. Finding the seedy motel we had made our base of operations was going to be nigh impossible. It rained a little harder. The army of droplets soaked through my jacket.

It wasn't too late at night, but the city was already quiet. I had spent time in many cities and this one was at its end. A few cars bumped up and down the crumbling paved roadways and a police siren wailed here and there, but other than that there were barely any signs of life. Even the vagrants were silent, lying on their cardboard mattresses asleep or staring up into the bleak night sky with blank idiot looks. None of them hassled me for change as I passed. Lining every street was a mixture of used and disused store fronts and the occasional skyscraping tower. There were lights on in dirty windows here and there, remnants of the nightlife the city had once hosted. I had felt alone walking the streets with Boar and now I felt like an abandoned child in a foreign land. I gritted my teeth.

Someone happened to be exiting a building and I caught a glimpse of the warmth and safety inside. It looked to be a bar though there was no sign mounted or hanging that designated it as such an establishment. I placed my hand on the door and pulled it open. It was in that unnamed bar where I had found my respite, my escape from the dying city that seemed to want to swallow me up in its labyrinthian streets.

The lighting was soft and moody though the black walls and ceiling tried to suck it up. There were panels of art dressing the walls, violent pieces that only served to remind me of Boar's broken and bloody body lying in the alley. The place wasn't very busy, there were a few patrons here and there staring into their drinks like glum gargoyles. One bartender and one waitress were sufficient to serve everyone in the place. The bar was to the left and lit up by dim Christmas lights hanging about the gargantuan mirror lining that side of the place. The center floor was filled with little rickety tables and the right wall was lined with booths. I took a seat in a dark booth facing away from the door. I had no intention of looking back out into that dreary night until I was good and drunk.

The waitress approached me. She was young and pretty, her eyes had a dangerous fire in them.

"What can I get you, hun?" She asked.

"I'll have whatever you got on tap." I looked around the bar, "Can I smoke in here?"

"You can smoke, hun. I'll be right back." She winked at me and I gave a weak smile.

I pulled out a cigarette and lit up. It tasted extraordinary. Over at the bar the haggard barkeep filled a glass for me. His eyes darted toward me and I averted my stare. There was something challenging in those eyes and I was glad I had chosen to occupy a booth rather than a barstool. The waitress came back with the glass of foaming beer, winked again, and walked off to check on her other customers. I followed her retreat with tired, lustful eyes. She turned, sensing my glare. A smile spread across her face.

I stared into the bubbling glass and breathed deep trying to gather my thoughts. Some movement at the back of the bar pulled my attention. A door opened, three men and a woman strolled out and threw back a red curtain in the corner that I had failed to notice before. There was a drum set, standup bass, keyboard, and saxophone. They all took their positions and began to play.

Their gloomy jazz washed over the room like a viscous liquid, slow and deliberate. They played their respective instruments as if it pained them, the woman most of all as she led the charge with her saxophone dirge. My mouth fell open as I listened. The music was my mood, the mood of the city—sad and dying. I shook off the spell they had cast on me to take a swig of my beer and tap the ash from my cigarette.

I thought of Boar again, his pudgy body lying there in a spreading pool of blood, his eyes staring up at me with an accusatory deadness. The truth was that I wasn't quite sure what had happened. He and I had made it to the designated alley in which the deal was to take place. Careful planning and days of preparation had gone into it, though events had still managed to go sour. The shadows cast by the abandoned vagrant barrel fire had come alive and danced down the alley toward us. I ran like a dog with my tail between my legs at seeing shadows moving without a physical body to cast them. I heard Boar shout once and then I heard no more until police sirens cried out in the night.

The waitress sat down across from me, startling me from my memories. She placed a hand on one of mine. It was warm and full of life.

"You okay?"

I realized that a couple of tears began to crawl down my cheeks for all to see. I pulled my rough hand from under her soft and delicate fingers and wiped the tears away.

"I'm okay, I'm okay. Just some bad memories."

She looked around a few times to ensure no one was paying attention to us, including the bartender, before she spoke again.

"If you've got bad memories, I have something that may be able to help."

I sniffed and downed the rest of the beer before I responded.

"Yeah what's that? More alcohol? Whatya fishin for a bigger tip? Get lost." I couldn't help my attitude. The gloomy jazz still droned on in waves filling the dark space around us.

She scowled at my rudeness, "There's a place, it's called the October Theater. People go there to forget. Or remember. It's a strange place, but..."

She was cut off when she saw that the bartender was looking in our direction. I waved to him and held up my empty beer glass. He nodded and filled another for me. The waitress slid out of the booth with feline grace and returned with the beer.

"Before you leave here, let me know if you're interested. I have a ticket."

I watched her walk away again, but this time she did so timidly, her previous coyness gone. I chugged the fresh beer and lit up another cigarette. My watch told me it was eleven. I had plenty of time to drown the memory of the death of my colleague.

I drank more, Boar's death still playing in my head. I tried to push it out. What could this October Theater be? I pictured it as a once-grand theater with a faded golden ceiling that had peeled and flaked, sending golden and plaster-white snowflakes down all over threadbare chairs. A relic of a time long-passed with rudimentary electrical lighting and a heavy wooden stage that couldn't help but groan and squeal as it was walked upon. I felt myself being pulled there, the October Theater was becoming another place, an escape from this universe.

I closed my eyes and imagined walking out from under the mezzanine toward the ancient stage. The players twirled about in silence in their strange costumes. I imagined looking down into the audience, scanning the smiling attendees faces, until I saw Boar, broken and bloodied, propped up in one of the throne-like chairs of the front row. I turned and ran back toward the entrance of the theater, nearly jumping from my seat, startled when the waitress touched my shoulder.

"Don't go there yet. Here."

She put a thick ticket stub that was lined with intricate gold designs onto the table. It was a ticket to the October Theater, but it didn't specify when or what show it was for, only that it was good for one show. I felt an anxious need to get there rumbling in my chest.

"When is the next show?" I asked, unable to keep the desperation out of my slurring words.

"There's one tonight. If you leave now you can make it." She said.

"How much I owe you?"

"Don't worry about it. Go out the door, take a right, and then another right into the third alley from here. Follow the alley until you can take a left. Before you get to the street, you'll find a side door into the theater. Enter only by that door." She was speaking in a hushed voice.

"But you need a tip, how much?" I protested.

"No! Go now. Don't worry about the tab. I'll handle it." She left before I could say anything else.

I glanced at the jazz band one more time. Their sound was still cold death. I slid out of the booth and steadied myself while I tucked the theater ticket into my jacket. I knew I was drunk, but I couldn't be as drunk as I felt, the mood of the bar and the music must have lulled me into an altered state. I took one more look at the grizzled barkeep and exited into the cool night. The sky was clear, and no more rain fell.

A beat-up taxi drove by, splashing dirty water onto the sidewalk. There were no other cars in sight except one parked across the street in a spot where the streetlight had gone out. There looked to be someone in it, but I couldn't be sure. I stood swaying on the sidewalk, my need to get to the theater dissipating as I appraised the dirty street, a street that should have been much busier. The city was dying.

I took a step forward and heard the parked car's door open. Out stepped an ominous figure cloaked in shadows. The dark figure began to cross the street to where I was standing. The entity's gait was silent and sinister, I didn't feel safe on that empty street. The other lights on the street didn't touch this phantom as if the light itself was frightened. Thoughts of Boar's assailants screamed at me to move. I turned on my heel and started for the theater. If the thing was coming after me, I hoped to throw it off in the twisting alleys.

I counted the alleys and ducked into the one the waitress had directed me toward. The alley stank like putrid garbage, I put my hand over my nose and my mouth and swiftly moved down it. As I approached the next alley, I was aware of something moving behind me. I spun and saw nothing, but still felt a presence. There had certainly been something there. It gave off the same energy as the shadows that had taken Boar.

I hurried down the next alley and found a door in the massive brick building on my right. A rusted sign hung over the door. I couldn't make out the words on it, but I knew I was at the right place. I yanked it open and hopped inside, eager to escape whatever had been following me.

It took a moment for my eyes to adjust, the hallway I stood in was lit only by the red exit sign above the door behind me. I could see another door at the end of the hall painted with the crimson light. The door led right into the seating area and I was struck dumb by the golden glory of the theater.

It was more magnificent and more decaying than I could have ever imagined. Loose tiles and intricate gilding hung from the ceiling like the dying foliage of autumn trees ready to drop. The seats were iron thrones with royal crimson cushions lit by great half-functioning chandeliers suspended overhead. This theater was old, a fact reinforced by the ancient dust smell hanging over everything. Some of the seats were occupied by lonesome figures and a few people peered over the mezzanine railing with pallid expressionless faces.

There was a nervous, anticipatory silence. The dark curtain fluttered, and the stage floor creaked as movement began in preparation for the show.

I found a seat away from the other patrons. As I sat, I spied the waitress entering. She looked around with a timid, twitching gaze and took a seat far down below where I sat. The lights were dimmed and there was nothing to hear but the creaking of the stage. Then the mechanism to raise the curtain whirred to life. Dread descended on me as the curtain made its ascent. I was aware of the iron grip that I had on the arms of my seat, but at least I was grasping onto something that was real.

I wasn't ready for what the curtain would reveal. The October Theater was, as the name suggested, a place of autumn. A place where the dying of all things was well underway, preparing for the full death of winter to come. The things on the stage down below me were nightmare abominations. Skulls, human and otherwise, decorated twisting wire bodies bent in unnatural shapes. Their appendages were leathery skin-like contraptions meant for some purpose unknown to all but the artist who had birthed the sedentary creatures. I held my breath and scanned the sculptures one by one as they sat in silence, their glare accusatory, judging the audience for their crime of living.

Someone in the theater screamed a crying scream that spoke of a broken psyche. I watched as a man threw himself over the backs of chairs in desperation, trying to get away from the things displayed on stage. Someone was weeping. My thoughts turned to Boar. The waitress had turned in her seat and was staring up at me, in her eyes was an unrestrained terror.

"Please, no more!" Someone yelled.

I looked back to the stage and saw Boar crawling about the floor under the looming statues. He left a trail of black ichor as he moved and wailed words that I could not understand. My heart beat faster and faster and I felt faint.

The curtains began their journey back toward center stage and I breathed a sigh of relief, the end was in sight. Quickly, the statues were covered and the lights grew to their former luminosity. A few people clapped. I didn't know how to feel about the horrors that had been revealed to me.

Aside from the man who had fled, all other patrons remained seated and quiet. Apparently, there was more to come.

The curtain rose again revealing a thin man in a moth-eaten tuxedo center stage under a glaring spotlight. He removed his ragged top hat and gave the sparse crowd a deep bow. He spoke with a soft voice, the acoustics carrying his words across the great theater.

"What you have witnessed tonight was a protracting of pain and horror from the depths of your unconscious. We here at the October Theater do our best to erase the hurt and the fear to leave your mind conscious and clear. Be off with you now as the hour is quite late. Or is it early? Very soon, I think, you will see the sun and with its rise, a rising of your spirits. Step lightly in life. Goodnight. Good morning. We hope to never see you again."

He bowed again, and the curtain fell. I had a vague feeling that if I didn't exit the theater as soon as possible I would be a witness to things more horrible than I had seen on stage. I had no wish to have any deeper understanding of how the October Theater's shows came together. I left through that crimson hallway without bothering to take a final look at the magnificent dying interior of the place.

The showing in the October Theater had come and gone and although I still mourned Boar, I had no bad feelings left about his death, no fear of the shadows that had hunted me. The tidal wave of feeling had faded as though years had passed and time had healed my wounds. I felt lighter just as the ragged man on stage said I would. The other theatergoers dispersed without a murmur among them. The waitress caught my eye and then was gone, back down the alley toward the bar. I stood just outside of the door watching people go.

I went to the front of the building to get a look at the main entrance to the October Theater. I expected a once-magnificent marquee and ancient lights that flickered and hummed. I made it to the street and gazed up toward the entrance, but instead of awe or wonder, I was filled with confusion.

There was no grand entrance, only the glowing fluorescent lights of a 24-hour laundromat. A fat man sat in a chair reading a newspaper as his laundry tumbled in the dryer next to him. There was a neon sign in the window declaring, "OPEN." I turned and retreated down the alley. There was no door with a rusted sign overhead, only an uninterrupted brick wall.

I stood staring at the wall, wondering if I had hallucinated everything. I plunged my hand into my pocket to dig out a cigarette with the hope of calming my nerves. My fingers touched the thick gold-trimmed ticket to the October Theater. I pulled it out and the word 'VOID' appeared across the ticket before my eyes. The words, 'Good for one show only!' turned a deep crimson color. I laughed and lit a cigarette. I let the ticket fall to the ground where it came to rest in a stagnant puddle.

THE END

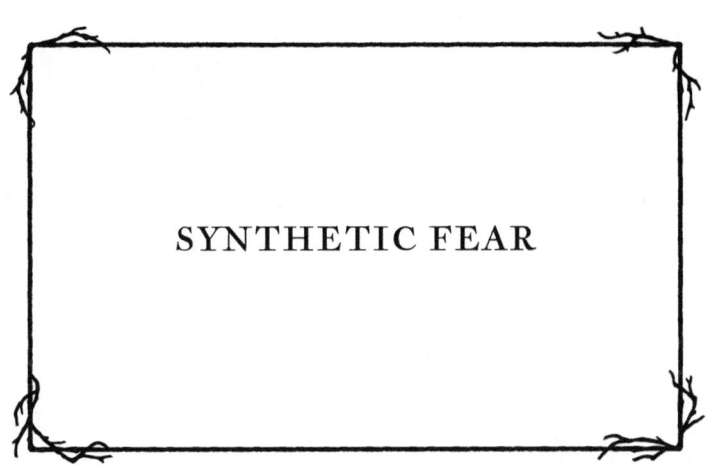

SYNTHETIC FEAR

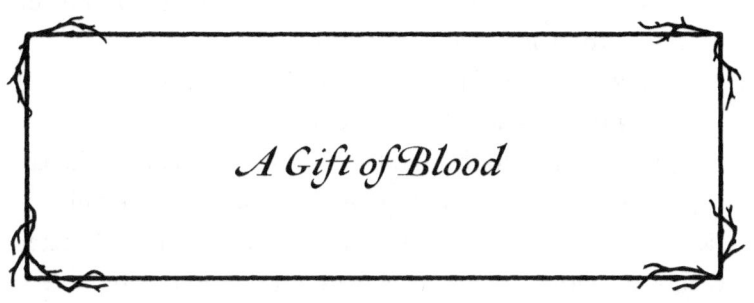

A Gift of Blood

THE DOCTOR'S OFFICE smelled like sickness. It smelled as if someone had tried very hard to banish the scent of decay and disease with some type of store brand cleaner. It wafted into his nose whenever the entrance door swung open to admit or expel another patient. The patients themselves smelled sick as they meandered by him. The patients spoke inane words and babbled about blood pressure or what bug was going around which nursing home. His head hurt as he listened. Against the subtle cacophony of the waiting room, he closed his eyes.

Names were called, and patients were brought behind the imposing oak door that sat as a barrier between worlds. Shuffling footsteps passed, and an elderly stink swirled. He kept telling himself he would be seen eventually. Finally, the number on his ticket was called out. His eyes opened to double check the number as the phlebotomist's gaze swept the room. She called out his number again. It was strange to willingly go to be pricked by a needle when one could have just as easily stayed in bed. It was stranger still to be referred to by number as if in some human meat factory. It was his turn to be processed. The smile on her face was beginning to sour when he stood and made towards her.

"How are you today?" Her smile lit up again.

"Alright." He said. That was a lie.

She motioned for him to have a seat as he handed the lab paperwork to her. She noisily typed away, confirming his patient information as she went. This new room smelled better than the waiting room. They were on the other side now, a sterile world rife with white lab coats fluttering about the halls. In his gut he felt dread rising. A terrible bubble of anxiety that set his heart racing as it expanded. He knew his face had grown pale and he could feel perspiration beginning to bead at his hairline. It didn't help to stare at the multitude of vials lined up neatly at his elbow. There was still a chance to run, to make some excuse to be away from those torturous instruments.

"Are you okay? You look a little pale."

"Anxiety."

"It's all mind over matter, kiddo. I'm gonna have you lay down while we do this, so you don't pass out."

"Ok."

He followed her into another room as a doctor hurried by with a tight, anguished look on his face. She motioned to the cushioned slab covered in paper, it crinkled as he sat on it. Her instruments of torture were laid out on the counter. He rested his back against the slab.

"Listen, if you can get a tattoo, you can handle this." She poked a finger at the elaborate tattoo on his arm.

"That took six hours."

"You won't be here for that long, kiddo."

"Let's hope."

The woman tied an elastic strip about his bicep coaxing a blood-filled vein out of hiding. He looked away, resolving not to witness the assault on the life-giving cord that throbbed in the crook of his arm. Some package was opened. The needle.

"Ok, deep breath in." He felt it go in. The thin little piece of steel punctured the soft skin cells that guarded his blood. "And breathe out. That's it. Nice slow deep breaths."

He felt the first tube being popped onto the needle and he felt the needle digging in a little more. The feeling made him want to squirm, to cry out and shrink away. He then made a grave mistake. His head moved mechanically, his eyes locking onto the action that was taking place at his elbow. Hot blood spurted into the little plastic tube. Immediately he felt light-headed. He tried to say something, but the world began fading into a darkness. A rush of sound flooded his ears like static on a television.

Everything was black. He had no body, he was only his consciousness. Time passed and he was aware of it, yet he didn't know what had happened. *You've passed out*, he said to himself, *just open your eyes, you're ok.* It didn't work. He began to hear sounds breaking through the static and he attempted again to rouse himself. It worked, and his eyes snapped open to take in the overhead light. *Say something, let her know you're okay.*

"I'm okay."

"Are you?" It wasn't the voice of the phlebotomist.

He scanned the room for the owner of the voice, finding a pale man standing in the corner. He wore an ill-fitting lab coat and had a surgical mask over his face. His eyes were unnerving, cold and dead. The man uncrossed his arms and moved closer.

"What have you got going on with your arm?" The words were carried on sour breath that smelled very much like the sickness that coated the waiting room.

"I'm having blood drawn."

"Are you sure about that?" The man's dead eyes narrowed.

The victim on the table swung his head to look upon his needle-pierced arm once more and his heart convulsed at what he saw. There was no longer a needle, only a pale white maggoty worm that was wiggling its way into the still-throbbing vein. The strange man seemed unbothered by the nightmarish screams that emitted from the patient.

There was an attempt to remove the worm, but it escaped the patient's fumbling grasp. It disappeared into his arm. It was unbearable, he just wanted to shrink away and cry. He fell off the table, scattering the phlebotomist's tools of torture across the room. The strange pale man had pulled down his mask to reveal something like a twisted rotting smile. But it wasn't a smile. The man had no lips, only ragged skin that fell partially over his teeth. He just stood and stared at the frightened patient.

"I need help, please someone help me!" The patient cried in vain.

He attempted to stay as far away from the dead looking figure as he made for the door. That pale ragged smile and cold stare followed him as he moved around the room, the stranger made no attempt to stop the patient. At last he reached the door and wrenched it open.

The hallway was different. It was dark and the paint was chipped and peeling. Dim light shone at the end and a thick vapor rose from the floor. His footsteps echoed strangely as he sprinted down the hallway. The dim light had entered the passage through a tiny window in a door marked as an emergency exit only. He threw himself into the door and spilled out into feeble sunlight.

The world was blanketed by thick fog and there was nothing to be seen save the sun, and even that was obscured by clouds. The patient righted himself and took stock of his surroundings. It didn't take long for black formless shapes to begin appearing in the fog. Hunched little shadows that moved in jerking movements. The patient started to hyperventilate. In his ragged gasps he could taste the mist that had engulfed the world. Sickness, vile sickness. A miasma of death and decay coated his throat and filled his lungs. He was suffocating, choking on the unbreathable air.

He turned back to retreat through the exit door, but it had closed. The window held the face of the ragged-lipped stranger. He had donned his mask once more and stood staring at the action unfolding outside. The patient banged on the door, his screams becoming desperate and high pitched.

"Let me in, open the door, please, please, help me!"

The door clicked open and the patient thrust his fingers into the crack that had appeared. He pushed by the sick-smelling stranger who pulled the door closed behind him.

"Am I the lesser of two evils?" The stranger folded his arms and appraised the panting patient.

"What is happening? I don't understand."

"I'm not quite sure if I do either. I don't remember how I came here."

"I was just having blood drawn and...and I passed out. I must be dreaming or something."

"Well, I guess you'd better wake up." The stranger turned to look out the tiny window again.

The patient backed his way down the hall, his eyes never leaving the stranger. The man never looked back at him. Once in the room, the patient paced trying to figure out how to wake himself up. He saw the phlebotomist's tools splayed across the tiled floor, he picked them up, continually checking the door for the return of the ragged-mouthed stranger. He laid back down on the table and closed his eyes, hoping this would return him to the waking world. He opened his eyes, finding three people standing above him and he wildly thrashed and cried out.

"You okay, kiddo?" It was the phlebotomist again.

The thrashing had pushed one of the nurses back, the other nurse and a doctor stood over him. The doctor held a stethoscope.

"That was strange, you passed out and I lost your heartbeat." The doctor hung the stethoscope around his neck.

"Don't get up, take it easy."

The patient's eyes darted around the room and fell on the door. In the window was a familiar face. The cold dead eyes of that stranger stared at him. The stranger winked and turned away from the door.

THE END

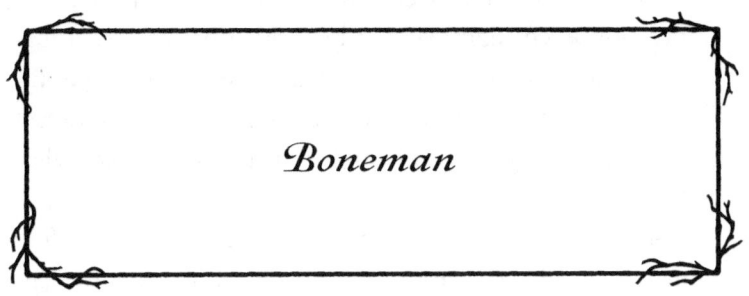

Boneman

THE PLACE WAS a ghost town. The wind rustled tattered curtains hanging in broken glass windows and shutters banged as exasperated gusts blew through the empty sidewalks. The streets were littered with debris attesting to the shattered existence that the place had come to know. The vibrant reds and oranges had been washed out of the desert by a deluge of ill grayness. The place was devoid of all life save the one man who had survived the storm.

Following that fateful storm, the dry desert weather had disappeared, replaced by a choking humidity and swirling walls of fog. Sunrise would clear away the murk for a time, but soon it would roll back in with stealthy, persistent silence.

The entire town had nearly been wiped from existence when the anomalous tempest had dumped its spectacular rains and struck with vengeful lightning. Being situated in the middle of a vast desert, residents were used to sand storms, but the sudden severity of this storm had taken them by surprise.

Quinlin often wondered if he had lost his mind in the storm. He had trouble recalling any memories from before the roaring winds and needle rains. The storm itself was a half-remembered nightmare and anything before was a forgotten dream. There were sensations of the past, but Quinlin could never hold on to them long enough for them to reveal themselves. His memories would return, at least that's what he told himself.

After the storm came the fog and the silence. The few animals that called the desert home had vanished. There were no more snakes, no more lizards, no owls perched atop the cacti—and not many cacti left either. The domesticated animals that belonged to the few ranchers still in town had been eviscerated by debris or drowned in flooding along with their shepherds. Perhaps some animals survived the storm, but if so, the fog had surely done them in.

The day after the storm he had gone out to look for other survivors and became caught in the haze. He was wracked with nausea and his head felt ready to burst as he choked on the mists. He managed to get back to his ramshackle home before collapsing into a fitful sleep. That was the last time he made the mistake of being caught out in the fog. Now, he always made sure to be back before the fog hit. He longed to leave the town and start over somewhere else, but that would have to wait until he found a way to make it through the choking gloom. He longed to be out of the vexing quietness that had settled around him.

When the fog wasn't busy choking everything, Quinlin would scavenge in what was left of the homes and businesses of this once-happy small town. He had taught himself to ignore the bodies strewn about the street, bodies that decayed very quickly in the fog. Most of the corpses were already showing bone beneath ragged patches of greenish skin. It hadn't been that long since the storm, but soon only clothed skeletons would be left.

During the fog, Quinlin did his best to occupy his mind with whatever books he could get his hands on. The first few days of his imprisonment were devoted to shoring up his storm-ravaged home to keep the haze out. After that project was finished, he fell into depression and went days without moving or eating. He poured what little energy he had into books, and it was always the books which pulled him out of the funk. The stories and histories he read were an escape from the horror that his life had become.

There was a library on the opposite side of town. He could make it there, grab a few books, and get back before the fog began its daily occupation. Quinlin was content with scavenging, eating canned food, getting lost in stories, and sleeping. As far as he was concerned he was the last person alive and he made every effort to have a good time within his means. He was at peace.

At least until a new neighbor moved in.

Quinlin awoke one morning to scraping and banging coming from the house next door. After so many days of only hearing the wind, the change in sound had jarred him out of sleep. He jumped out of bed wide-eyed and strained to hear the muffled clamor. He wanted to believe that there was someone else alive, but he also tried to prepare himself for a sudden realization that madness might have finally overtaken him.

He pulled on his threadbare jeans and a dirty white shirt as he hustled to the door. He cracked it open and slipped out like a cat trying to avoid notice. There was whispering floating on the breeze, but he could not discern the direction it was coming from. There was excitement welling up in him and his eyes were watering at the joy of finding another living being. He wanted to squeal.

There was a great bang and he whipped his attention to the house that had once been his neighbors. A shadowy form loped by one of the broken windows and Quinlin called out.

"Hello!?" He shivered at his own voice as it sounded so alien and wrong.

There was no answer. Quinlin crept to the home and knocked on the cracked front door with a timid, shaking hand. There was movement inside.

"Hello? I'm not going to hurt you. My name is Quinlin, I was beginning to think I was the only one who survived the storm. I have food and books."

Quinlin let the silence hang overhead as he waited for a response. His feelings sank when he realized it could just be an animal. His hand went to the door knob and he heard more movement inside the house. Then a wavering liquid voice floated out to him.

"You survived?" The voice said.

"Uh, yes I did. It seems you have as well."

Quinlin wasn't sure, but he thought that the voice had stifled a laugh.

"May I come in?"

"No!" The voice shouted, startling Quinlin.

"Well, you are welcome to visit me in my home. It's just next door."

"Can you do something for me, Quinlin?" The voice asked.

"Uh, sure. Anything you need."

"I need bones."

"Excuse me, I don't think I heard you right."

"Bones, Quinlin, bones, the skeletal structure that supports the meat of a being." The voice said.

Quinlin still didn't understand. He stood in front of the door grasping for an answer as to why this other survivor would want bones. Perhaps he was an artist and he needed somewhere to focus his energy, like Quinlin with his books. All of a sudden a memory came to him. He recalled seeing an art showing once, long ago, on one of his trips across the desert with his parents. The artist had rigged up grotesque hanging structures made of the bones he had found exploring deserted ranches. It was a dark and morbid exhibit set in a derelict gas station. A grim experience for a child.

"May I ask why you need," Quinlin paused with unease creeping up his spine, "bones?"

"You may not. You will bring them to me, Quinlin, whether you do so willingly or by force remains to be seen."

Quinlin backed away from the wind blasted house and retreated to his own. He locked the door for the first time in ages. This other survivor was unstable. Quinlin felt ill thinking about looting even the animal corpses to get the bones that his new neighbor seemed to want so badly, never mind the human corpses, that was unfathomable. The other survivor's banging and scraping started up again and Quinlin was eager to go about his scavenging for the day.

He hurried past the other survivor's home without bothering to glance at it. He headed for the library to find a few more books and maybe some food in the refrigerator in the staff break room. He hadn't touched it yet not wanting to let out the cold air that it held. His mood lightened a little as he strolled under the bright sunshine and he closed his eyes letting it wash over him.

Quinlin stumbled over something and he snapped his eyes open in enough time to grab onto a twisted mailbox. Regaining his composure, he hazarded a glance at the debris that tripped him. It was a body. The corpse's face was turned up at him and an idiot smile showed through the remains of the thing's cheeks. There was not much left of it besides the damp and moldering clothes on its back and tough, leathery skin.

Quinlin glanced around to make sure no one was watching him and felt silly—there was no one left alive to watch him. He bent close to the remains with a hand over his mouth and nose. There were no insects. Remains like this should be crawling with beetles and maggots, swarming with flies, circled by vultures. It seemed only the heavy fog had eaten away at it.

He reached out a steady hand and placed it on the cheek of the thing. He almost expected it to move, to wake out of its permanent slumber. There was an itching urge to pull the skull from the remains. A morbid urge that grew so rapidly that Quinlin gasped and stumbled away from the corpse.

He stood and hurried in the direction of the library pushing the thought of desecrating the dead from his mind. He heard a shout echoing in the distance. Quinlin only made out his name and the word bones. He was sure that the shout had ended in laughter. His new neighbor must have yelled something to him.

The library was one of the largest buildings in town and it greeted him with jagged shadowed mouths for windows and a tattered flag that stirred in the slight breeze. The library had become a sacred place to Quinlin. The peace and the bounty of knowledge held within left him in awe. He held a deep reverence for whatever force had spared the books from the storm's damage.

He closed his eyes and gave the building a slight bow before he entered with blazing flashlight in hand. Enough light got in through the windows to see most of what the book temple had to offer, but darkness held sway over the basement and that's where Quinlin was going. The older books were held there, the ones that weren't allowed to be checked out and had to be handled with the utmost care lest they fall apart.

Quinlin went to the desk and rifled through the drawers until he found a pair of cotton gloves, which he donned. The book he meant to look at was a history of the desert town in which he was imprisoned. Nowhere in its two-hundred-year-old pages did he find any mention of a storm like the one he had lived through. Sand storms and dramatic heat lightning made the annals, but nothing like he'd experienced. He closed the book, letting it rest and peeled off the cotton gloves. He left them on the desk to use the next time he needed to handle one of the older books.

The staff lounge happened to be in the basement as well, so he went there and raided the fridge and cupboard. He came away with some bottles of water, a can of tuna, and a sealed box of crackers which were all zipped securely into his backpack. He clicked the flashlight off as he ascended the steps. He heard movement that broke the silence and he froze in place.

"Bones, Quinlin, bones. Not silly books. Where are you?" The other survivor was somewhere upstairs.

Quinlin began to back down the stairs taking care to be as quiet as possible. When he reached the last step, he felt an arm snake around his neck, a steel grip seizing his right wrist in a painful grasp. The arm and the hand were cold and clammy.

"You're my creature now, Quinlin. If you do not deliver even one bone to me today," the cold hand slid down Quinlin's wrist and found his pinky. "you'll hurt a lot worse than this."

The cold hand twisted and snapped the bone of Quinlin's pinky. He cried out and the cold arm around his neck disappeared. He clicked the flashlight on and whirled around, but the beam revealed nothing save the bookshelves and door to the staff lounge. He investigated his broken pinky and saw it jutting out perpendicular to the rest of his hand. His breath came heavy through clenched teeth as he grabbed it. On the count of three he snapped it back into place releasing a screech of pain.

Quinlin quit the library, his plans of book-exploration extinguished. A cold sweat beaded upon his brow as his eyes darted around looking for any signs of his assailant on his way home. His searching gaze caught only the grinning corpse he had stopped to view on his way to the library. It lay there in the same position, though it seemed to beckon him closer.

Quinlin wheezed, he had been holding his breath. He moved closer to the corpse. He compulsively scanned the area to see if anyone was watching before stomping on the brittle neck of the thing. There was a dull thud and a crack that resounded through the ghost buildings lining the empty street.

Bile crawled up Quinlin's throat as he kept the corpse pinned with his foot and pulled at the skull with his uninjured hand. The pulpy flesh ripped and tore, most of it sloughing off the skull and staying attached to the remains on the ground. Putrid gray liquid poured from the base of the skull splashing his shoes.

He gagged and vomited. Tears flooded his eyes. He moved mechanically back to his home with the skull held outstretched in front of him, its empty black sockets gazing into his watering eyes. The jaw was still attached to it, making it seem like the thing was grinning wildly at him.

Before he knew it, Quinlin was standing outside of his neighbor's house. With a cry, he hurled the skull into one of the broken windows clipping some jagged shards of glass. He panted in the silence until he heard the familiar quiet laugh. Quinlin stormed into his house, threw himself on the bed and wept until he fell asleep.

He woke in the middle of the night to the sound of something being dragged outside. Moving to the window he tried to peer through the swirling fog lit by a glowing full moon. There was a shadow out on the street dragging a large object toward his neighbor's house. The light revealed little, but Quinlin decided it must be his neighbor dragging another one of the inert bodies from the street. He glanced down at his broken pinky and was surprised to find himself angry rather than fearful. Without a second thought he pulled open his front door to confront the other survivor.

"Hey! If you're gonna loot corpses yourself, why threaten me into doing your dirty work?" Quinlin shouted.

The person dragging the corpse let out a moan, dropped it, and loped off into the shadows of a house across the street. Then he heard his neighbor's voice clearly from inside the house next door.

"Do not interrupt the others in their work, Quinlin." His neighbor said.

"Others? There are other survivors?" He choked on the fog billowing around him on his front step.

"Shut your door, Quinlin, lest you become like them."

Quinlin's heart began to beat faster and he slammed the door. He stared out through a half-boarded up window at the abandoned corpse on the ground and the person that had been dragging it appeared again to finish the job. Another shadow appeared dragging another body. Then another and another. Quinlin could do nothing but lay down and press a pillow over his ears to shut out the myriad of morbid dragging and the occasional muffled speech from his neighbor. He managed to fall asleep again through it all.

Morning came, and it was like nothing had happened. The streets were clear, and the town had gone back to the same lonesome stillness that had pervaded it since the storm. Quinlin made the decision to attempt escape from the town, from this personal hell.

He threw some canned food into his bag, a flashlight, some water, a multitool, and some warm clothes. After he was packed and steeled to go, he snuck out the front door. In an instant his neighbor's door flew open and the sound that came forth could only have been the sound of bones rattling. Dry, dull, and hollow knocking and clanging echoed out and into the street. Quinlin only stopped long enough to see a less-than-human shadow shape in the house approaching the door. The bone noises rolled from the shadow with each step the thing made.

Quinlin sprinted as fast as his legs would go towards the library. Many of the remains that had lain in the streets were gone, including the body he had pulled the skull from. It made him uneasy to think that there were others in the town hiding away until the boneman called them. He made it to the library and continued past it, redoubling his sprinting efforts. He had never been past the library in his scavenging, but now he planned to be well past it and off into the gray wash of the desert.

Evidence of civilization quickly fell away and Quinlin found himself fleeing across the cracked ground. The far-off hills began to manifest in the shimmering heat and Quinlin believed he was going to make it. He slowed his pace and looked back towards the small town to see how far he had gotten.

The library was only two feet behind him.

He shuddered and began to walk backwards. He felt himself moving, but the library never got any farther away. Instead he ran to it and pounded its walls with his uninjured hand, crying out in distress.

"This is your hell, Quinlin. You live here now. Did you really think the gods would have saved a sinner like you from the storm? You are going to collect bones for me for all eternity my friend." His neighbor's voice said. "A fitting punishment for a monster like you."

The neighbor ceased speaking and Quinlin strained to hear more as his breathing became heavy. His mind worked to understand the sentence that he had been given. A sudden rattle of dry bones sounded out nearby and Quinlin shrieked in terror.

THERE WERE ONLY a few casualties attributed to the freak storm that had rolled through the little desert town. An elderly woman had suffered a fatal heart attack, a man fighting the wind had been impaled by a fence post, and a rancher had drowned trying to save his cattle. There was much work to be done in the town and when volunteer cleanup crews went to Quinlin's house, they were shocked to find the friendly bookworm dead. It seemed he had hit his head and drowned in the two inches of water that had flooded his place.

As the crew sifted through his ruined home, they discovered jars filled with bones, plaques with human skulls mounted like trophies, and the beginnings of what seemed to be some type of bone suit. The bones were collected and sent out for testing. All had belonged to various missing persons or otherwise cold cases. The town's residents buried his remains in an unmarked grave out in the desert and razed his house. The people were eager to forget the serial killer who had hidden among them for so many years.

THE END

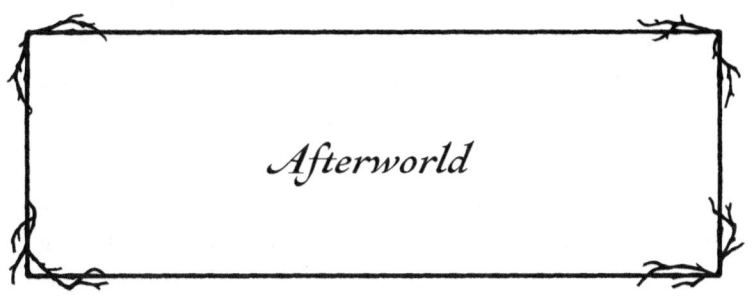

Afterworld

"**W**HERE DID YOU GO?**"** Came a voice. My eyes opened to the darkness of my room. The curtain-less windows were a painting of the moon and stars dancing on the whitest snow. Fresh snow that had fallen for two days. It held me in the tiny mountain cottage with no company but the tiny footsteps of mice in the ceiling. The snow was undisturbed save for two footprints. I closed my eyes, willing the paranoid thoughts away. Then came a tap. Tap. Tap. Uniform on the cold pane of glass. Tight-chested and breathing hard, I didn't dare look out the window again. I began to count. One, breathe in, two, breathe out, three, breathe in. By eighty I had entered a dream state.

Something came to me and grinned, with what mouth, I do not know. It extended a branch-like arm and beckoned me to follow. My consciousness left my body and drifted towards the thing. As I got farther away, I grew colder, chilled to my soul. I turned around and saw the window open. I flew back screaming at myself to wake.

My eyes opened again to the darkness of my room and darted to the window. Icy death whipped through the house coming from the sitting room and I bolted out of bed, pulling the blankets with me. The bedding would serve as my armor against the icy intruder. Slowly, I opened my bedroom door. Into the living room I looked, and was gripped with a deep terror.

The front door of the cabin was wide open, inviting snow and wind into the front room. The wood stove had battled valiantly but the flame flickered and failed, my heart convulsed almost failing with it. I bounded forth and slammed the door, pushing it through the snow that had accumulated. I shuffled to the stove to administer aid to the fading embers. More wood and kindling went in and I threw the vent wide open. The stove blazed to life flinging an unearthly orange glow about the cabin's front room. Turning my attention to my room, I saw movement at the window.

Against my fear, I moved to my room to investigate, hugging the blankets closer despite the renewed warmth. There were more footprints now. They were in a line from the original set to the window. Something had been peeking in. "Where did you go?" I said, releasing the fear I clung to. It had no hold on me now. Not with the world in this state. Sleep. I needed sleep.

The black void welcomed me as I dozed. That thing was back. I knew it wanted me to follow. One single malignant eye rolled as it turned towards our destination. I did not let myself look it in the eye. Again, I drifted, not knowing if I went willingly. The thing had gravity, a tugging I felt in my bones. They ached as I drifted, just watching the black mass move about the starless void.

Suddenly a slash of blinding light was ahead of us. The thing forced gruesome fingers into the slash and pulled. A door. A soft moonlit and snow-covered wood stood before us. Not a whisper sounded, trees stood like sentinels under the bright moonlight. A lone figure moved out in the distance. The crunching of snow drifted into my ears. A clammy hand closed itself around my wrist. I looked down in horror as my guide slowly pinned my arm against my back. Unseen lips touched my ears, whispering, urging. Words of slaughter rolled from its tongue and burrowed themselves within me.

My body heaved and the gateway into the void closed behind. I stood in the woods, nude, but felt nothing. There was a jagged knife in my hand, black as the creature that had armed me. It was a strange thing, it did not reflect the moon and it felt hot in my hand. Crunch, crunch, crunch. Boots compacting snow ahead of me pulled my attention from the blade. Death, slaughter, whatever the thing asked, just as long as I would get some sleep. My bare feet were silent in the frozen powdery hell.

It was a man that I stalked. He, dressed head to toe in warmth, was unaware of his impending death. Closer and closer I crept until I could reach out and touch him. My left hand made for his shoulder, my right thrust the knife into his back. My eyes blazed with hunger as I stabbed and stabbed. The figure collapsed to the ground. I cried out at my victory, at my chance for a good night sleep until I noticed there was no body within the clothing. I crouched and pushed the pile of cloth around. A pile of clothes only, no body within.

There was blood on the knife. I could see spots of blood on the ground. I dropped the blade and it hissed steam in the frigid snow. Then I felt them in my back. The stab wounds ached dully. I reached my hands back and felt the sticky sanguine fluid leaking from ragged wounds. I cried out in pain,

I cried out at the betrayal. I went to my knees in the snow. I went to my knees in the snow and...I went to my knees in the snow and...

"Where did you go?" I nearly fell out of the bed when I heard the voice. It was not my own I do not think. How long had it been since I last spoke aloud? Was my sanity fleeing? There was a knock at my bedroom door. I was here alone, was I not? There was no one left alive. The bombs had fallen and there was no one left alive. Knock, knock. Deliberate, urgent. I was here alone, was I not? I WAS HERE ALONE, WAS I NOT?

"What do you want from me?!" Ragged scream, my throat was bone dry and full of fear. The door swung in and in the moonlight stood the creature of my dreams. A mouth that was not a mouth grinned, the malignant eye locked its cancerous gaze on me, and branch-like limbs reaching out with gruesome, crooked fingers. I turned to the moonlit window to see another of the creatures peering in. It had left the tracks before.

Then I felt the jagged knife slip in between my ribs. It boiled my blood and melted bone. The window exploded inward to admit the second creature. They had me. When my screams died out, all was peaceful. No sounds disturbed the sentinel trees or the immaculate snow. There was no one left to be alone. The bombs had fallen and no one was left alive.

THE END

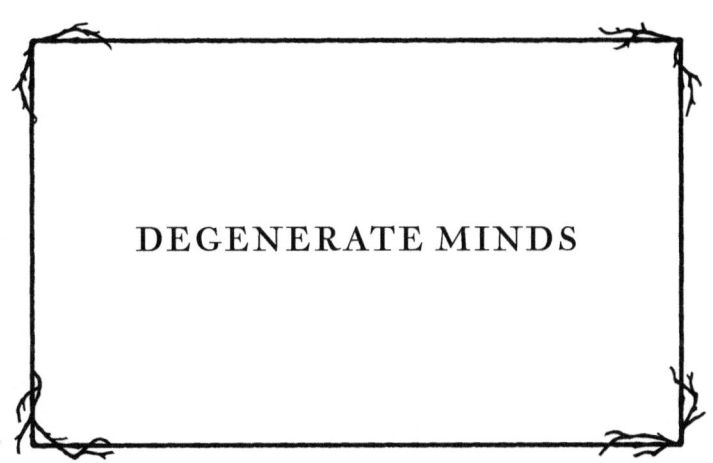

DEGENERATE MINDS

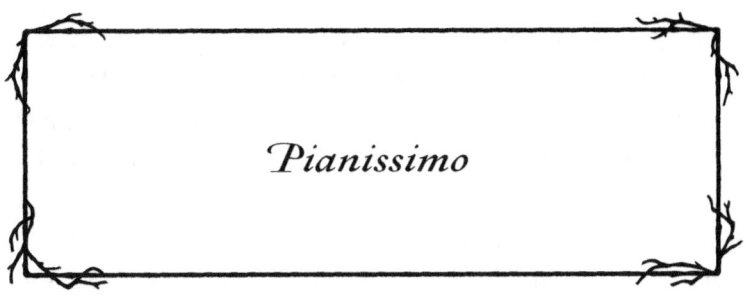

Pianissimo

IT WAS DARK, I was awake, and I heard it again—the delicate tapping of piano keys, soft notes floating through the still night air. They came more evenly, forming a melancholy song that tugged at my heart. Whoever was playing that piano out there at this time of night knew the pain that I was suffering.

I got out of bed and opened the window to its fullest extent. The air was humid but it felt good. The stars twinkled over the sleeping little town. The screen came out easily and I stole out and onto the roof overhanging the porch that wrapped around the inn. The music flowed from somewhere in town, perhaps a pub or someone's private music studio. I laid myself out on the roof and relished the heat that it still held from the daytime sun.

I lay there thinking and listening for a long while, my thoughts always returning to the same place—Sarah was gone and I was alone. I was alone in the world that night, along with whoever was playing that beautiful and sad melody. I made the choice to find the source of the music instead of attempting to fall back to sleep.

This strange little town truly slumbered after sundown. The gas street lamps were on and not a single window was lit on the streets that I walked. My shoes on the cobblestones sent echoes that almost drowned out the soft piano. I stopped often and strained to listen for the source. It seemed to be ever deeper into town.

I came across a mangy dog who merely growled at me and disappeared down an alley when I tried to approach it. At first the quietness of the night was peaceful, but then it became overwhelming. The daytime held such life and gaiety that I began to think I had wandered into a different town altogether on my stroll. I feared that my footfalls on the cobblestones were going to wake some curious beast that would chase me as though in a nightmare. The sad song became louder as I twisted and turned toward the center of town.

Sarah played piano. I would slide myself onto the bench and snuggle up to her with a glass of wine in my hand. She'd take my hands and spread my fingers to play bass chords while she played her heart out on the higher keys. The last time we spoke was seated at the piano together. I didn't know what she wanted from me. The tears still caught me by surprise whenever I cried.

I wiped them away, realizing that the piano music was coming from the building across the street. It was a three-story u-shaped brick structure with a sweet little courtyard in front of the entrance. A fountain gurgled softly next to a massive tree. In the flickering pale gaslight I could see that its sick gray bark was split and flaking away at the urging of some strange mold that had begun to grow about it. As I approached it, I began to feel ill. The gnarled and twisted branches were reminiscent of skeletal lightning strikes. No leaves grew on the thing despite the fullness of summer that was upon the town.

Even in the warm dead air of the night I shivered at the tree and to my horror I saw it shiver back. There was no breeze. I took a step back and it shivered again. The piano music had stopped. I felt like I was descending into some mad dream. The rising horror in me receded as the melancholy song started up and the tree stood still.

I told myself it was only my lack of sleep, that trees did not move independently. I approached the building, keeping a skeptical distance from the tree. Judging by the directory, the building was full of art studios, workshops, music studios, doctor's offices, therapist's offices, and who knew what else.

I tried the massive glass door that led into the lobby and to my surprise it was unlocked. There was some dim lighting from the ceiling, enough to show me ornate tiled floors and exotic potted plants lining the walls. A gilded staircase wound up into the darkness of the upper floors. I approached it, terrified to break the stillness of the night and chase away the beautiful music that came from somewhere above. The stairs were carpeted and made stealth an easier task. I took them slowly, running my hand up the smooth banister.

Sarah would have loved this place.

I reached the second floor and still the music was above me. Once on the third floor, I followed the notes left as though I could see them beckoning me. I found the door the song was escaping from, slipping between the door and the frame. I took the knob and turned it slowly so as to not startle the sad soul at the keys.

The room was lit only by moonlight, but I could see clearly enough. Two windows looked out on the courtyard with the dead tree dominating the one on the right. Between them was a grand piano with a young woman seated at it, her delicate fingers sweeping over the keys, pushing out the melancholy song that was filling the barren and disused room.

"Sarah?" I choked back a sob.

The young woman spun in terror and fell back against the keys, creating a jarring and abrupt ending to the song.

"No. I'm so sorry, no. You're not Sarah. I'm sorry to scare you, please continue." I said trying to smooth things over.

The girl let out a scream, but she wasn't looking at me anymore, her eyes were on the tree looming outside of the window.

"I shouldn't have stopped, I'm sorry! Please." She cried out and fell prostrate in front of the window.

I watched in horror as the tree shivered. I *had* seen it move before, just like it moved then. It listed toward the building and pushed against the window until the glass exploded inward. The girl screamed and I fled back down the hallway to the stairs. Through the doors I saw something tearing itself out from the inside of the tree. It had limbs like a crab and its pale body was pulsing like a maggot. The dead tree was giving birth to a horror that shouldn't exist in any imagination.

I scrambled to the nearest office door and threw my shoulder into it. I fell into the dark room, kicking the door shut just as the glass of the front doors shattered. A rapid clicking and wet, gushy sliding echoed from the walls and floor of the lobby. Then the sad piano music started up again. The playing was jerky and less composed than before, but she was doing her best to play the same dismal song.

"It's too late." I heard a voice say from somewhere in the lobby.

The girl screamed and all fell silent. Then there was a soft knock on the door to the office where I hid.

"Mr. Helger?"

I cracked the door open and saw the innkeeper standing there in her nightgown with a heavy coat draped over her shoulders. Her silvery hair gave her a celestial appearance in the dim light. She held a hand out to me.

"Come, let's get you back to the inn. I'll make us some tea."

I took her hand like a frightened child feeling comfort in her boney grip. We walked hand in hand out of the building. We passed the listing, half-uprooted tree and the innkeeper clicked her teeth in annoyance at the sight of it. I was terrified, I couldn't help but stare over my shoulder expecting to see the thing that had exploded from the tree.

"She should not have been playing that song, Mr. Helger, she knew better. You can stop looking over your shoulder, you're quite safe with me." She said.

"What..." Was all I managed to say.

"Hush. Tea first."

She guided us back through the darkened streets of the town with composure. I didn't doubt that she could have gotten us back to the inn blindfolded. We encountered no life but our own and the streets were quiet except for our footsteps. I was thankful for the silence.

Once back at the inn, we entered the common room. A fire was blazing in the great stone fireplace, the sight of it melted away my anxiety. She ushered me to a comfortable chair in front of the blaze and disappeared into the kitchen. She returned after some time with two steaming cups of tea. I breathed deep and found to my surprise that it was fennel tea—my favorite. She sat in the chair opposite me.

"Tell me Mr. Helger, why are you here?"

"This place was to be the first stop on our honeymoon, but she's gone now." I gazed longingly into the tea. "It's strange, I don't quite remember the name of this town."

"That's not uncommon. Do you know where we are?" She asked.

"Only vaguely, come to think of it. I remember catching the bus north from Ashland, but after that, I'm not sure." I replied.

"I don't want to alarm you Mr. Helger, but you may be staying here for quite some time."

"Why?" I asked.

"They and their children are everywhere, and they have a way of keeping people here. Hold on to the memories of your Sarah, as painful as they can be. They'll keep you grounded and present here."

I took a sip of my tea and meditated on all that the innkeeper was implying.

"That thing I saw was real?" I asked.

"Yes."

"And there are more?"

"Yes. It'll be safer if you stay in at night. Finish your tea and then get back to bed."

Halfway through the cup of tea I began to feel drunk. I steadied myself and looked into the innkeeper's eyes. The flickering fire gave her a strange appearance as she gazed unblinking over her own steaming cup. After that, all was a blur.

I AWOKE TO THE SUN streaming through the blinds and the sound of a violin energetically playing a shanty somewhere down on the street. I sat up and shook off the grogginess. My first thought was that last night must have been some terrible nightmare, but then, I could still taste the fennel tea on my tongue. There was a quiet little knock at my door.

"Yes?"

"Mr. Helger, I've got some breakfast for you!" Came a cheery young voice.

"Come in."

A youthful maid entered with a tray full of steaming morsels. She regarded me with a genuine smile and set the tray up on a stand next to my bed.

"How much do I owe?" I asked.

"It's on the house, Mr. Helger." She said with a wink.

She ran from the room before I could offer a tip.

The smell of the eggs, bacon, pancakes, and coffee hit me and filled me with a ravenous hunger. I grabbed a plate and shoveled pancakes drenched in maple syrup into my mouth. After my first helping, I got out of bed and threw the windows open to let in the fresh air and sunlight.

Across the street was the man playing violin as passersby dropped coins into the bowler hat at his feet. He nodded and bowed a little at each tip he received without slowing his pace. I could smell the salt in the air and soon I heard the bell of a ship ringing. It was strange, I could have sworn the city was farther inland.

I made myself another plate and continued to watch out my window while I feasted. Children skipped about while their parents lagged behind, conversing with other parents. A fancy horse-drawn carriage bumped by with some lordly passengers aboard by the looks of it. The town seemed perfect in the happy morning sun—a stark contrast to the previous night.

After finishing nearly the entire tray that had been brought to me, another soft knock sounded at the door and I pulled it open. It was the maid again.

"When you're good and ready, your presence is requested in the office downstairs." She smiled and moved off down the hall following her message.

I shut the door and went about tidying myself up. Perhaps the innkeeper could explain to me how I lost track of time drinking tea and ended up back in my room. I dressed in fresh clothing and headed downstairs to find out what I was wanted for.

The office door was ajar. I peeked through the crack and knocked. The innkeeper whisked the door open and regarded me with a jovial smile.

"Mr. Helger, good morning! I have a book here that details the history of the town, I think you'll appreciate it. I think it will shed some light on your curious situation." She said.

I glanced around the office behind her before entering.

"Did you drug my tea?" I asked her without hesitation.

"My dear, I merely gave you something to help you sleep. How did you sleep?"

"Like a rock, I'll admit." I was secretly thankful for the sleep I had gotten.

"Well, have a seat while I find the book. I didn't expect you so soon." She motioned to a cozy chair in front of her desk.

I sat and noticed an opened letter laying out on the otherwise immaculate desk. The beautiful curling script caught my eye—It looked so very much like Sarah's hand. The innkeeper's back was still turned as she scanned the bookshelf for the text she had been speaking about. I leaned forward to get a better look at the letter and my breath caught.

The signature at the bottom *was* Sarah's. *Mrs. Sarah Helger*.

I sat back in the chair as sweat broke out on my brow. Impossible. Sarah was gone, we had never been married. My eyes darted around in a frantic attempt to calm myself.

"Ah, here it is." The innkeeper said in a singsong voice.

When she turned around, I flashed a smile.

"Are you okay Mr. Helger?"

"Indigestion. The pancakes and syrup." I said, swallowing audibly.

"You poor thing. Take this and I'll send a maid up with an antacid. You'll have to excuse me, I have a busy day ahead of me."

I nodded and took the book. I kept my pace steady until I was out of the office and then quickened my step back to the relative safety of my room.

I threw the tome on my bed and went to the window for air. My mind raced, I felt as though my sanity were slipping. There was only one thing that I could do: get back into the office and read that letter.

I contemplated trying to go outside to enjoy the day, but I couldn't bring myself to. I stayed in my room pacing the floor or staring at the wall trying to process my thoughts. Sarah was gone. She was gone and that's all there was. I was alone. I was to be alone forever after. It was frightening to have no control over my own thoughts.

I ignored several knocks on my door, one no doubt had been the maid with an antacid. A few times I picked up the shabby book the innkeeper had given me but dropped it back onto the bed. I couldn't distract myself with anything.

I spent the day agonizing until the sun finally dipped below the horizon, plunging the city back into its dead slumber. I slipped my shoes off, treading as carefully down the hallway as a cat. I winced whenever the stairs creaked under my weight, but the common room was devoid of any life to hear. The fire had dwindled to almost nothing—a good sign that no one had been in for a little while at least. I moved as an apparition through the common room and laid an ear against the office door. Not a sound. I tried the handle and the door opened up for me.

There seemed to be no one in the darkened office. I moved to the desk and found that the letter had remained in the same spot. Without a second thought I grabbed it and retreated out of the room. Another guest was coming down the stairs and I brushed past him ignoring his 'good evening.'

Once back in the safety of my room, I wedged a chair underneath the doorknob and stared for a long time at the crumpled letter I held clenched in my fist. After a series of deep breaths, I brought it to the tiny desk I had taken the chair from and smoothed it out under the buzzing lamplight.

> *To whom it may concern,*
>
> *I'm writing to you to plead that my husband be taken care of as humanely as possible. He has no concept of what he's done or what he's been a part of. I do still love him very much, but I cannot be with him any longer. Especially after the inci-*

dent. For myself, I shall try and move on with life. I will always have the good memories we shared, though I'm sure they will be painful for some time. The doctor assured me that your people were the best at what they do and I'm putting the life of the man I love in your hands. I pray he forgets me as quickly as the doctor says he will.

Sincerely,
Mrs. Sarah Helger

Incident? What incident? We had never married. She still loved me. What had I been a part of? What was wrong with me to have doctors involved?

I tried to sit back in the chair, my legs feeling like liquid, but I forgot that I had wedged it under the doorknob. I hit the floor with a grunt. My mind was shattered, and the letter was real—it was her handwriting. I hugged my knees and did my best to keep my breathing even. Too much breathing would throw me into a panic.

And I heard it again—the delicate tapping of piano keys, soft notes floating through the still night air.

It was the same damned melancholy song, but the keys were slightly out of tune. Each note throbbed in my head as the out of tune piece entwined itself with my thoughts. I stood and left my room. I left the inn, ignoring the innkeeper's warning to stay in after dark and let the night swallow me up.

As I headed toward the building I had visited the previous night, I was aware of the nightmare tapping of those creatures moving about. The tapping, sliding sounds reverberated through alleys as black as the void. The sounds slowly grew, though I could still hear the melancholy piano.

I marched into the building through the broken glass door with God knows how many of the monstrosities trailing me in the dark. I climbed the stairs and went directly to the room I had visited the previous night. I threw open the door.

There stood Sarah, beautiful Sarah. Next to her stood the innkeeper with one motherly arm around Sarah's shoulders. Sarah had tears in her eyes.

"Sarah?" I began to cry myself.

Then I felt the cold crustacean-like appendages gently closing around me. I felt the sluggish, pulsing bulk of the thing pressing against my back. Sarah shut her eyes as tears fell.

"I told you that it was best to stay in at night, Mr. Helger. Didn't I?"

THE END

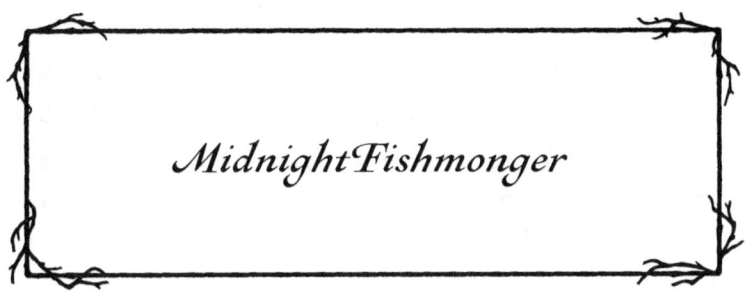

Midnight Fishmonger

A RUSTED STREET LAMP dumped its light onto the bus stop, its pale orange glow keeping away the dark. The light flickered as I approached. I feared that the bench and the grimy glass enclosure might disappear into the darkness along with the pale glow. There was a thick fog about that only rose to my knees. I couldn't see my feet below me, though I knew that there was nothing to worry about. The worry would come at the end of the bus ride.

I took a seat on the bench and looked out into the darkness. My eyes could find nothing, and there wasn't much to see anyway, but I knew what lay across the street. The bus stop was well off the beaten path on a lonely country road that served as a border for various farmlands. A strange place for a bus stop indeed, but it was the one that I was meant to be at.

I dug a cigarette out of the crushed pack in my jacket pocket and stuck it in my mouth. The taste of it was enough to relax me, but I lit it anyway. If anything were out in the field watching me, they'd see a tall lanky man with a briefcase in his lap and a little orange ember lighting up his face. I grinned at the thought of something watching me out there in the night.

In my briefcase, underneath all the necessary documents for the meeting that was to take place, there was a hidden compartment for my pistol—just in case the deal went rotten. I patted it, resisting the urge to crack it open for the hundredth time to check that all was in order. All *was* in order; my mind just couldn't help itself.

Overhead, I heard the swishing of massive wings. A feather floated down, landing on my briefcase. It was large, probably from some kind of violent bird of prey. *What was it doing out at this time of night?* I brushed it off. A shrill call echoed from one of the fields. I couldn't make out what vermin or creature it might have been from. The bird of prey must have gotten something.

I mused on the nocturnal struggle between predator and prey until my thoughts were interrupted by two faint points of light appearing in the distance. My heart leapt. I breathed out slowly, trying to stay calm. The bus was on its way. The points of light grew and refracted through the mists, painting the fog in fluorescent light. The engine rumbled, the exhaust choking once or twice as it slowed to a stop in front of me.

Its chrome bullet-shaped body was of a different age. Really, the whole vehicle was, from tires to headlights. The doors clacked open. I stared up into the eyes of a bulbous old man who didn't seem quite awake or like he had taken a shower in quite some time. I flicked my cigarette away, stood up, and climbed onto the bus. I was the only passenger.

I took a seat toward the middle after dropping some coins into the payment slot. The driver closed the door and the bus chugged until it was rolling again. There was some kind of religious service playing on the radio, but it was warbly and hard to make out with the interference of static. The driver seemed to grunt in agreement with the speaker every once and awhile before falling silent again. I planted my head on the window to look out into the nothingness.

The bus bumped along for a time and then jolted onto the relative smoothness of a paved road. I had begun to doze off, but the transition from dirt to civilized infrastructure had shaken me awake. In the distance I saw the warm twinkling lights of the city, a bastion emerging from the emptiness of the night. The bus picked up speed as we entered onto a highway.

Drizzling rain started to dot the windows and built up until it could no longer cling to the smooth surface. The city loomed closer as the bus twisted and turned on the serpentine highway. I checked my watch.

"Excuse me." I said.

The driver didn't acknowledge me.

"Are we running on time? I have an important meeting at midnight."

The driver looked at me in the mirror and looked back out onto the road.

"Yes." He said after a moment and then he turned his radio up to drown out any more of my questions.

We made it to the outer limits of the city. I stared out at the cramped ghettos unable to imagine life in such congested neighborhoods. I caught the sight of a man slumped against a doorway, desperately trying to raise a bottle covered with a brown bag to his mouth. It slipped out of his hand and shattered on the steps. He slid down to a crouched position and cradled his head in his hands. I felt for him, I had been in much the same position at times in my life.

The bus rolled on, ignorant of the struggling poor, and we entered the city. There wasn't much traffic and our progress was halted only by lonesome red lights swinging in the breeze of the meager rainstorm. Somewhere in the distance a siren sounded, but the city was almost as quiet as the nothing farmland I had walked along earlier in the evening. The lack of commotion felt wrong somehow.

The bus turned toward the waterfront district—a rusted strip of corrugated iron buildings housing everything from fisheries to "luxury" apartments. The bus shuddered to a halt at a bus stop sign that hung upside down by its remaining bolt. I stood with my briefcase and made my way to the front of the bus. Anxiety was beginning to grow in my stomach.

"Thank you very much, sir." I said, nodding to the driver as he glared at me from the mirror.

I stepped down onto the sidewalk and narrowly avoided a stagnant puddle swirled with a nebula of motor oil. The air smelled of diesel and the stale saltiness of a place populated by fresh and rotten fish. It was a heavy smell that my senses didn't particularly appreciate. I hoped the smell would improve once I had entered the building I was looking for.

I walked in the opposite direction of the bus as it shuddered away. My contact hadn't given me the name of the person I was to meet, only an address. I didn't see any numbers on any of the buildings and my anxiety was quickly turning to frustration. I spotted a mailbox overstuffed with yellowing pieces of mail. I went to it, looking around to see if anyone watched. I pulled a few pieces out and to my surprise the number on the envelopes was that of the building I was meant to enter.

I looked up and saw only a few dim lights in windows half-covered by broken blinds. I shoved the mail back in and tried the door. It opened with some effort and I entered, leaving the rain and silent city behind me.

The air in the lobby of the place was heavy with humidity and smelled of fresh fish. My stomach relaxed a little in the absence of the harsher, rotten scents that had polluted the streets. I climbed the stairs to the second floor and went down the dirty carpeted corridor as I was instructed. I counted the doors until the fourth and I placed a hand on the knob. After a deep breath and quiet words of encouragement, I went in.

The place was a fish market. A glass case ran the length of the room with all manner of exotic looking seafood fileted up for those looking to buy. The ceiling and walls of the room were painted an ugly yellow accentuated by the glaring fluorescent lighting. A dirty ceiling fan made its lackadaisical circuit and the blue tiled floor was slick with moisture. No one manned the counter.

I approached and appraised what the place had to offer. White, pink, and orange-colored butterfly filets, cutlets, steaks, and loins were laid tenderly on beds of white ice. Farther down there were more exotic delectables being offered—urchins, squid, and whole octopi were clustered together in neat little colonies along with other creatures that I didn't quite recognize. At the opposite end of the counter were the crabs, shrimp, lobsters, mussels, and clams. Little paper signs sat in front of each product denoting the price per pound.

I had never been much of a seafood eater living so far

from the shore and all, but something about the cuts of meat and the fresh salty smell caused me to salivate. Perhaps if the deal went well, I'd endeavor to purchase and cook up some of the fish. I pulled my now-hungry eyes from the glass case and looked around for some type of bell to ring for service.

Before I could call for anyone, a man appeared through the swinging door behind the counter. He was tall, thin, and wore an apron covered in the reds and pinks of new and faded blood stains. He held a fileting knife in one hand and a mass of guts in the other hand. He looked me up and down before disappearing back through the door.

I stood there with my mouth open in the sudden awkward silence. I wanted to run from that place, but I was frozen. I could only wait for what was to come. Out from the back came the tall man, a short man, and an older man. All wore matching blood-smeared aprons and all had the same smoldering blue eyes.

"You're late." Said the older man.

I glanced at my watch. It was two minutes after midnight.

"I assume you have the paperwork?" The older man again.

"I do." I said.

"Good. But first I'd like to show you something. Follow me please and indulge an old man." He said.

He went back through the swinging door. The other two men waited for me to make my way around the counter and through the door before they followed. They weren't quite menacing, but their presence felt heavy behind me. The back-room was cool and smelled of even fresher fish. There were steel counters covered in blood and scales upon which the men had been butchering their products, a large metal freezer at the back of the room, and a stack of cardboard boxes with ice spilling out from damp compromised corners.

"Do you know of the ribbon worm?" The old man said while pulling the top box off the stack in a shower of ice.

I only shook my head.

"It's an amazing little creature."

The old man placed the box on the counter, took the lid off, and extracted a small styrofoam container about the size of a large fist. He placed the lid back on the cardboard box and shoved it to the side. He beckoned me closer and I went. He donned a pair of latex gloves and cracked the styrofoam open. I raised my head to try and get a peak at what was inside without stepping forward, but the man's hand was already in the box.

His gloved hand appeared again with a fleshy pink squirming thing that he laid out on the blood covered counter. It extended itself to almost a foot long before contracting in an attempt to get away from the gloved hand. My skin crawled watching the glistening little monster slink through fish blood and scales.

"The worm has a proboscis which it keeps inside itself until it finds prey. It then inverts the proboscis, sending it out to catch its prey in a venom-laced web. It's quite amazing to watch them feed."

The man placed a gloved finger in front of what I assumed was the head of the worm. It bumped into his finger and recoiled. Then, out of the thing's head, shot a spiderwebbed lightning length of what I can only describe as mucus-like goo. It went out for about a foot and then was withdrawn back inside the creature as suddenly as it had appeared.

"Neat, no?" The man smiled at me.

I cringed.

"Should we get down to business?" I asked.

As I finished the question, the two men behind me each seized one of my arms. In my surprise I dropped my briefcase and cried out. The taller man had his arm around my neck restricting the movement of my head.

"Now, the interesting thing about this particular breed of ribbon worm is that the toxin it uses to immobilize its prey is actually a powerful psychedelic. We have your employer's documents and my employers would like me to be rid of you. I'm not one for killing, so don't worry about that...but this ribbon worm's toxins will completely fry your mind. I'm sorry to have to do this."

I struggled and kicked at the men who held me as the old man picked up another of the creatures from the styrofoam box and approached me. He held its body in one hand and kept the thing's head gripped between his thumb and pointer in the other hand. I watched helplessly and thrashed with the rest of my body. I closed my eyes and felt the cold slimy thing's body touch my nostrils.

And then I felt the horrible viscous web shoot into my nose and make its way into my throat and sinuses. I gagged and screamed. I could feel the venom seeping into my nerves and blood cells. The old man backed away with the thing in his hand, but I still felt the web embedded in my skull.

"Oh, and when the worm feels threatened, it'll detach the proboscis in an attempt to escape its enemies. Perfect for letting the toxins absorb into the brain tissue. Get him out of here."

As the two men dragged me out of the backroom, the world began to move in odd ways. I coughed and choked on the intruder in my head and managed to spit chunks of it out. The men spoke to each other, but the language was foreign. I looked from one to the other and then we were approaching the front door of the building. The door anticipated me, it breathed in ecstasy knowing that it would have me for a meal. I shouted and thrashed against the two men again, but they fed me to the door.

I fell out onto the sidewalk into the belly of the beast that was the world of night. The mouth-door shut behind me and the silence began to whisper. I sat and glanced up and down the street. Only what was illuminated by the streetlamps existed, and each meager conical shape of light beckoned me toward its comfort. I blew my nose as hard as I could onto the street to purge the remaining substance and watched the writhing chunks of proboscis in disgust as they fell onto the street.

It was snowing out. Thick clusters of the stuff floated down through the light cast by the streetlamps and I approached one of them. The snow was as red as a rose and the flakes that I caught in my hand melted into blood, it smelled like fish. I stuck my tongue out and caught a few of the flakes. They tasted of iron.

My employers weren't going to be happy, they were expecting me back in the morning with payment in hand. I tried my best to focus, but there were others on the street now moving just outside of the light like swaying shadows. I wanted my gun. I spun to find the building I had been thrown out of, but the territory was unfamiliar.

The salt-diesel and mixed fish smell was its own presence looming behind every corner just out of sight. I steadied myself and moved to the safety offered by the next street lamp.

The snow was beginning to accumulate, and my footprints were horrible black scars in the bloody powdered landscape. I leaned against a phone booth that wouldn't quite stay still.

Some ways down the street I caught sight of a figure that had dared to enter into the light. I rubbed my eyes and suddenly it was closer. A bent man with a comically large grin on his face stood in the light only a few streetlamps down. He wore a suit of rags that was built with a dizzying array of colors. His wicked curving fingers were clasped together in front of him and he tilted his head to the side, the toothy smile undiminishing. The strange otherworldly jester turned my skin to gooseflesh with his gaze.

"Stay away." I squeaked.

The grin opened to let out a gust of child-like laughter.

"You there, how came you to this place?" Said a voice from the dark behind me.

I spun and looked out into the pulsing blackness trying to find the source of this new being, instantly regretting turning my back on the jester. The new being's words were powerful and sweet like those of a benevolent queen. I pictured her standing a head taller than me, dressed in reserved opulence. Another figure stepped into the light of the next streetlamp. I couldn't quite make out the face of the person, but they wore a ridiculous glittering outfit. It disappeared out of the light again and I rubbed my untrustworthy eyes.

Then the figure stepped into my little circle of light. She had no face that I could speak of, only a roiling mess of features that wouldn't quite stay still. Her form-fitting outfit was full of colors I had never seen—it dazzled me as it caught the light. She did stand a head taller than me, but her looming presence caused me no distress. She reached out with long cold fingers and caressed my cheek. The flakes of red seemed to shy away from her.

"Child, you do not belong here."

At her singing words I fell to my knees and closed my eyes at the magnificence of her presence. I felt as though I didn't deserve to be living and breathing in the same space. She placed a spidery hand on my head. She spoke nebulous words out into the dark over my head and I heard a monstrous hissing from right behind me—the jester had almost gotten to me.

"They did something to me, they robbed me and shattered me and when my employers find me they'll do worse." I said.

She ran her hand through my hair.

"Do not worry, I will guide you." Her words swirled around me.

I stood, and she took my hand. Without another word we moved out of the safety of the light. Her hand was chilly, and her long fingers clasped around mine like the spindly legs of some sun-bleached crustacean. Her grip was comforting and made her presence all the more real. Now that I walked with her, the crimson snow avoided me as well and though my feet still left prints, hers did not.

The nightmare queen's garments had their own luminescence or at least retained some of the light that shone on us as we moved through the circles of streetlights. Each time we entered a darkened area, the glittering clothing glowed soft and warm. I found it hard to keep my eyes off of her as we walked. When I did look out into the dark, I regretted it—there were things moving out there, but they respected the queen and kept their distance as the jester had.

We found the right building standing there alone in that strange world. She strode up the steps with her swirling head held high in her perfect posture. The door opened before she touched it and she turned to beckon me to follow her. I took a last look out into the strange dark and noted the silhouetted creatures before following.

The interior looked much the same. The stench of fish was still pungent, though my nose now detected sulfur as well. She turned and held a finger up.

"Wait here."

I stood dumbly and watched her ascend the stairs and disappear around the corner. The silence was complete. I thought about following the queen, but shuddered to think of what would happen should I disobey her—the shadows, the jester, the dark, and the snow all feared her.

She reappeared holding my briefcase loosely at her side. She descended the stairs and held it out to me. I took it and she placed a hand over my face.

"You do not belong here. I'll see that you are gone now."

There was a flash of pain in my sinuses that caused me to squeeze my eyes shut and cry out. When I opened my eyes again the silence was gone and replaced by the humming of electricity in the building. The queen was gone. I crashed through the front door and saw that the city was back to the familiarity of the night. A siren wailed in the distance, there was no more red snow.

I didn't stop running until I was in a more populated part of the city—relatively speaking. I found a pay phone and called my employers to let them know what had happened. Then I found the nearest bus stop, studied the route map and sat down, eager to put the night behind me.

THE END

Addy's Song

JWAS COLD. I shivered under my cocoon of a thin blanket. The pipes in the wall knocked as the heat kicked on. I wasn't sure that it could warm me sufficiently. It was morning and almost time for the orderlies to bring me to the cafeteria for breakfast. I hadn't slept at all and I wasn't hungry. Someone knocked on the door.

I swung my legs over the side of the creaking moldy cot and hesitated before touching my bare feet to the frigid tile floor. The cracking, chipping green paint on the walls seemed to smile at me. My head swam. The knock sounded again.

"Come in." I mumbled.

The lock clicked and the door swung open to reveal a big orderly painted in the glaring fluorescent light of the hallway. My room suddenly felt very dark with only a tiny window letting light in from outside. The orderly stood and stared at me like an idiot child. If the way they treated me was any indication, I was supposed to be the idiot. But, had I the chance, I could outwit any of the lazy jumpsuit-wearing men. This particular specimen had stains running down his chin.

He snorted mucus into the back of his throat and swallowed audibly as I sized him up. Jacob was his name.

"Breakfast." He growled.

"Let me dress."

The blanket fell and the big man threw clean clothes at me. I caught some of my outfit but had to collect the rest from the floor. I donned the pale blue hospital-like garb, very careful not to disturb the new dressings over the surgery I had sustained the previous day—they had removed much of the flesh from my right forearm and taken large samples of my right calf muscle. The clothes were starchy and ill-fitting, and I found that the muscle removed from my calf had given me a limp. Strange that there was no pain.

"No shoes?" I asked.

"No."

I approached the orderly who stood a foot taller than me with his arms crossed, unmoving in the doorway. I looked at him and he looked at me. He swung himself back to open a path for me like some giant fleshy door. I felt his impatient steps behind me as I limped down the hall toward the cafeteria. One of the fluorescent lights flickered and went out. I stopped under it and looked up, inspecting its blackened tube. The orderly shoved me and I shuffled forward, nearly falling.

The cafeteria was empty. No one stood behind the counter and no food had been laid out. I sat at the closest table and watched as the orderly continued toward the counter. His footsteps echoed in the cavernous room. He disappeared behind the counter and into the kitchen and reappeared with a steaming tray clutched in one hand.

He dropped the metal tray in front of me. It clattered and added its own echo to the room. Whatever the yellow soupy substance that one compartment of the tray held splashed all over the table and me.

"Eat up. Doctor will be in soon."

I turned and watched the man leave. When he was on the other side of the cafeteria entrance, I heard him lock the door. I turned back to the food, or what passed as food in that place. A spongy block of meat, yellow soup, mushy boiled greens, and a hard heel of bread. I wasn't very hungry, but the doctor would force feed me if I didn't eat.

I picked up the heel of bread and a few maggots fell out of their hiding places within. I knocked it on the table and a few more fell out. I went to work tearing it apart to find all of their kind and expelled them from my breakfast. A dozen or so wiggly white maggots inched about on the table. One by one I smashed them with my thumb. I wiped their juices on my pants. The food wasn't so hard to swallow if you mixed it all together. I shoveled it all into the biggest compartment and let it all blend and soak into the meat and the chunks of hard bread. I glanced around the cafeteria while I waited for everything to soak.

The large room was lit by skylights dispersed around the ceiling randomly. It was as if they had purposely tried to eschew putting the windows in any discernible pattern. One of them only held ragged shards about the edges, the glass had been broken ever since I had arrived. On rainy days, half of the cafeteria flooded. It was a dull gray day—sunless, cloudless, skyless. I was just a crippled being, in a decrepit building, in a feeble gray void of existence.

And then I shoveled the concoction into my mouth as fast as I could. They never gave me utensils and they never gave me anything to clean my hands with. I wiped them on my pants. They always reprimanded me for getting so dirty before my appointments. It didn't seem to matter though, they always proceeded with their procedures whether I was clean or not. I gagged it all down trying not to breathe in the process, lest I find out the tastes of what I had just eaten.

As if on cue, the cafeteria door unlocked and in stepped the doctor flanked by two orderlies. One was Jacob and the other was new. The new orderly was skinny and short. He didn't blink and reminded me very much of a starving coyote. Doctor Herbert had his hands in the pockets of his spotless lab coat. A stethoscope dangled around his neck like jewelry. His tie was a strange fractal pattern of birds.

"How are we this morning?" He removed a hand from his pocket and adjusted his glasses.

I gave a wry smile and nodded.

"Unfortunately, we're going to have to run a few more procedures on you today. Will you please accompany us?"

I stood from the table and before I was fully upright, the orderlies had moved to either side of me and gripped my upper arms as if I were trying to flee. I did my best to walk between the two of them, one nearly slouching and the other nearly tiptoeing to match my height. The doctor led our party with his hands clasped behind his back.

We passed other rooms, empty rooms that had the same abandoned look as mine, though unlike mine, no one was occupying them. Old dusty gurneys and rusted bed frames decorated the cramped spaces. Water poured from the ceiling in one of the rooms, the putrid liquid had begun to pool out into the hall. The doctor avoided the puddle, but the orderlies marched me right through, soaking my stockinged feet with the brownish muck.

The hallway seemed as though it would never end and time slowed in my mind. Things became a swirling blur. They had drugged the food.

I was back in my room, shirtless and shivering on the bed. I looked down and saw a large blood-stained bandage covering my abdomen. I sat up straighter and winced as whatever they had used to close the wound pulled at my flesh. Carefully, I undid the bandage to reveal messy stitches and yellow blood plasma leaking out from between them. My gut felt as though something had been removed. I retched, and the stitches pulled tight again.

I stared down at the mess I had made and watched as a couple maggots squirmed their way out of the vomit. I gagged at the sight but composed myself—I didn't feel my sutures would stand up to a second convulsion. I lay back on the bed. Two days of procedures in a row was something the staff had never subjected me to before. I couldn't get to sleep with my abdomen throbbing the way it was.

They left me alone for three weeks, or at least it felt like three weeks. It could have only been hours or maybe a month or two. They showed up with meals here and there for me to eat in my room. They never came at regular intervals. The sky had remained a dull gray for that amount of time and I had lost track of the day and night cycle despite barely sleeping. It must have been some time, because my abdomen was healing up nicely.

I sat on the edge of the bed wrapped in the thin blanket,

letting my head loll forward onto my chest. I was still cold, and the room smelled rank. I realized it was my wounds that smelled. I didn't dare remove any of the dressings—I was terrified to find the gangrenous flesh surely lurking beneath. I opened my eyes to look at the dried spot of vomit on the floor. The maggots hadn't made it very far from the pool before dying. They looked like beings that had fled from a blast zone only to succumb to radiation poisoning.

A knock sounded at the door.

"Come in." I said as if I had any authority over my accommodations.

The door opened to reveal a figure dressed in coveralls and a respirator. I couldn't tell who it was, but they approached me and hauled me off the bed with some strength. They half dragged me out into the hallway and pushed me into a room on the opposite side. The door slammed in my face and I heard the lock click.

My new room looked much the same as the last one—small window, cracked green walls, a tiny toilet, and a moldy cot. There was a folded stack of clothes and blankets on the cot. When I approached I felt the freezing draft emanating from the window. I quickly dressed in the new clothes. They gave me a sweater which I pulled on eagerly. I wrapped a thin blanket around me and then a thicker one that they had left as well.

From my old room across the hall I heard much movement and muffled voices. After a little while they were gone, and I was left alone in silence again. I resumed what I had been doing—sitting on the edge of the cot and meditating. I sat for a long time ignoring every sensation that I felt. A soft knock snapped me out of my trance. Knocking. Always knocking on the door as if I had any authority.

"Come in." I said with a sigh.

Whoever was coming in had trouble with the lock. It clicked and chunked a few times before the great door swung open. I glanced over and was hit with confusion. A young girl, maybe only eighteen years old, stood in the light wearing only a thin paisley hospital gown. The gown had blood stains on it. Her face was disfigured. It was only then that I realized I had been sitting in complete darkness.

"Please, folla me." She whispered almost pleading.

"What..."

"Shush! Hurry." She put a finger to her lips.

I stood and limped to her. She took my hand and I stared down into her ugly face. They had taken her nose off and her left eye was sunken and stitched shut. She blinked or maybe winked, I couldn't tell. A small secret smile spread on her face.

"I thoughta was alone." She whispered. "Let's go, we gettin' outta here."

I couldn't place her accent.

We moved down the hallway stealthily like vermin trying to avoid hunting wolves.

"I shouldn't be leaving, they haven't finished with me yet." I said.

"Well ya finished with them. They no good, ya know what they doin' with ya body?"

I shook my head.

She pulled a folded piece of paper out of the pocket of her gown and handed it to me. I unfolded it. It was an advertisement for a rejuvenation clinic.

'Surefire rejuvenation using real human cells!'

'The future is now!'

'100% Safe and 99.9% effective!'

'Get a free quote today!'

A beautiful woman smiled a perfect smile underneath the claims.

I looked at the girl, but she was still walking ahead of me.

"This place? No. I'm here for..." I tried to protest.

"What ya here for?" She asked, spinning to face me.

I stopped abruptly. "I...I don't know. To tell you the truth. I'm just in need of procedures is all. I'm sick."

"Old lady needa new eye. They gon' an pop mine out an put it inner. We just living storage for replacement parts, ya." She snatched the advertisement out of my hand and stuffed it back into her pocket.

I followed her in silence. Maybe we were. It was true that I didn't know why I was there. That line of thinking led me to the awareness that I couldn't remember anything before coming to that place. The girl was right, we had to leave.

"Do you know how to get out of here?" I asked.

"I saw where they take bodies. We goin' out like the dead." She said.

We rounded a corner and saw two orderlies walking down the hall towards us. They were too busy arguing with one another to notice us. We dove into the first room on the left and shut the door behind us. The room had a dense humid smell of rot about it. The girl gasped, and I followed the direction of her gaze.

In the corner were the huddled remains of someone. Skeletal structures showed through grayish flesh. Mold covered the body. The corpse's head was buried in its knees. A spider descended from the ceiling and alighted upon the thing's wispy-haired head. A dead thing. I feared that the orderlies were en-route to that very room to retrieve the body and take it to the exit the girl was talking about.

I opened my mouth to say something and shut it again when I heard the orderlies walk past. Their voices faded, and the girl was back out into the hallway again. I followed. We went off down the hall at a quicker pace.

After many twists and turns of the similar-looking run-down and forgotten hallways we arrived at a door marked 'Morgue.' The girl pushed the door open and the same dense and humid death smell hung about the room. There were bodies on slabs in bags. Each was tagged. I resisted the urge to unzip the bags to find out the fate of each individual corpse. As if reading my mind, the girl spoke.

"Don' worry 'bout em. We ain't goin' be like em, we outta here." She said taking my hand again.

She led me to another door at the back of the morgue room marked with an unlit exit sign. She pushed through the door and we were greeted with blackness. She reached into her other pocket and withdrew a flashlight. She clicked it on and shined it down the hallway. It was a long hallway.

"This where they roll bodies out. Come on." She said.

I followed close behind her. There were stains and rubber skid marks on the cracked tile floor. The walls were brick and undecorated. Eventually the flashlight beam revealed a set of double doors that had pieces of cardboard taped over the windows. We closed in on the doors.

"Ya ready?"

I nodded.

We pushed through the doors together and the first gray light of dawn lit the outside. We stood on a concrete platform where transports could back in to retrieve corpses. A little way beyond the path was a stream. We both ran to it.

Garbage floated lazily in the murky water, careening off slimy rocks poking out of the water. Looking at the dirty water made me realize how thirsty I was. I stooped to take a drink and the girl grabbed my collar.

"Ya crazy? That's water'll make ya sick."

I stood straight again.

"Sorry." I mumbled.

"Well. Ya got anywhere to go?" She asked.

I shook my head no.

"Come on then."

She marched off into the woods by the stream and I followed her. I turned back only once to gaze at the building we had escaped. The main structure sat up on a hill with vines growing all over the outside of it. There were holes in the concrete and broken windows. I shivered at the ghostly structure and turned back to follow the girl.

We plodded along in relative silence. The girl began whistling once or twice and when I tried to join in she stopped. I stopped when she stopped. It was easy going through the woods. I even began to feel hungry. Leaving the place had had an immediate effect on me—I already felt more like a human.

We stopped when the sun began to dip below the trees and tried to throw together a makeshift camp. The girl went about collecting wood for a fire while I did my best to construct a lean-to in the event of any rain. Dark was settling in and we had a modest fire for warmth and a simple structure that both of us could fit under.

"What's ya name?" She asked.

"Miller." I said.

I rolled myself underneath the shelter to settle in for the night.

"What's yours?" I asked.

"Addy. I'm Addy. Nice to meetcha Miller." She smiled in the firelight.

Addy wiggled herself into the shelter and snuggled herself right up to me. I flinched away at first, but she pushed herself up against me. She reached behind her, grabbed my arm, and wrapped it across her stomach.

"For warmth." She said.

I relaxed a little. She was warm. I felt safe with my arm around the girl and a fire crackling in front of us. I had been so used to the dreary innards of that building that I had forgotten how important these little moments of joy can be. I let the joy drag me down into a peaceful sleep.

In the morning we set out again following the gurgling, garbage-choked stream. Addy skipped and danced along the water's edge in the sun-dappled dirt, whistling a tune that I didn't attempt to match—I feared she'd stop whistling and the warbling notes eased my mind. Empty faded cardboard packages floated between little rocks jutting out of the murky water. Plastic bags clung desperately to branches reaching into the water. Somewhere overhead a bird cried out, but other than the water, whistling, and lone bird call, the day was as silent as could be.

"Where to, Addy?" I asked, making sure to annunciate her name.

"We gon' get some clothes first. Change outta this dirty stuff." She took up her song again.

"What's that you're whistling? I like it."

The girl whirled around to face me while still skipping backwards. "My ma sang it to me." She turned back.

The trees thinned out and revealed a heavily pot-holed parking lot laying out behind a crumbling brick building and a wooden one that seemed to be falling in on itself. The little stream fell into a storm drain in the lot, half-clogged with debris that had made the journey to the end. I hesitated to leave the safety of the trees and Addy marched right across the parking lot as if it were exactly where she was supposed to be. I gave a cursory glance around the silent property and followed in the girl's footsteps. She took up whistling again and I relaxed a little.

We crept along and entered the tight little alley between the crumbling brick building and its termite-rotted neighbor. The air smelled like stale garbage and forgotten bins full of rusted recycling. I slowed my pace as we neared the exit to the sidewalk and the street. Addy turned around to check my progress and I saw a car roll by out on the street. She came to me, took my hand, and dragged me along with her.

"Come on Mill, they's gotta be a store here." Addy said.

I let her lead me, she had ceased whistling, but the song still echoed in my head.

The street was empty. Not a car was parked between the faded white marks lining the road. The rotten wooden building seemed to be a laundromat. The lights were on, but none of the machines spun. The brick building had large glass windows, a few of which were spiderwebbed with vicious cracks. Big chipped letters reading KENO were painted across each glass panel. The place was dark. The other buildings up and down the street seemed to be just as vacant and decrepit.

Addy pointed across the street to a building marked TAI-

LOR, though the O was missing from the hand-lettered sign. We crossed the street, looking both ways despite the absence of traffic. A dog barked somewhere off in the distance.

Through the glass windows we could see the lights were on. The shop looked to be well-stocked with materials and finished pieces of clothing. Addy pulled the door open and the hinges squealed with rust as a bell dinged at the top of the door frame. I froze in the door and Addy walked up to the counter.

"Hello." She called.

There was no answer.

She went to a rack, pulled off a flannel shirt, a pair of repaired but faded jeans, and threw them to me. I caught them, shuddering at the memory of the orderlies throwing clothes at me. Addy let her gown fall to the floor. I averted my eyes as I felt my face flush.

"Let me know when you're dressed." I said, closing my eyes.

"K. I'm dressed."

I opened my eyes and found her nude, staring at me with her one good eye. A grin spread on her lips. I saw the scars that she carried on her body, permanent reminders of whatever procedures she had endured. I shut my eyes and she let off a burst of giggling.

"Ha-ha." I said.

"Ya face is red!" She said between laughs. "K. Okay. I'm done."

I let my eyes open and saw that she had put on a t-shirt and a frilly yellow skirt.

"Turn around so I can change."

She complied and to my surprise, didn't sneak a peek as I dressed in the stiff jeans and itchy flannel. I pulled the garments on with care not to disturb the yellowing bandages on my arm, abdomen, and leg. I had forgotten about them, but underneath I still felt a dull throb. The bandages needed changing very soon.

Then we heard something in the back room of the store. Addy shivered and backed toward me. I stood paralyzed until she stepped on my bare foot and I yelped. Something heavier crashed. The two of us launched ourselves through the door of the shop and sprinted back to the safety of the alley we had exited to stare unblinking at the shop.

Nothing followed us out of the store.

"Come on." She let her eye linger on the store for another second and then moved off to the right following the crumbling sidewalk.

I followed. We walked in silence in the quiet afternoon until we passed a hardware store. Addy went into the darkened building despite my protests. I stood outside with apprehension growing in my stomach like a cancer. It was too quiet. Addy returned with a rusted ax in one hand and a pry bar in the other.

"Pick one." She said.

I reached dumbly for the pry bar.

"Clinic's nearby, I think." She continued down the sidewalk.

I followed. She hefted the ax and took practice swings into the air in front of her. I'd have preferred she whistled rather than wield the ax. I looked at the pry bar in my hand. There seemed to be dried spots of blood on its chisel head.

She stopped. I looked up to see what had checked our progress. Addy stood there in the golden afternoon sunlight holding out the flyer from the rejuvenation clinic. The building she checked it against sat up on a hill away from other buildings. A meandering driveway connected the property to the main road. The decay that had seemed to have taken over town had touched the once-shining white clinic too—even sitting up there above the lesser buildings. Addy let the flyer fall and it floated to the ground.

She began to climb the hill and I could do not but follow.

We could see that the lights were on through windows of the place, but like the other buildings it appeared to be vacant. Addy went right through the front door, her skirt swishing, and the ax hanging loosely in one hand. I looked back down on the quiet strip of vacant buildings and saw a figure walking leisurely down the street in the opposite direction of the clinic. I breathed deeply and entered.

There was a thick layer of sick gray dust covering everything in the waiting room. An old CRT television mounted on the ceiling in one corner played silent static on it. A bell chimed, startling me. I turned to see that Addy had smacked the little silver service bell sitting on the front desk.

"I weren't gon' say nothin' before, but I got a bad feelin' about this town, Mill. Ain't no one here." Addy said.

I nodded and swallowed hard.

"I figure we come in here, kill them rich people usin' us, and disappear together. Happy ever after, ya know?"

"Let's check the exam rooms." I said.

We walked through the door adjacent to the reception desk and entered into a long hallway of doors. Addy took the left side and I took the right. The first room looked much the same as the waiting room—disused and dusty. I looked over my shoulder and caught a glimpse of the room Addy was entering. Somewhere down the hall a door closed.

We looked at each other wide-eyed and peeked back into the hallway simultaneously. The hallway looked much the same. Addy took quick stealthy steps and joined me.

"Mill, if this place ain't used, what they doin' to us in that place? Why they take my eye, my nose, why did they...did they." Addy began to cry.

My breath caught, and I took her into my arms. She sobbed quietly against my chest. I felt shaken. With all her confidence, I'd had no doubts about following this young woman. Her whistling had even eased my anxiety. But here she stood, stripped of her confidence and force. A small part of me wanted to be back in my room at the facility where I knew what to expect from the doctors and orderlies. It made me want to cry. Out here in this dead town the future seemed just as bleak.

"Addy." I whispered.

She sniffled, rubbed her eye and looked up at me.

"We heard a door. There's someone here. Let's go find them." I said.

She smiled, stood on her toes, and planted a kiss on my cheek. I smiled too.

We left the room brandishing our weapons, ready to confront whoever was in the building. We found the rooms were all as abandoned and dusty as the first. There was one final door at the end of the hall marked SURGERY. Addy looked at me, I nodded, and she pushed through the door.

The surgery room was clean and smelled sterile. Nothing was out of place, nothing was broken, it was a perfect room in a world of broken-down structures. Scalpels, bone saws, and other surgical instruments were laid out on a tray next to the freshly made-up operating table. There were leather restraints hanging loosely from it.

A door on the opposite wall opened to reveal Doctor Herbert in a spotless white lab coat, a hand in one pocket and the other holding open the door nonchalantly. He took us in and I saw a brief look of surprise pass on his face, but it was gone in an instant.

"Ah, there you two are. You've caused quite a ruckus at the facility. My men searched over the entire complex frantically. Of course, they only did so because the punishment for losing my two favorite specimens was to be terminated. I only lost two of them before we figured out where you had gone."

Addy screeched in rage and launched herself at the doctor with the ax raised. She knocked over the tray of surgical instruments and the room was filled with a hateful clattering of metal. The doctor sidestepped into the room and a large orderly appeared from behind him and caught Addy's ax mid swing. It was Jacob. He yanked the ax from her hand and brought a knee to her stomach. She crumpled and fell to the floor gasping. I watched as Jacob delivered swift kicks to the helpless girl on the floor.

"Miller, drop the pry bar and come here." The doctor said over the violence.

I looked at him and then down at the cold length of metal in my hand. I crouched down and placed it on the floor. There was a scalpel at my feet. Addy cried out as she was kicked. I winced at the blows. I snatched the scalpel up and concealed it in the sleeve of my shirt, not knowing fully what I intended to do with it. I stood and went to the doctor. He held an arm out to me and I stared down at Addy who was unconscious.

I saw my chance when Jacob bent to pick Addy up. The doctor put his arm around my shoulders and I slashed with the scalpel. His other hand went to his throat trying to keep his lifeforce from leaking out of the wound I had given him. Before Jacob could react, I threw myself onto his back and slashed at him with Scalpel. I succeeded in getting his throat too, though rather than sitting down and trying to staunch the bleeding like the doctor was doing, the big man flailed about trying to remove me from his back.

I held tight and soon Jacob's movement became sluggish as he stumbled and fell forward into the operating table. I jumped back as he went to the floor. A pool of red spread out from underneath him and bile crept up my throat.

Doctor Herbert watched me wide-eyed as I picked Addy up and cradled her in my arms. He attempted to say something, but he couldn't. His face was pale and his eyes grew dull. I left the clinic with the unconscious girl.

I walked off down the road away from the main strip of vacant buildings with Addy in my arms. The sky was ignited with a dramatic sunset. She stirred, tensed, and relaxed when she saw that it was me who held her.

"They're dead." Was all I could say.

She put her arms around my neck and gave me an awkward hug.

"Can you walk?" I asked.

"Ya, I think."

I put her down.

"Can you whistle that song?" I asked.

"Ya."

The two of us walked off into the approaching night with Addy's song lightening the heaviness of the darkening world.

THE END

STYGIAN HORROR

City of Ghouls

𝔄 LARD THE WITCHPLAGUE found himself stripped to the waist and chained frontside to a wall in a damp basement soon after he had entered the village. He had arrived at dusk and the clouds spat rain as he attempted to make his way to the church that stood taller than the other structures in town. There was a disquieting silence swirling among the fog that hung about. He encountered no one until he was jumped by two powerful men and then dragged away like a corpse.

A single candle burned low on the table trying to hold up the considerable weight of the dungeon dark. The wet coppery smell of his own blood filled his nose as the men had nearly flayed him with a whip. Unsatisfied with Alard's answers, they had gone. In the silence he elected to make an escape.

His arms were outstretched, and the chains helped support his exhausted body. With a little concentration he rearranged the bones in his left hand until the manacle let go of his wrist. He hung limp from the remaining manacle and breathed a heavy sigh as he corrected the form of his left hand. When he was ready, he reached up and undid the iron encircling his right hand.

Alard stumbled to the table where the candle flickered in fear of the approaching warlock. The table held his shirt, coat, cloak, boots, and rune-marked shortsword. The sword had drunk the blood of countless practitioners of witchcraft and almost shuddered at Alard's touch, himself being versed in certain mystical arts. Donning his shirt caused him to suck air through his teeth as the cloth settled into his wounds and began to soak in the uncoagulated blood. With boots and jacket on, cloak wrapped about his shoulders, and sword sheathed at his side, Alard lifted the candle and began to search for an exit.

When he found one and moved toward the door, the dim light in his hand revealed a youthful girl standing in the corner, eyes shining and mouth smiling.

"You shouldn't be down here child."

"And *you* shouldn't be out of those bonds." With a laugh she pranced towards him and gazed up in wonder. "I'm sorry they've treated you roughly."

"I find that the common folk are very superstitious and have an intense dislike of foreigners in these uncertain times. I usually have a day or two before I'm threatened or thrown out of town. I'll admit I was surprised to be jumped so quickly. Who might you be?"

The girl walked in circles around Alard, appraising him. "Oh, I can't give you my name. That knowledge would leave me powerless."

The girl was a witch, a vile sorceress. He could now feel the dark charge of magical energy in the air. Instinctively he reached for the blade at his side, but didn't draw it.

"Are you going to kill me? I knew you were a witch hunter."

"I don't do that anymore."

"Do you still help people?"

"No."

"These people need your help. You saw the barrow next to the church, so many are dying that they're running out of room to bury people."

Alard let his gaze linger on her for a moment before reaching for the door.

"I wouldn't go out into the night if I were you. There are things far worse than me lurking about. Horrors birthed from myth and superstition stalk forth on drizzly nights like these."

"I'll take my chances."

The door led to a moldering staircase which led to a hatch. Water trickled in through the cracks and promised a horrendous rainstorm. Alard threw the hatch open and rose from the dungeon like a revenant cadaver. The rain was heavy and cut visibility, but the shining white church spire was still apparent in the lightning flashes that chased away the dark.

He still planned to make his way there despite the rough treatment he had been given by the town's residents. The priest would hear his words and hopefully shelter him for the night. The churches and monasteries dotting the countryside were always willing to give what aid they could to a witch hunter, even a retired one.

The rain had turned the dirt roads into a mess of sloshing mud. Every home and shop he passed was dark. Strange that not a soul was awake, even though the hour was late. The man continued his slog and made it up the modest hill which the church sat upon.

To Alard's horror the building looked abandoned. The cemetery next to the church was a haphazard mountain of earth that surely covered hundreds of coffins. The girl was right—they were running out of room for burials and had begun building upwards. The heavy rain was sloughing off great chunks of grass and earth as it rolled down the monstrous barrow.

Alard moved to the great oak door of the house of God and lifted the iron knocker. It fell with a deadened thud. Almost in unison with the thud, a great chunk of the burial mound gave way, revealing a coffin. Alard caught the motion out of the corner of his eye. A flash of lightning later and the wooden box came loose and tumbled down the hill. It broke open on a headstone and spilled the corpse out into a pool of mud. The heavens seemed to rain harder as if trying to wash the grotesque thing away.

The witch hunter let the knocker fall again, praying that someone was in the building. He heard a sound, but it did not come from the building. He turned to the hill again just as a pallid-faced something peered over the peak.

"Hello? Who's there?" Alard's hand strayed to his sword. He had not drawn the thing in three years and was not sure that he could, should the need arise.

The thing climbed fully on top of the hill, presenting itself to the man. It was humanoid. The figure crouched low, gnashing its crooked teeth. The ghoulish thing was dressed in decaying rags that barely covered its nudity. It began to descend the hill, not taking its milky eyes off Alard the Witchplague.

"You stay there, fiend, or I will put you to death."

The ghoul did not heed the man's warning. It made its way down to the carcass floating in the mud and crouched close to it. Then began a sluggish feast. Alard threw his shoulder into the church door attempting to force his way in as the ghoul noisily slurped down the rotting vital organs of the corpse. The door gave way on his second try and he stumbled into the dark antechamber.

When he turned to shut the door, a flash of lightning lit up the forms of three more rancid ghoul-things standing out in the darkness with staring milky eyes. The trees waved behind them as if celebrating the feeding frenzy that was to begin. Alard slammed the door closed and replaced the bar that his efforts had knocked loose.

The church was quiet, and water dripped somewhere inside. The man dug around in the pocket of his coat and produced his flint and steel. After a few strikes, candles were lit, and the pews and altar were embraced by a warm glow. Dust covered everything. It was apparent now that these people had abandoned God. Or perhaps God had abandoned them. From a window Alard could see the ghouls pulling out more chunks of earth and breaking open other coffins.

"I told you there were terrible things out in the night."

Alard spun to see the same youthful girl he had encountered in the dungeon cellar. She was completely dry while he was soaked in comparison. How had she staved off the rain? This one was a very talented witch.

"What are they?" He asked, regaining his composure.

"I don't know. People started dying of plague and then those things showed up. On stormy nights they pull bodies from the pile and feed. The townspeople wake up to find half-eaten loved ones which they can do nothing but rebury."

"I believe they are ghouls. I've heard of such things, but never have I encountered one."

"Will you help this town, witch hunter?" The girl was very sincere in her plea.

"What would you have me do? Kill these creatures?" Alard asked.

At that suggestion a third voice joined in on the conversation. A croaking, sick voice.

"You may kill them, but they are innocent. You kill them and there will be more."

The witch and the Witchplague both searched for the origin of the voice and found it as another one of the ghoulish creatures shuffled from some hidden back room. The same rancid face, gnashing teeth, and milky eyes, but this one was dressed in the vestments of a priest.

"They are those who survived the plague. They have come together to search for the shroud-eater, the one who is buried and keeps the plague alive and spreading. These wretched creatures think only of stopping the spread of sickness."

"Father, you yourself have become one of them." Alard gripped the hilt of his sword until his hand hurt.

"Well so I have, my son." The priest cackled a dry papery laugh. "Very soon I will succumb to the same fate as them and you will see me pulling apart the very bodies I gave last rites to."

"What do you suggest I do, Father?"

"Help those forsaken souls find the shroud-eater and put an end to the plague."

The ghoul had nothing more to say and retreated. Alard tried to speak further to the priest, but he would not listen to the witch hunter. So, he turned to speak with the witch, but she was gone. Alard looked about, searching for her. He was alone again.

He had a decision to make—fight or flee. He could escape into the dark of the night, shrug off the rain and continue on his journey or stand shoulder to shoulder with grave fiends and desecrate the remains of God's children. To be a witch hunter was to walk a fine line between God and the damned. The townspeople would not understand the desecration of the graves, but they would be cured of the disease that plagued them. Alard turned the notion over in his head. After only three years, Alard the Witchplague decided to step out of retirement.

Alard stepped back out into the storm and the four ghouls that had gathered to feast stopped chewing to stare up at the witch hunter. He had the runed sword in his right hand and a sigil of divine protection dangling from his left hand.

"Step aside fiends and I will find your shroud-eater!"

The ghouls froze and focused in on the witch hunter with their dead eyes. They crouched lower and moved away as he strode forward. They seemed to be taking great effort to show deference to the man. He sheathed his sword and donned the sigil. There lay a shovel on the ground. How convenient, he thought.

Alard went to work digging into the soft ground that made up the hill. Great swaths of the barrow tumbled down with each coffin the witch hunter pried from the earth's grip. Each shovelful of soaked earth became agony and the man's whip wounds opened again as he worked his back muscles to the brink of total exhaustion. He opened coffin after coffin, but each body still retained a complete grave shroud bundled about them. When the ghouls moved in on the bodies Alard had unearthed, he chased them off with his sword.

"You shall only have your shroud-eater, fiends. Let these bodies rest."

Grey dawn began to peek between the storm clouds

when Alard found what he and the ghouls were looking for. The body that lay in the coffin he had pulled had a hole in the death shroud wrapped about its head. A meager flash of lightning showed a gruesome grin framed by shriveled lips.

"Here you are ghouls."

Alard gave the coffin a swift kick and dumped the corpse down the hill. He sank to his knees, breathing heavily. The ghouls stared at it and then back at him before descending upon it with gluttonous greed. As they bit, chewed, and pulled, a dreadful scream emanated from the shroud-eater. A flash of lightning showed him the carcass struggling against the ghouls, its head jerking back and forth.

Alard averted his eyes as the ghouls pulled the shroud-eater apart with a sickening crack. The screeching of the thing died. That's when the witch hunter noticed the witch again. She sat on the front steps of the church watching Alard.

He moved towards her and she made no attempt to flee.

"My hero." She said with a childish grin.

"What are you playing at girl?"

"You've done this town a great service and you seem to be just the individual I am looking for. I have another job for you witch hunter."

Alard let his gaze linger on her for a moment before his curiosity got the better of him. That flame for hunting the supernatural had been ignited again.

"What did you have in mind, witch?"

𝕬FTER THAT NIGHT the ghouls never returned to town. The villagers spent the following days cleaning up the atrocious mess that was left of their graveyard, but not another person contracted the plague and those suffering from it miraculously recovered. Then, of course, there was the question of where the man they had captured entering the town had gone. Not many correlated his appearance with the disappearance of the ghouls and the plague, but those that did thanked God. They elected not to search for him nor question how he slipped his bonds. Life got back to normal in that town and Alard the Witchplague moved on with rekindled purpose.

THE END

The Runes of Dead Men

I.

AUDAX WAS DYING. He had spent weeks on an uncomfortable cot suffering from a relentless fever. His lungs burned and burned as he coughed and choked. The healers tended to him, but there was not much they could do. Audax had been the tribe's greatest thaumaturge in a hundred years. If he could not help himself, then no one could. He whimpered and prayed to Yaalon each night, but his words went unheeded. It seemed doom was in store for Audax.

"Oh, great Yaalon, have mercy on my old bones. I, your humble and most devout disciple, ask for this insignificant boon. Mercy! Oh, how my body burns."

The healers knelt at his side. One burned incense while the others moved their hands over the old man, trying to ease his suffering. Another night was beginning and still Audax suffered. Little did Audax know, Yaalon heard and Yaalon in his mysterious omnipotence made the decision to come to Audax that night.

One by one the healers left, weeping for their master. His

death would bring about the end of a golden age of magical arts. Audax was too paralyzed by his sickness to mete out the dark secrets he held, and the healers wept for the impending loss of knowledge. Audax quieted as darkness became complete. The candles flickered as they burned low and a form manifested out of the shadows.

Yaalon stood above the old man who was dying before his eyes. The god had taken the form of a beautiful young man with black eyes and a shock of equally black hair. He wore clothing from an unknown alien age. He knew the man by the prayers he had sent up, a very devoted disciple indeed. There was nothing for the god to do but end the old man's suffering.

Yaalon knelt next to the old man who stirred weakly.

"I have come for you, child. I thank you for your service and your devotion. I grant you the boon of mercy. I will speed you into the afterlife to live for all eternity."

As the god moved his supple hands to caress the old man, the old man spoke.

"Yaalon, please." Audax said in a weak whisper. "It is a trap. My body burns in the clutches of Cygnus. He is making a play for power and plans to kill you right here and now in your mortal form. I fear he is moving through the village as we speak."

Yaalon froze and his eyes went wide. He spun to face the door, ready for an attack. Cygnus, The Ashen Swan, son of Yaalon and now his betrayer. Before Yaalon could flee, he felt a sharp dagger pressed to his throat from behind. Audax had an arm around the god's waist and a golden ceremonial knife pressed to his throat.

"I did not lie when I said this was a trap, but it is a trap of my own design. Cygnus still sits among the stars, cozy and sleeping. I am the one making a play for power." Audax coughed harshly.

Yaalon stood pin-straight. "Is it also true that you are dying?"

"It is."

"You fool of an old man. You have just damned yourself to an eternity of suffering." Yet Yaalon remained frozen, for a slit throat in this form would nearly kill him.

"I have a better idea, Yaalon, I wish for you to grant me power and in return I will serve you for all eternity as your right hand. You would have my unswerving loyalty and an agent to act on your behalf. Think of all the plots that your children have made against you. Think of the benefits of having a hidden spymaster to foil them and protect you."

"You make this offer as you press a knife to my throat, mortal. Why should I trust you?"

"Think of it as a display of what I can do for you. I just deceived the great Yaalon, master of all that is and will be. Can you afford to have me working for anyone but you?"

The god remained silent for a moment.

"Very well."

Audax laughed until it turned into a coughing fit. He released the god who turned to face him. A single drop of night-black blood rolled down from where the dagger had pricked his neck. Audax dropped the dagger onto his cot and waited for what would come next. Yaalon placed a hand on Audax's forehead.

"From now on you shall be known as Kebalinos, The Deceiver."

Audax smiled a crooked smile until searing pain shot through his body. In a flash of light, the two divine beings disappeared from the hut and reappeared in a grove of twisted black trees bearing strange fruits. The sky swirled with black clouds. Audax, now called Kebalinos, stood in awe of the realm he had been transported to. He whirled to find Yaalon and saw that the god had left him alone. Momentary panic gripped him.

"You will find my library and you will study. I will not set you against anything until you have learned all that I need you to learn. You are no longer a mortal, Kebalinos." The echoing voice sounded from everywhere. "We will speak again when the time is right."

II.

𝕴 CAME HOME to a hastily scrawled note taped to my door.

Meet me at the athenaeum. I have something very important to show you.

The signature at the bottom of the page was messy, but I still recognized it. Doctor Theodoric Fletcher taught all my favorite courses when I attended college. He was a gifted historian, anthropologist, psychologist, sociologist, and linguist. There wasn't a lot he couldn't do, and it showed in the plethora of degrees and titles he held. During his time in England he was even knighted—I'm not sure if that makes him a Sir Doctor or Doctor Sir.

We formed a close bond, I was his most devoted disciple and he my benevolent god. I loved the old man like a grandfather. We kept in touch after I graduated, in letters, postcards, and photographs. The note on my door was strange because that meant that he was here in town. Last we spoke he was across the pond teaching as a guest professor at Oxford.

I placed my briefcase on the floor and wrapped a scarf around my neck. My work was done for the day and I made the decision to walk over to the athenaeum. The twilight sun peered at me through the gothic spires of the buildings along the skyline, seeming to try and hide itself as I moved closer. The ancient Romanesque library stood before me in all its glory. I had spent many hours there perusing the shelves.

As I hung my overcoat and scarf on the coat rack, I spied Theo in a nook on the second floor, a pen sticking out over his ear and his mustache working as he read quietly to himself. I smiled, I had missed the old wizard. He spotted me as I approached the stairs and excitement was ablaze in his eyes. I held out my hand to shake and he pulled me into a bear hug. Surprising strength for a frail old man.

"My son, it is so good to see you."

"Likewise, Theo. What are you doing back in the states?"

He looked around suspiciously as if to see if anyone watched us. He motioned for me to follow him and we made our way to a private room in the back. The sign on the door read *Reference Room, please see front desk for key*. Theo produced said key and pushed the door in. He checked outside once again before shutting and locking it behind us.

"My boy, I was having a holiday over in France. I was outside of Marseille in a park, strolling about when a deranged man approached me. Of course, I was very wary of him, until he called me by name. I thought maybe he had been a student of mine at some point. He took my hand and placed a folded scrap of paper into it and whispered to me, '*Djedefre* dances.' I had no idea what he meant. The scrap of paper contained symbols I had never seen before."

The doctor reached into his coat pocket and produced a

yellowing scrap of paper. He held it out to me and I studied the symbols. They were runic and a few almost looked like letters out of the Greek alphabet.

"What are your first impressions, boy?"

"I see Greek and Roman influences. Maybe an alphabet adapted to a certain tribe of barbarians? We know Ulfilas took the Greek alphabet and modified it to write his Gothic bible. It was probably used somewhere between 150 CE and...I don't know, 800 CE?"

Theo just stood there smiling at me, almost shaking with anticipation.

"Oh, it's far older than that. Think Greek dark ages, somewhere between 1100 BCE to 800 BCE."

"That's impossible. There was no writing, everything was oral tradition in that age."

"Was it? How do we know for sure? My theory is that the ancient Greeks and Phoenicians had contact with a very early Germanic tribe. One that has yet to be discovered, most likely due to cultural appropriation and lack of archaeological evidence. Somewhere, however, their written word still survives."

"Theo, someone could have made this up, and they're putting you on."

He laughed. "Then how do you explain this?"

The old man moved past me and donned a pair of cotton gloves. He pulled out a box from the wall and unlocked it with a key. The book he lifted out looked ready to fall apart. He held it up for me to see. It had a plain hide cover that was mold-eaten and flaky. He opened it delicately. I shivered when I saw that the first page was filled with the same symbols the doctor had just shown me.

"What...where did they find that?"

"A reclusive old collector left his library to this particular athenaeum about a year ago. I was here helping to sort and identify books when I came across this one. I had them lock it away for me to study when I had some free time. Then I was handed that note in France last month. I didn't think I had seen the symbols before, but two days later I understood their vague familiarity. I took a leave of absence and came right back here. You are the only other person who knows about this."

"So, are we going to decipher it?"

"I already have." He winked at me. "I didn't want to call you until I had cracked it, turns out it was rather simple. It reads a little something like this I believe;

Djedefre donre/ opu lore/ mam bore/ beba slore/ bleq sta roros/ bleqen koros/ chuf allos/ frega Ibykos.

It's a poem. I believe the literal translation is;

Djedefre dance/ on snow/ men break/ heartbeat slow/ black star rise/ blackness grow/ cry all of us/ fear Ibykos.

Djedefre and *Ibykos* are names, but of who or what I do not know. Pretty grim piece of writing, yes? I believe that the black star the note is referring to is a black hole that returns to the night sky every winter. I'm not sure how the author of this piece would know that though, if it's as old as we think it is. I'm no astronomer, but I know you need a telescope and you have to know exactly what you're looking for."

"This is amazing, Theo. This all needs to be studied. I'm going to take some time off from work and we can pursue this, that is, if you're willing to work with me again."

Theo smiled and nodded his head.

We worked for a week straight, deciphering the ancient

book page by page. The farther we got into it, the less it sounded like any known language. It seemed to be a religious text as it was full of rites and incantations to appease a certain pantheon of gods. We puzzled out a few more of their names; *Cygnus, Xanthe, Kebalinos.* Just saying the names out loud caused me to shiver. Not with fear, but with anticipation.

III.

Kebalinos began his search for the library. He no longer felt the weakness of age or the flame that had been in his lungs. Born anew, the man-made-immortal was ready to serve Yaalon.

It seemed like he had walked for weeks before a great black tower appeared on the horizon. He laughed and quickened his pace. The forbidden knowledge called out to him.

The tower twisted up into the clouds and caused trauma to the eye if looked at for too long. Kebalinos disappeared into its mouth for a thousand years. He spent every moment absorbing and learning all that Yaalon kept locked away. The knowledge changed him. It shaped him and nourished him. Kebalinos began to lose his humanity. He would never fully lose it, but he was more god than man by the time he had absorbed every word in that place.

It was then that Yaalon contacted him. They held court in a room at the top of the tower. Kebalinos was now dressed in dark robes and the shape of his face had shifted, his eyes retreating backward and his mouth protruding forward. He now resembled a snake, a face fitting of a deceiver. Yaalon sat regal in a throne made of unidentifiable bones bleached bright white. The throne shone in the darkness of the room.

The god had taken on the form of the beautiful young man again, a favorite of his. Next to Yaalon sat Xanthe, a bubbling mass of eyes and tentacles. Xanthe, The Deep One, Lord of Oceans. His form was smoke-like and threatened to disperse at any moment.

"Kebalinos, you have made great strides in your learning. Of all my children I trust only Xanthe. He is here to bear witness to your entry. Never has an outsider been admitted to our family of gods, but here you stand. Welcome."

Yaalon waved his hand and a skulking little ghoul moved toward Kebalinos with a tray. On the tray stood three goblets filled with a black liquid. Kebalinos took a glass. The remaining two were brought to Yaalon and Xanthe. The two gods raised their drinks to Kebalinos in a toast and all three drank the putrid liquid.

"Thank you for being here, Xanthe." There was a grunt and the mass of eyes and tentacles disappeared.

"Thank you, Yaalon." Kebalinos said with a flourish.

"It is time that we get to work." Yaalon said.

IV.

ONCE, WHEN THEO was out getting us some fresh coffee, I heard an echoing whisper sound when I spelled out a name; *Yaalon*. Everything in my study seemed to shy away from me as I searched for the source of the whisper. *Yaalon* was the one who begat all others. Those who practiced this pagan religion feared almost all of the deities, but all of the deities feared *Yaalon*. Even *Ibykos*, the so-called *Champion of Moonless Nights*.

The doctor's weariness seemed to grow as we made progress with the text. I felt the opposite. I had more energy than ever, I had barely slept since we embarked on our journey through time. A new language, a new culture, new gods, I couldn't bring myself to stop thinking about them!

The professor's demeanor took a turn for the worse when I reached a section of the book that expanded upon the note he had been handed. If my translation was accurate, it spoke of two heralds who would tell the world of the coming of *Djedefre*, who in turn would herald the coming of *Ibykos*. I half-jokingly suggested to Theo that maybe we were the heralds. He became angry. I was surprised at his outburst, but he apologized and left without saying another word. I assumed he went to get some fresh air as he was staying with me in my home.

When he didn't return after a few moments, I gave chase. I didn't want to leave our work for the night on a sour note, I intended to cease translating and treat the old man to a beer or two. I followed his footprints in the newly fallen snow. A second set of prints suddenly appeared next to his. The prints were human-like, elongated and dainty. The thing that left them seemed to have been dancing from foot to foot, twirling about. The prints crisscrossed Theo's prints here and there as if it danced around him.

I didn't really believe what I was seeing, but the name *Djedefre* kept sneaking into my thoughts. *Djedefre* dances upon the snow. Their prints stopped at a third pair of prints. I shivered as snow settled on me. The new set was claw-like. I wanted to laugh as the name *Ibykos* began to creep into my thoughts. I wanted to laugh, but at the same time I was scared. The prints terminated at that spot, Theo was just gone. I continued on a little further, but I couldn't pick up the trail. I crossed the quiet street, nothing on the other side.

When I came back to my home, the front door was wide open admitting little swirling squalls of snow. I called out and no one answered. I found my study in ruins. The book was gone, the note was gone, and all the work we had compiled was gone. I righted my desk chair and dropped into it, defeated. I called the police and reported the break in, but they told me I had to wait twenty-four hours before I could report Theo missing.

"I'm sure Doctor Fletcher is sound asleep at home, it *is* pretty late." One of the cops said.

I told them he was staying with me, so I don't know where he could have gone, but they didn't care. I didn't bother them with the details about the footprints, as much as they bothered me. I grabbed a blank sheet of paper as the police exited and began to write down that ancient alphabet from memory. I refused to be intimidated by whoever had ransacked my study.

The next morning, I searched for him. I followed the footprints again, but the sidewalk was muddled with others. The snow had turned a dying brown color all along the road. It was always a shame to see pure snow decay away with mud and salt. I didn't find him at the athenaeum or our usual breakfast spot. He had disappeared with his footprints. I came home with a coffee, ready to make some phone calls.

There was another note taped to my door, more hastily scrawled than the first.

They're more horrible than you could ever imagine, they do not adhere to any laws of science or nature. She came to me and danced and he came to me and spoke and I was captured. I don't know what I can do, but they are coming. They call me herald.

There was a drop of what looked to be dried blood on the bottom of the note, but it was shaped like a wax seal, as if something was pressed into the blood which dried it into an inane family crest. I squinted at it closely and I could make out some of the runes from the forgotten alphabet. I sat down with the note and read it over and over. Where was he?

That night I had bizarre dreams. There were words on the tip of my tongue, birthed of that forgotten language and the name *Yaalon* was like a cyst in my skull. I stood after waking and pain shot through my eyes. I took some aspirin, but it did not help. I stumbled out into my study with great effort holding my aching head and sat. I picked up a pen and scribbled the runes that spelled *Yaalon* on a scrap of paper and read it aloud.

There was whispering again, moving through my home and dancing across the curtained windows. I caught two words of the hushed voice, if it could be called a voice. It sounded like; *en beld*. I rubbed my exhaustion filled eyes as comprehension crept into my thoughts. *En beld* was 'in blood.' *Yaalon en beld.* The pain in my head peaked and I gritted my teeth against it. Before I could stop myself, I was tracing the runes of *Yaalon* into my arm with a penknife.

When I finished the last rune, my vision began to fade, and I felt my body going limp. I put forth great effort into staying conscious, but I lost the fight. When I opened my eyes again, I was in a strange place. I seemed to be in the middle of a grove of twisted dark trees, and dark clouds covered whatever type of sky was above me. Before me was a circle of rough cut marble blocks surrounding an obelisk. I approached the obelisk and lightning struck it. There was no thunder, but I felt the heat of the strike.

"Welcome to *Yaalon's* realm, adept." Said a papery voice.

A robed figure stepped out from behind the obelisk. A cavernous hood hid half a face. The figure threw its cowl back revealing its snake-like humanoid countenance. It grinned with daggered teeth. I told myself I had to be dreaming, but it all felt so real.

"Who are you?" I asked.

"I am *Kebalinos, Yaalon's* chosen one."

V.

*T*HE WORLD LOOKED very different to Kebalinos, but he was ready for it. He wore a face that wouldn't attract any attention as he moved through the city's crowds. There was a festival being held that day, a phantasmagoric celebration of a goddess named Ukaleq. Effigies made of woven twigs danced up and down the street as small fires burned within their hearts. There was singing and chanting.

Ukaleq had been birthed when Cygnus had set fire to a large swath of forest to punish the practices of a certain tribe. The tribe had hunted to extinction the swan, the sacred bird beloved by Cygnus. Out of the ashes of the conflagration rose a daughter. Cygnus spurned her, and she made her own way into the hearts of the people that now populated the area. They cast aside the old gods for this new one, becoming monotheists.

Great wars were fought with religious connotations. Followers of the old gods made attempts to convert the heretics, but these new people stood tall and resisted the onslaught.

Their religious fervor and love for Ukaleq only grew. In time, a small cabal gained power with intent to persecute and put down any followers of the old gods. Yaalon took notice as his dwindling human followers died out one by one.

Kebalinos shrugged his way into an alley and watched as the swirling multitudes danced and sang by the opening. It was time to pay Ukaleq back for all the souls damned in her name. The door the wizard sought was locked securely. He took great care in exercising his new power and in moments he was on the other side of the door, the lock still intact. The building was dingy and old, dark and musty. Muffled voices sounded from above. A meeting was taking place on the upper floor.

The wizard moved past rotting tapestries and climbed a staircase dimly illuminated by a single candle in a wall sconce. He placed his ear to the door and heard the cabal speaking heatedly about a nearby village. Kebalinos took a moment to translate, he recognized the language from his time in the library.

"They must be harboring more of those Yaalon-loving dogs." Said a voice.

"Even if they are, Yaalon is old and dying. His followers lack the strength to oppose us now." Replied a sultry woman's voice.

"It is true. In time, their beliefs will wither and die. Ukaleq will be the only god in the hearts of the land." Said a third voice.

Kebalinos appeared in the room with them in a flash of silent lightning. Five regally dressed nobles stared at him in surprise. He let his face drop and their surprise turned to terror as they looked upon his serpentine smile. The wizard licked his sharp teeth before he spoke.

"My master is not happy with you. He is disturbed by your cruelty towards his flock and he wishes to have a word with you." Kebalinos spoke with folded arms.

One of the men drew a dagger and lunged at the wizard. He sidestepped the attacker and held him by the throat. He brought the man's ear to his mouth and he whispered into it. The attacker fell to the floor writhing. Insects began crawling from his mouth. He choked and gasped as they continued to push their way out and scatter along the floor. The other nobles were paralyzed in their seats.

One by one Kebalinos moved to each and whispered into their ears and one by one they bared their forearms and laid them on the table. Kebalinos picked up the attacker's dropped blade and began to carve his master's name on each of their arms. Their bodies went limp and disappeared into Yaalon's realm, never to be seen again. The vomiting man started to choke, the swarm of insects suffocating him, his breathing slowed until his chest no longer rose. Yaalon would take care of that lot. Kebalinos left the building and headed back into the streets, ready to implement the next part of the plan.

As he moved down the alley, he donned a new face, hiding his serpentine glare, so as not to spark any more interest from the revelers. The common people were easily swayed. They were uneducated and superstitious, the very foundation of any organized religion. Kebalinos sneered and wove his way through the masses to seek out one of the effigy holders. He found a tall woman stamping her feet and rattling the twig image of Ukaleq on its pole. Tiny embers sprayed out of the thing's ribcage with each jolt. They settled and died within the dust cloud kicked up by the woman.

Kebalinos came close to her and slipped a hand onto her shoulder. She took no notice as people were bouncing off one another everywhere on the tightly packed street. But, she did notice when the wizard's other arm wrapped around her waist. She spun to push her assailant off and was met with the deadly mesmerizing stare of Kebalinos.

"Well hello there my beautiful angel, you shall help me finish the task at hand with that beautiful image of your beautiful goddess."

The woman's face softened and she bent slightly to plant a kiss on Kebalinos's forehead. He kept his half embrace on the woman and snaked a hand up the pole to where her hands held tight. He whispered into her ear and the twig effigy with the embers burning in its heart exploded with a force that sent those close by sprawling. The woman still stood with the wizard's arm around her waist looking dazed.

"Tell them." Whispered Kebalinos.

The woman's shrill cry went up and she began to proselytize to the crowd. Music and singing still went on in the distance, but all those close by heard the powerful woman lamenting the iron grip Ukaleq had on them. She played to their fears of an eternity of suffering if they did not turn to Yaalon, the one true ruler of all that is and will be. Ukaleq, the daughter of genocide, unwanted by her ashen mother or her scorching father. Ukaleq was a goddess without friends. Yaalon was the only friend the people would need.

A fight broke out as one commoner fell to his knees and pledged himself to Yaalon. Followers of Ukaleq had dragged him upright and began to pummel him. Kebalinos laughed as more peasants joined the fight, each proclaiming for Yaalon or Ukaleq. The wizard shrugged off into the next crowd that was only half-paying attention to what was happening in the street. Their plan was working.

VI.

THE GRUESOME MOUTH moved, "Had the others left the book, you would have soon found that I was once what you would call human. I was a disciple of *Yaalon* in a time beyond remembering. When I was close to death, I swindled him into accepting me into his cabal of god beings. I watch the maneuverings of the others for him. Not many of them know who I am."

"I'm looking for someone." I said.

"I know you are, why do you think I granted you passage to this place?" *Kebalinos* laughed. "It has been so long since we have held court with humans. I myself have grown lonely in the company of the immortals. Events were set into motion for the revival of these forgotten gods, but a few act out against us. *Djedefre* and *Ibykos*, incestuous brother and sister meddling in my plans. They came for you, but I prevented them. *Yaalon* can put a stop to it all, but you must do something for him."

"I'm not doing anything for anyone. I'm dreaming right now, aren't I?"

"I assure you that you are not dreaming. But for now, I release you. You will know what to do when the time comes."

The wizard creature placed a hand on the obelisk and he disappeared in a flash of lightning that shot up into the clouds. My vision clouded, I felt limp.

I awoke with a start, blood all over my desk. The runes still oozed on my arm, but the pain in my head was gone. I went to the bathroom and smeared antibiotic cream on the fresh cuts and wrapped my arm with a bandage. I was losing it. I was having a psychotic episode, right? I called the police again and told them about the note left by Theo. An officer showed up to collect it as evidence and take down my missing person's report. The officer eyed me suspiciously as she took down my account of that night.

I was starting to wish Theo had never shown back up. He wouldn't be missing right now, and I wouldn't be losing my mind. It snowed again that night. I could swear I heard singing outside of my house. There were those dainty footprints in the snow, but no one nearby. All was quiet outside. I didn't sleep, every tiny noise caused me anxiety. When I went to change my bandaged arm, I noticed it had stopped bleeding. When I unwrapped the gauze, all that was there were faded scars of those runes. My fingers played across them and they felt cold.

I laughed to myself. It all had to be a bad dream. I contemplated getting evaluated. A knock sounded at my door, I didn't move. It sounded again and slowly I made my way towards it. I cracked it open and saw a vagrant standing on my front steps. He pushed a black lacquered box through the space and I took it without thinking. He turned and strode away.

The box felt heavy, I traced the intricate carvings with my eyes as I moved to my study. I placed it on my still bloody desk. I opened it. On moldering silk lay a withered hand with a symbol tattooed onto the palm and a candle. The contents smelled foul, like burning dung. I stared at it. I was surprisingly calm. A hand of glory and a candle made from the fat of the same malefactor. I had read about them, but I never imagined I'd ever see one.

I placed the hand delicately among my dried blood on the desk. I found matches in the kitchen and when I returned, I lit one to soften the bottom of the candle. It emitted a sickening smell as I fastened the base of the candle into the palm of the hand. The match burned down as I stared at the thing and blackened my fingers. The pain pulled me out of my trance and I sucked on my burnt fingers. I do not know how long I paced back and forth staring at the thing. It was dark out. I could swear that I heard jovial singing somewhere in the distance.

I steeled myself and struck another match. I lit the candle and the lights in my home dimmed. The atmosphere went hazy with some kind of miasmic fog. The world felt as though it were a dream, swirling itself about me. The candle dripped wax onto the hand of glory and the flame flickered fitfully. My front door opened slowly, and heavy footfalls made their way to the study.

There in the doorway stood Theo, pale-faced and blind. He raised his arms toward the ceiling and began to speak in a weak voice.

"My son, you have made a grave mistake. They are here now, you have given them entry to your home."

$VII.$

REBALINOS LAUGHED to himself, the people danced at his fingertips. He took great pride in the abilities he now possessed. As the night wore on, more and more people were convinced of the weakness of Ukaleq and the strength of Yaalon. He cut puppet strings, re-tied them, and pulled on them until they were ready to break. When he felt good and tired, the wizard retreated to a dark rooftop to watch the chaos unfold, his word spreading out like thawing ice.

As he sat and pondered his new existence, feet dangling from the edge of the rooftop, something snuck up next to him. He gave a start when the shifty thing turned out to be a beautiful young woman. She sat innocently next to him making no effort to hide her nakedness. Her skin was olive and her hair done up with flowers.

"You have wounded me, yet I do not know why. You are no mortal. What then, are you?" She said in a playful voice, rich with the sounds of summer.

"You must be Ukaleq. Your people persecute those who are rooted in a religion far older than you, girl. Your father may have been The Swan, but your mother was a poor forest, infested with human scum. I fear you will not hold much sway over these people anymore, see how the doubt spreads like a disease?"

"You have taught me a lesson, stranger." Ukaleq smiled at Kebalinos.

Before he could move away, she pounced on him and her body became a blaze of fire, her eyes went from emerald to ruby. As his robe caught fire she pressed herself against him and kissed his mouth hard. His mask melted away, the heat revealing his serpentine face, but she continued to ravish him anyway. He attempted to push her off but she was stronger than him.

"This is how it happened to my mother, stranger." She said as his clothing burned away to nothing.

Before she could take advantage of him, Kebalinos teleported through the roof and into the room below. He landed with a thud and heard a screech as the wild demi-goddess searched for her quarry. With all the concentration he could muster, the wizard flung himself back through time and space into the realm that had become his home.

The desolate landscape was a treat to his eyes. He began walking immediately to find an obelisk. The runed structure brought him right to the doors of the library he had become so familiar with. Yaalon was waiting for him in his boyish form, idly leaning against one of the black gnarled trees that stood as a sentinel guarding the entrance.

"You did well, my spy. It is a shame Ukaleq found you, but fortunately she was not able to take advantage of you. A child would cause problems for you. I fear she will search for you as long as her followers are in disarray, but we must keep them plunged in chaos until they abandon the goddess altogether. You have earned this tower, I give it to you with the task of guarding its knowledge." Yaalon spoke as he slowly made his way up to the doors. "It shall now be known as the 'Tower of the Deceiver.' I hope the residence suits you, I can't have my right-hand moping about the planes of this realm, awaiting my orders."

"Thank you, my lord."

Kebalinos bowed deeply. When he stood erect, Yaalon had disappeared. He looked around before entering his new abode. It was then that he noticed his pale bony body was still naked. In a moment his twisted form was covered again with a dark robe and he stood there in the entry hall admiring the place. A small ghoulish thing crept out from behind a door. It came up to his chest and had a face like a goblin.

"My lord, I am Kesh, a gift from Yaalon. I am here to serve whatever needs of yours may arise." Said the impish thing.

Kebalinos smiled. He was ready to make use of his powers, his servant, and his new castle of knowledge. Schemes multiplied in his head as he wove his thoughts together. He waved his servant off. It was time to retire. Infinity would hold plenty of chances for secrets to be bought and sold and subterfuge to be executed. Kebalinos was happy in his new position. The gods had no idea what was coming.

VIII.

$\mathfrak{M}$Y BREATHING BECAME heavy as the once-distant singing approached. A low bassy sound accompanied it now. The sounds mixed and grew until it was all I could focus on. Theo fell to his knees and his mouth moved soundlessly as if praying. I backed away. What had I done? Was the hand of glory not the thing I was waiting for? Had I been tricked?

Lightning lit the window, but no thunder accompanied it. *Kebalinos*? The singing ceased and was replaced by a terrible screech. The house shook for a moment and I thought I heard a word in the screech; *Yaalon.* The miasma suddenly lifted, and Theo was gone. I could still feel a presence. Into the study waltzed the wizard *Kebalinos* in his swaying dark robe. Thankfully, he kept his hood up and I wasn't forced to look upon his gruesome face.

"You were a beautiful pawn. Thank you." The hand of glory and what was left of the candle disappeared into his robe.

"So, what now? Where is my friend?" I asked.

"Now? Now, you believe. You've experienced the power

of gods that are very much alive. Spread the word or keep it to yourself. Regardless, we are gaining strength. I fear your friend is lost, he has become a pawn on the losing side." He reached into his robe as he spoke and withdrew the ancient runic book that had vanished from my study. "Take this. Learn it, reproduce it, spread it."

As my hand touched the book he offered to me, there was a blinding flash of lightning and a blast of heat. When I opened my eyes, the thing called *Kebalinos* was gone. The world was dim and quiet. Theo was gone, that hurt, but in a way, he would live on with me and my work.

The knowledge within the book changed me. It shaped me and nourished me. It wasn't long before I left my little town and settled into a remote cottage close to the northern border. I couldn't bring myself to interact with regular humans anymore. My purpose was greater. There I worked and prepared to spread the holy long-forgotten word kept alive within the runes of dead men.

THE END

ACKNOWLEDGMENTS

Special thanks to Trevor Vaughan for getting this whole thing started, Nick LeBlanc for helping me bring these visions to life with Domesticated Primate, and Dean Forsythe Jr. for taking care of art and layouts on the original texts. I'd also like to thank my friends for all their support and my lovely wife for pushing me to keep these stories alive.

A.C. Perry is a musician, poet, and author of *Forgotten Nightmares and Sullen Fantasies*. A lifelong fan of fantasy, science fiction, horror, and any kind of speculative fiction in between, he took the plunge into the abyss and began writing his own stories in 2015. Described by some as a Renaissance man, A.C. Perry is interested in everything. From identifying edible wild plants to studying the decline and fall of the Roman Empire, A.C. is always getting up to something. His musical pursuits include the fantasy synth project Trädvarelse and his industrial/ambient noise project CRUSHER CONVEYOR. When he isn't writing, making noise, or dabbling in some new hobby, A.C. is overseeing the electrical production of industrial control systems for an engineering company. He currently lives with his wife in Pawtucket, Rhode Island, and is hard at work on his first novel.

Instagram: acperryfiction
Email: acperryfiction@gmail.com